The Lottery
Murders

DEAD GIVEAWAYS

RHONDA A. COLIA

ISBN
978-1-959314-79-0 (Paperback)
978-1-959314-80-6 (eBook)
978-1-959314-78-3 (Hardcover)

The Lottery
Murders

Table of Contents

Chapter One

The Hit

Profuse sweat was beading on Rory Phillip's brow as he tried to think his way out of his situation. With an intruder's gun to his head, he had few options.

"Drop it," The intruder muttered. Rory was eye-to-eye with a man who was clearly on a quest to hurt him. He saw it in his eyes. Rory hard elbowed him in the ribs, but it barely fazed the intruder. They briefly scuffled, but the gunman gained control and Rory dropped the gun. Little did he know this was his last chance to physically overtake his opponent.

His attacker was responsible for the recent break-ins in the area to throw off suspicion of Rory's pending demise. 'Make it look like an accident' were his instructions from his contact, Florida State Attorney General, Mark Stein.

The assailant destroyed Rory's cell phone with the heel of his tennis shoe and picked up the gun. He had done his homework and cased Rory's tractor-trailer repair shop for days until a cabover unit was in the shop. The Tallahassee shop was owned by Rory Phillips and his wife, Beth.

Cabover engine units work like a flip-top cap on a tube of toothpaste. The entire cab of the truck flips over and hangs open above the ground exposing the engine for maintenance and repairs.

The infiltrator had previously tampered with its safety system and would have to move quickly. He'd already raised the cabover to tipping center, so that it was suspended in midair. With one safety release damaged, the other one would soon fail beneath the weight of the massive cabover. All he had to do was use a pipe to strike the one remaining safety release and, *voila*, instant accidental death.

Rory never thought his life would end violently. Although a gun aficionado, he'd never had a gun drawn on him and he wasn't prepared for this. He quickly jerked back into the moment, focusing his thoughts on how to extricate himself from the situation.

The assailant didn't speak much but motioned him to the cabover. "Climb," He grumbled and nodded toward the truck. With a gun at Rory's back, he walked him towards the truck.

Rory climbed the small distance to the top of the engine and tried back kicking the gun from his attacker's hand, but it was no use. The gun went off and clipped Rory in the inside of his of thigh, and it bled profusely. The bullet nicked his femoral artery and came to rest in his thigh bone. He felt the hot, sticky red fluid flow out of him, and he panicked. His mind was impaired, and pain was overtaking him.

His captor paused briefly to retrieve the bullet casing from the accidental shooting. Despite Rory's bleeding, the assailant forced him towards the center of the huge hood of the cabover. Rory wondered, 'is he going to shoot me again or crush me to death?'

Knowing these could be his last thoughts, his mind bolted to his wife and a way out of this. How was this happening? Why hadn't he called the police when he had the chance after hearing something suspicious? He thought he had his whole life ahead of him, but now he wasn't so sure. What about his wife, Beth? In seconds, he recalled their last conversation.

"I'll be home about 7:30 p.m.," he told her.

"Why? What's going on?" Knowing that arrival time would be later than usual, Beth was concerned.

"Nothing, honey. I heard a noise in the shop, that's all. No big deal." Rory assured her.

"What noise? What'd it sound like?" Beth questioned.

"I don't know. But I'm the only one here, so I need to check it out." Rory informed her as he retrieved his favorite pistol from a false bottom drawer of his desk. "It'll only take a minute. Besides, I have my gun with me." He spoke as the alarm went off. "I have to check the cabover anyway. It's that new mechanic, Tim. I wanna know if he's the hotshot he thinks he is."

He continued talking as he walked into the shop. He wasn't overly concerned because the alarm had a habit of going off when tripped by a cat or rodent, so he wasn't about to panic before checking things out. He was a hands-on kind of man and had barely finished speaking before Beth cut him off.

"Rory, you know how many recent break-ins we've had in that part of town please, just call the cops and come home." Beth was pleading with him. "I have really important news and I can't wait to share it with you." If only he'd listened, he would have been home with her now, but how could he have known his actions would mean life or death?

"I'll be home in a minute. I just have to check this out first, and whatever important news you have will be better because you had to wait to tell me. You know, anticipation and all," he teased.

The alarm was sounding. Rory's mind swirled. What's taking so long? Is there a way out of this? What will happen to Beth, Janice, and John, not to mention his parents? Could his dad's heart handle the shock of his death? What had Beth wanted to tell him and why was it so important? These were a few of the thoughts darting in his mind like a pinball machine as he desperately glanced for something to defend himself.

Rory tried to reason with his killer. "Please! Just take whatever you want, but I have a wife and family to care for and I really need to be here for them. It's our anniversary today and she's waiting for me right now." Rory heard the desperation in his own voice. "I'll give you anything you want. You don't have to do this." Rory pleaded.

The man he was pleading with was Jason White, or 'Whit,' as he was known by law enforcement and Interpol. He was one of America's top-ten most wanted fugitives and had a two-hundred-thousand-dollar bounty on his head. He never missed a target, but that didn't mean that occasionally things went wrong. He was just so good at his game that he never got caught. Whenever he couldn't kill from natural causes, he made it look like an accident, just like tonight.

Whit's track record was impressive by the standards of his world, but he had a few quirks. He whistled under his breath while committing his crimes. He found a perverse pleasure when victims begged for their lives. Tonight, was no different. He briefly toyed with Rory, making him think he had a choice of taking a bullet or being crushed to death.

"How do you want it? A bullet from your own gun?" he quizzed as he examined it, noting it looked like a WWI vintage weapon. "Or one from mine?" he sneered.

Whit instantly knew it was an antique gun and figured he'd keep it as a souvenir. It made no difference to him if the police found the bullet in Rory's leg. Given the mess he was about to make of him, he doubted they'd even find it. But no matter. By the time they did, he'd be long gone, out of the country until his next job, besides, without a gun for comparison it was a moot find.

"Maybe you'd prefer to be crushed to death?" He taunted. He paused as he brandished Rory's gun around again, admiring its authenticity. "Either way, you're gonna die here, tonight. I'd prefer to shoot you, but I have to make this look like an accident. Those were my orders," Whit informed.

"Shooting you is much more humane and less painful, but if I crush you to death, people *will* remember it, including that little wifey of yours." Whit purposely let it slip that he knew about Rory's personal life, implying that he was being targeted for murder rather than interrupting a would-be thief.

"Wife? You know about my wife? Who are you?" Rory fired questions hoping to buy some time while trying to talk his assailant out of murdering him. He zoomed in on a wrench just left of his feet. If he could just distract

Whit long enough to lunge for it, but it would be the equivalent of bringing a knife to a gunfight. A wrench wasn't any better.

His thoughts continued pinging. "Why me? Why do you wanna kill me? Who wants me dead?" Rory was dazed and trying to wrap his mind around the fact that this gunman was definitely not there to rob him, but to murder him. "*Beth!*" His last thoughts were consumed with grief knowing she'd have to face life without him; he worried for her safety.

"I got my orders and I never ask why," Whit responded, whacking the remaining safety release, and the three-thousand-pound cabover came crashing down on Rory. While standing on the ground adjacent to the cabover Whit bolted out of the way, avoiding the mess, and splatter. He was whistling "My Way," as he struck the safety. The last thing Whit heard was a long drawn out "Noooo ..." followed by a quick groan. "My work is done here," he uttered with a smirk and continued whistling.

He'd prepared an exit strategy. He stuck around in the shadows of his grand finale until the police arrived. He knew the alarm would soon descend the authorities, so he hid until the police arrived and then casually left the scene as he walked right by the other men dressed in blue.

No one noticed the flecks of arterial spray that barely landed on him due to the dark coveralls he wore over his cop's uniform. He remembered to bring along a spare pair of job-appropriate shoes to avoid suspicion. While hiding and waiting for the police to arrive, the assassin merely wiped off the little blood splatter that had landed on him, slipped off his coveralls and tennis shoes and put it all inside a brown evidence bag he'd brought with him. Then he strolled right out of the building agreeing with the first responders about how gruesome the death must have been.

Meanwhile, Beth was sick inside as she hung up the phone. Her heart was pounding so hard, it felt like a panic attack. She'd dialed 911 and reported an intruder at her husband's business. Then she called her sister, Janice, and brother-in-law, John, to come over and drive her to the shop.

When they arrived, the detectives had already secured the scene. The police tried to shove them back behind the crime scene tape until they identified themselves. Beth's mind was jumbled as she concluded it was their turn to experience a break-in, but deep inside she suspected more. She kept trying to calm the nagging whisper in her mind that things weren't all right.

She recalled the muffled conversation and scuffle she'd heard, but figured it was because Rory had surprised a thief. So far, the break-ins had been free of violence and no one had been hurt. To date, it was only missing inventory, tools and electronics that had been taken, all were items that could sell for a quick buck. However, her heart felt like an anvil as she read the officer's body language and her hopes plummeted. She readied herself for bad news.

"How's my husband?" She was staring at the officer as he delivered the news.

"I'm so sorry to inform you, Mrs. Phillips, but there was an accident and I'm sorry to say your husband did not survive. He was killed in an accident about a half an hour ago. I'm so sorry for your loss." Officer Jenkins hated informing families of fatalities. It took a toll on him. He'd been on the beat for twenty-three years and it never got any easier.

Beth blinked twice and swallowed hard. "He can't be dead. I just spoke with him." She was in denial but had to know more. She asked the obvious questions in disbelief. "How did it happen? Are you sure it's Rory? Are you sure it's not the intruder?" Her voice was cracking as tears floated in her eyes.

"Yes, ma'am. I understand your concerns. But we found his wallet, so we're sure it's your husband." He hesitated briefly. "And regarding the accident, we don't know everything yet. It appears the safety releases on a cabover failed and it fell on him." The officer was as gentle as he could be, given the circumstances.

There it was. The gut punch that nearly buckled Beth's knees. If it hadn't been for her sister, Janice holding her by the arm, she would have hit the floor. Her heart went deaf the minute she heard the words, 'I'm sorry to inform you.' She was in shock, and everything was a blur. She was functioning on autopilot.

"Mrs. Phillips, are you all right?" The officer was showing genuine concern, but she couldn't focus on his words.

"What? I'm sorry, I didn't hear you. Can you repeat the question?" Her eyes were glazed.

"I asked if you're all right. I think all of you need to speak with Captain Denton. He's the lead investigator in charge of your case." The officer wanted to answer her questions, but the only way to do that was to get her to the right person.

"Yes. I'll be fine," Beth answered as she looked past him, seeing nothing. Beth and her family were escorted to the police station and ushered into Captain Gene Denton's office. He had already left the crime scene to CSU investigators and was ready to question the victim's wife.

Denton was seated behind a well-worn, heavy walnut desk and sipping at a steaming cup of black coffee. His desk sported a large glass ashtray littered with cigarette butts. "My deepest apologies fer your loss, Mrs. Phillips. I can't imagine what thoughts and feelinz' you must be dealin' with right now. But rest assured, we'll get to the bottom of all this."

He cleared his throat before continuing in his pronounced Southern drawl. "But, in order to move things along fast as possilb', I need to ask ya some questions," he started.

"Okay," Beth responded, nodding her head yes. "What do you want to know?"

"Well, first of all, where were ya tonight between the hours of 6:00 and 7:45?" he asked.

"I was home preparing a special dinner for us. Today is, well it *was*, our eighth anniversary." Beth choked as she corrected herself to say *was*. She continued. "I was on the phone with him for about five minutes or so."

"What time did that call take place, Mrs. Phillips?" Denton pressed.

"I know it was about 7:15 p.m. because I called him so I could time our meal to be done when he got home. We had decided to celebrate at home rather than fighting the crowds at the restaurants since our anniversary is Valentine's Day," She tapered off as that thought consumed her.

"Mrs. Phillips, you're doin' fine. Just a coupl' more questions and you can go home and get ya some rest." Denton reassured her as he came around his desk and half sat on the edge of it right in front of Beth. "What, if anything, did ya hear, Mrs. Phillips?" Denton asked, knowing this was the all-important question of the interview.

Beth began. "Well, he told me he heard a noise in the shop, and he was going to check it out, along with the work of a new guy. I warned him not to do it since in past several weeks there have been so many break-ins in our area."

Beth briefly paused to clear her throat. "He said he had his gun with him, and he could handle things," she concluded without showing emotion. She was in a fog and answered in a matter-of-fact fashion.

"What happened next?" Denton inquired.

"He stopped talking and it sounded like he dropped his phone. He didn't say he'd call me back, he just stopped talking. I could hear him speaking with someone, but it was muffled and I couldn't make out what they were saying. Then the phone went completely silent." Beth took a drink of water. She was simultaneously thirsty, tired and wired.

"Did ya hear anything else, Mrs. Phillips?" he nudged.

"No. I told you everything I heard, and then I dialed 911 and my family brought me here. I'm not supposed to drive right now. I'm newly pregnant and I'm high-risk," she said as she patted her slightly swollen belly. She said as she patted her slightly swollen belly.

"Congratulations on yer baby, Mrs. Phillips. By the way, was anyone home with ya at the time of yer husband's death? Can anyone corroborate your story?" He asked as gently as he could.

"Corroborate my story?" Beth was blindsided by the insult.

She sighed deeply and shook her head. "No. I was alone preparing a full course dinner for the two of us. I was planning to tell him I'm pregnant. We'd been trying for a long time and had nearly given up. I wanted to surprise him with the good news tonight," she waned.

Janice chimed in. "She called me around 7:30 to tell me what happened and that she'd dialed 911. That's when we drove over, picked her up, and came straight here. So, in a way, doesn't that corroborate her story?" Janice was disgusted at the insinuation of Capt. Denton, but realized he was just doing his job.

"I think so," Denton replied. He would verify Beth's information with the time of the 911 call. He looked down at Mrs. Phillips and said, "Thank ya fer yer cooperation, Mrs. Phillips. Rest assured, if there is any foul play, yul' be the first to know. Please don't leave town as we may need to talk with ya again as the investigation progresses. Thank ya, again, Mrs. Phillips, and I sure do hope you get to feelin' better." Denton's Southern drawl was simultaneously charming and annoying.

Immediately, Beth jumped in. "What do you mean, foul play? I thought you said it was obvious that he was crushed to death in an accident. Are you saying the robber did this?" Beth was overcome with surprise and suspicion.

"Oh no, ma'am. It may well be that yer husband's accident and the break-in were just coincidental. We didn't find anyone at the scene. So fer, all the evidence points to it being an accident, but we have to cover all the bases since there was a break-in and this was an unattended death.

Ya know, he wasn't under a doctor's care and all, so that makes this as an unattended death. The fact that ya said ya heard an intruder makes us extra thorough." Denton informed.

Denton continued, "We don't believe it's anything but an accident at this point, but we have to explore all possibilities. We think yer husband surprised the intruder. The accident appears to be a separate incident." He tried to halt her disquiet but could clearly see he wasn't effective. Before he could speak again, she interrupted his thoughts.

"Before I go, I have a question for you, Captain Denton," Beth said, still strong enough to keep her composure while reeling in shock. "Were you able to get any images from our surveillance cameras?" she asked hopefully.

"No. I'm sorry, but they weren't working properly at that time of the break-in. They musta malfunctioned. It's something else we'll be investigatin.'Can ya tell me if you'd been havin' any trouble with your surveillance system, Mrs. Phillips?" Denton quizzed.

"Not that often. We've had our share of vandals from time to time. But most of the time it worked well. I think Rory had it serviced recently due to all the break-ins. Why? Did you find anything?" Beth asked, puzzled.

"No, ma'am. As I said, there wasn't any footage. The cameras were on, but they malfunctioned around 7:00, actually, 6:57 to be exact." He was sorry he didn't have any good news for her.

The information deadened her inside. She'd been holding out hope that whoever did this would have overlooked the security system. She knew it was foolish, but she hoped anyway. If only he had listened to her. If only he had called the cops. If only Rory had come home. If only…

Chapter Two

Marty

B*uzz. Buzz. Buzz.* The phone vibrated several times before Marty was roused enough to answer it. Marty Saunders, an ace reporter, had fallen into an unusually deep sleep, which she considered a rare and blessed event, since she was a light sleeper. She mumbled under her breath as she picked up the phone.

"Wouldn't you know it. I finally get to sleep and some idiot wakes me up." She fumbled with her cell phone. "What is it?" she grumbled into the speaker while propping the pillows underneath her back.

The voice on the other end of the phone was her boss, Joel Cleveland. He completely dismissed Marty's tone of voice and went straight to the point. "Marty, there's been an accident at a tractor-trailer repair shop on the northeast side of Tallahassee and apparently the owner's dead and I want you to cover it. Catch the six o'clock Delta to Tallahassee. It doesn't get there till 7:00 a.m., but that's the earliest flight there is. You're already booked and your ticket is at the counter."

"Why do you want me to cover a local story?" she asked sleepily. "What's the significance of a national coverage?" she was yawning now.

"Because you covered this story a couple of years ago when the victim was one of the winners of the Mega Millions lottery, something north of seventeen-point-three mil and the locals are all over it," Joel explained.

He was rather annoyed with her as it was so early in the morning and his temperament was short, but he continued undaunted. "His wife is newly pregnant with their first child and I want you to do a follow-up to cover this as a human-interest story. You know, are lottery winners really lucky?

Supposedly, they tried for a long time to have a family and she's high risk, so go easy on her."

Marty had scrunched into a sitting position as soon as she recognized Joel's voice. She blinked long and hard one time, then stared at the clock, trying to focus on Joel's instructions and this ungodly time of the morning. The large red numbers glowed 3:43 a.m.

"Marty are you listening?" Joel snarled with growing impatience.

"Yes. What kinda accident did you say it was again?" Marty stumbled with her words as she recalled what he just said. "Some tractor-trailer repair shop? What's the address?" she queried sleepily as she strung her questions together.

"It's Rory's Tractor-Trailer Repair Shop at 26345 Miccosukee Road," Joel replied. "They think the owner was killed last night in an accident. I texted you everything," he grunted.

"Oh yeah, it's coming back to me now. They were gonna donate some of the money to build a shelter for battered women and abused children," she said with fond recollection. "That's what makes this a national story. That's right, they were one of several winners." Marty was remembering the details of her first story with the family.

"When I say it's a national story, it's a national story," Joel growled into her ear. He figured after all their years together, she'd know when to question his judgment.

"My God, how awful," Marty exclaimed as she pushed back the hair from her face and shook her head in disbelief. "I can take it from here. I'll be there first thing in the morning. What about the camera crew?" Marty asked as she realized it was going to be another long day.

"Already on their way. They're taking the van for an uplink," Joel told her. "I called them first so they could meet you on location. Be ready for at least the nine o'clock lead-in, sooner if you can break in ahead of other media. Spend most of the day getting the widow's story. Then wrap up with the latest on the candidates. Got that, kiddo?" He questioned.

"Yup!" Marty responded with as much enthusiasm as she could muster at that hour of the morning. "I'll be in touch. Thanks, Joel." She hung up the phone with some effort. She sat silently for a moment and watched the time on the alarm clock change to 3:59 a.m. Then she threw back the covers, stretched, yawned out loud, and planted her feet on the floor. Her day had begun.

For Marty, a hot shower and a cup of coffee had become the equivalent of magic beans. Although they're simple pleasures, for a field reporter they sometimes were often as elusive as a Pulitzer, especially in foreign countries. Living out of a suitcase had its challenges.

Marty took advantage of the early hour and lingered in the shower for almost thirty minutes. She was dressed and ready by five o'clock. Her carry-on bag was already packed. She just had time to stop by the coffee shop before rushing to the airport about fifteen minutes away.

Relaxed inside the airplane, Marty prepared preliminary questions for the interview with the story's widow. It was such a tragic one. Life sucks, Marty thought to herself as she sipped vitality from her third cup of over-priced coffee she'd brought on board.

Now that she had a new assignment, it would take a lot of her personal resources to land the interview with his widow. Getting in to see her wouldn't be easy. She wasn't sure if she'd remember her from an interview two years ago. Marty had to sell herself to Rory's widow and convince her that she was the right reporter for her exclusive interview.

The plane landed a bit early, thanks to a tailwind, and Marty caught a taxi to the location.

When she arrived, the site was buzzing with crime scene specialists, police detectives, on-lookers, reporters, and camera crews. The yellow-and-black crime scene tape stretched around the perimeter of the building and the press were apparently still waiting for a statement from the medical examiner.

She put on her press pass as the taxi came to a halt. She paid the driver and bolted from the car with her carry-on and headed straight for the CNB unit's van. She dumped her bag inside and caught a quick briefing from the crew of three, Max, Sam, and Howard.

Howard was the seasoned one, 47, and getting tired of field coverage, whereas Max and Sam were both in their early thirties. Sam was an outgoing people-person, but Max was the polar opposite. He was self-absorbed and liked living in his own world.

Howard daily defined the line between tasteful journalism and tabloid sensationalism. He knew sometimes getting the human-interest side of the story meant knowing when to stop the camera. He had a sixth sense for knowing when more wasn't better. His moral journalism still appealed to the baby boomers but was fading fast in modern reporting. It was what Marty most admired about him. Anymore, it seemed the more salacious the story, the better it's reception.

"What's the scoop?" Marty asked to all in general as she shielded her eyes from the sun and looked from face to face, waiting for a response from one of them.

Howard spoke first. "There's not much to tell. We're still waiting for the second statement to give us a positive ID on the body. They think it's the owner, Rory Phillips. All I know for sure is that whoever it was, he was smashed like a bug when the cabover fell on him. I dunno. At any rate, a man's dead, very, very dead," he trailed off.

Sam interrupted. "Yeah, guess that's what's taking so long. It's the clean-up of all that mess and trying to gather evidence if there is any."

Marty cringed and turned her face away from the thought of the scene that Sam continued to describe from supposition.

Max was sitting inside the van, playing with the uplink and appeared to be only half-listening to the conversation. This was normal since Max always seemed more interested in electronics than people. He glanced up at the three clustered just outside the van's open door and apathetically shrugged. He grunted as he kept his hand on his earpiece and readjusted some frequencies.

"Well, anyway," Marty interjected. "I get the idea. Not a pretty sight. Do they know how it happened?" she asked as they waited for the pending update.

"Not a lot of details on that end either, Shorty." Howard gave her that nickname years ago when she was younger and as green as they come. He was the only one who called her that, but she liked the term of endearment and all the history they shared together. As far as their story went, they had to play the waiting game before they'd get their answers.

Marty had been in Miami covering the general election campaign and the vetting process of illegal immigrants and refugees coming into the U.S. before Joel reassigned her to Rory's death in Tallahassee.

On the evening of her second day in Miami, Marty went straight to her hotel room. She opened the door with her plastic card key as quickly as possible and collapsed inside the door as she momentarily shut the day out of her mind.

She dropped her purse on the floor next to the bed. She ran her fingers through her hair and grasped the back of it for a long moment before letting go. About five minutes passed while she slowly moved to her closet to change into her favorite oversized blue-and-white-striped lounging shirt and matching solid blue shorts. Leaning against the wall, she pulled off her bone-colored slings and massaged her toes with obvious relief.

She slipped on her soft, white scuffs and shuffled over to crack open the mini bar. She grabbed two cylinders of bottled water and a yellow package of peanut M&Ms and set them on the coffee table in front of her. She then approached the executive business desk and searched the center drawer for a directory of the hotel's amenities.

After finding it, she sank onto the sofa with one foot tucked beneath her and reached for a bottle of water and the M&Ms from the coffee table. She jerked open the pop-top valve of her water, tossed her head back and guzzled the chilled mountain stream down her parched throat.

She paused only for a quick breath and continued eagerly drinking, this time squeezing the bottle, allowing the water to rush into her mouth. It caused overflowing trickles to spurt out of the corner of her lips and flow down her chin. She didn't care. She was thirsty from the humidity of the Miami heat.

She ripped open the bag of M&Ms and began nibbling on them one or two at a time while she browsed through the hotel's amenities and menus. Her stomach was slightly nauseous from the day's events, which left her with an apathetic appetite. She stopped munching on the M&Ms, set them back on the coffee table and finally made a reasonable selection.

She ordered room service from the hotel's main fine dining restaurant, The Reef. After reading the menu, she realized she was hungrier than she thought. She had the chef's special: chicken teriyaki, asparagus tips, seasoned baby potatoes, a croissant and, for a treat, she ordered cherries jubilee, her favorite dessert. After the day she had, she felt she earned a few extra calories.

She picked up the remote, clicked on the TV and flopped onto the bed, flipping mindlessly through the channels. She finally selected an episode of *King of Queens*, lowered the volume and closed her eyes.

She was covering the story of illegal immigrants and refugees. It was physically and mentally challenging. Both sides of the story made sense. Marty was looking for a re-run, no-brainer show that would ease her mind, which was seared with images of pleading eyes and the desperate cases of immigrants, some whose cultures are barbaric compared to the culture in the United States.

But keeping our country safe is paramount for all who live here, and it was argued that allowing too many illegal immigrants into our country would raise crime rates, overwhelm our welfare system, and take jobs away from Americans. Legal immigration is purposed for refugees from countries with civil uproars.

It was an election year, and immigration was the primary hot button issue of the race.

One opponent was for immigration, wanting to keep America's boarders open, allowing the 'poor and huddled masses' into our country. Whereas the sitting president was against it to the point that some would call it an extreme. He was wanted no illegal aliens and didn't support an easy path to citizenship either.

But to look at all the refuges from poverty-torn lands left Marty hollow and disturbed. She lay motionless on the bed for several moments as she let go of the day's fatigued depression. She subconsciously allowed her mind to drown in the voices of Carrie and Doug, who was plotting once again to keep something from Carrie.

She reached across the bed for the remote and flipped to the preview channel to the see what else was on. She desperately hoped to find a familiar movie. However, after watching the choices scroll by, she muted the sound and emptied the rest of M&Ms into her mouth and started for the bathroom.

She couldn't help but notice the tanning effects of the sunshine state. She curled her thick hair into a loose knot and secured it with a large clip at the back of her long blonde hair. She unbuttoned her nightshirt with quick ease, as it was so well-worn from constant use that the buttonholes were now larger than normal and, consequently, nearly unbuttoned itself.

She checked the water temperature, adjusted it slightly to a lukewarm rain and stepped inside. Ahhh, she thought to herself, a simple shower is the cheapest form of therapy on earth. She lathered and rinsed quickly, then massaged her muscles as the pulsating water revived her.

Knock. Knock. Knock. "Room service." A masculine voice announced himself.

"Damn! I forgot about dinner," Marty muttered to herself as she shut off the water and reached for a towel. "I'll be right there. Just give me a minute," she shouted as she hurriedly finished drying herself.

The towel slumped to the floor as she hopped into her shorts, having to stretch them over wet patches of skin here and there. She then reached for her shirt and was still buttoning the bottom of it as she opened the door.

"Good evening, Ms. Saunders," the server greeted her with a low sexy tone. It was hotel protocol to greet the guests by name as often as possible. The personal touch often spelled the difference between stiffs and tips in the hospitality industry and a wise man knew which side of his bread to butter.

"My name is Seth and I'll be your server this evening. Would you like me to set this on the table for you?" he inquired as he eyed her up and down.

"Yes, please. That'll be fine, thank you," Marty acknowledged, as she glanced up from buttoning her shirt. She noticed that he had an extraordinary smile and pretended rapt attention as he began presenting her dinner selection.

Seth continued, "Next, we move on to some lovely side dishes, seasoned potatoes and a fresh croissant. To complete your dining experience is one of our evening specialties, flambeed cherries jubilee. It's one our finest desserts. I can flambé it now or leave the matches with you."

"That sounds wonderful. Please go ahead and light it," she replied and shot him a coy smile.

She remembered she still had paperwork to do. "Just let me sign for that," Marty said as she tried to shut down the conversation. She leaned forward in her chair and reached for the pen in Seth's hand. Their fingers twisted together briefly before she shot him a 'nice try' look and he relinquished the pen into her hand.

Marty smiled with satisfaction as she locked the door behind him and thought to herself, *I've been lonely too long.* She crossed the room and began her meal with the cherries jubilee.

Chapter Three

The Call

The scene was buzzing with reporters waiting impatiently for confirmation of the victim and the facts surrounding his death. It was almost time for the live report. Howard patted Marty on the knee twice, trying to calm her nerves.

"God, does anyone know how wife and the baby are doing?" Marty questioned. She was a bit nervous about her possible upcoming interview. "Has anyone heard anything from her yet? Has she broken her silence?" she queried, hoping for a new response.

"Haven't heard," Sam mumbled. "You know everything we know at this point. Didn't the guy win some big lottery over a year or so ago and was gonna donate money to build a shelter or something like that?" Sam inquired as he stepped out of the van to stretch his legs.

"Just think, you finally win all that money and then wham," Sam smacked his leg for emphasis, "You're dead."

"Well, at least his wife and baby won't have to suffer financially." Marty put her two cents in.

Howard added, "She's set, for life if she invests wisely," Howard concurred with sympathy in his voice. He was thinking about how his wife would cope with financial consequences should this situation ever befall his bride of twenty-three years.

"You're so right," Marty agreed. "Geeze, she's got so much to deal with, I can't imagine how much worse it'd be if she had to worry about money right now."

"I'm going for coffee," Max said as he stretched his arms over his head and yawned. "Anyone comin' with me?" he asked as he looked at Sam.

"Sure. I'm in. Who wants what?" Sam responded more out of habit than from unfamiliarity.

"Where ya headed?" Marty urged.

"There's a quick mart down the road a couple of blocks on the left," Sam informed them. "We spotted it on the way in. You want the usual, Marty?"

"Yes, please." Marty lightly patted Howard on the back as a gesture of comradery. "You goin' too?" she questioned, knowing it would be a first. The crew had a routine, and it would be unusual for Howard to leave the site whenever a story could break at any moment.

Sam and Max almost always made the run together and were never gone a minute longer than necessary. Everyone needed each other and they all worked well together. As a team, they had worked together off and on for the better part of four years. And so far, none of them had experienced any serious ego infractions.

"Nope." Howard spoke with his usual matter-of-fact candor. "I'm waiting with you, Shorty."

"I know." Her voice was just above a whisper as she watched Sam and Max disappear around a corner. Marty glanced at her watch. It was already 8:15 a.m. She sat down next to Howard and began to fidget with her phone as she eyed the building's exterior for movement.

"Can't rush leg work, kiddo. We'll be live at nine with whatever we have, so relax," he advised.

"Oh, it's not that. I'm just wondering about his wife and baby. How do I interview her, *if* I interview her?" she pondered while thinking out loud. "I can't fathom how devastating this must be for her. What kind of thoughts must be flooding her mind? How overwhelmed she must feel." Marty sighed deeply and shook her head no.

"I hope her baby is okay. I wonder if she has family here," she questioned to no one in particular. Without warning, she sprung to her feet and was pacing back and forth in front of the van.

Suddenly, she spun around to face Howard. She had that look in her eye that he had become accustomed to over the years. It was sort of a dauntless, light bulb idea look that he knew meant subjugation was certain and soon.

"Whatcha' up to, Shorty?" Howard looked puzzled. "Checkin' your messages?"

She almost always had her phone in her hand or on her person. "I can't sit here anymore. I need answers," she stated firmly. Her voice now harbored aggressive propensity.

She scrolled quickly through her contacts. She wasn't angry, just frustrated with herself for not thinking of this obvious source when she first arrived. After all, any first-year journalism student would have already done this by now.

"And no, I'm not checking my messages, but I'm about to leave a few." She quickly scrolled through her phone list, found the number she needed, dialed it, and anxiously listened for an answer. Once again, she began pacing in front of the van when, surprisingly, a voice answered on the fourth ring.

Marty locked eyes with Howard as she began to speak. In a moment, Howard knowingly closed his eyes, smiled confidently, and mimicked her sigh of relief as he made the connection too. She would have her answers shortly.

Chapter Four

Marguerite

The room inspired and rejuvenated the senses. It was immaculately clean but not sterile. The shades of green in the room ranged from soft pastel to vibrant rain forest. One wall was painted a soft peridot green, while the rest of the walls were knotted pine. A terra cotta flagstone fireplace was the focal point of the room. It was trimmed with milk-white, hand-hewn, polished stones which glowed warm hues of red, orange, and blue reflections when the fireplace was burning.

Positioned in the center of the mantle was a first edition of *Uncle Tom's Cabin*, which was braced by a silver antique book holder. A pair of wireframe spectacles and an old-fashioned pipe were set in front the book. The tranquility was shattered by the ring of a cell phone.

Marguerite Montanez ceased her dusting and searched for her phone. Let's see, she thought to herself. She didn't leave it in the guest room or her pocket as she checked her apron. She glanced around the room and momentarily spotted it on the black baby grand. She retrieved it by the third ring but couldn't answer it until the fourth.

"Hello," she answered. Marguerite was in her early fifties, of Mexican descent and cleaned distinguished homes of Tallahassee's wealthy elite. She was well-educated and well-spoken but with a heavy accent. She made a very good living, and even had a waiting list for her coveted services. She was formerly employed by the state capital as director of domestic engineering before the new administration moved in. Prior to that she worked as a nanny.

"Hello?" Marty's voice was hopeful as she heard someone pick up after placing the call to her former nanny. She was banking on Marguerite's information, which to date had a flawless track record. "Will wonders never cease? I thought you fell off the planet," she responded in welcomed surprise. "It's been a while. Is everything all right?" Her voice was filled with true concern.

"Yes. Everything's fine at my end," Marty said as she returned concern. "Is everyone in your world doing okay, too?"

"Absolutely. They're all great," Marguerite assured.

"I'm calling because I need your help," Marty said while she continued to pace.

"Sure. What's up?" Marguerite asked.

Marty swallowed hopefully as she looked at Howard, who was still sitting in the van's open doorway. She drew in a breath and began. "There was an accident last night here in Tallahassee and a man is dead."

Marguerite's gasp interrupted her. "Who is it?" she queried. Because of their special relationship, Marguerite had been a confidential informant for a few of Marty's stories before, but they never involved a death. It was usually your typical moral scandal. They were serious issues but nothing on the level of homicides or suicides. Therefore, her curiosity was piqued, but so was her caution.

"Yes. I'm afraid so, Marguerite. It happened last night at a place called Rory's Tractor-Trailer Repair Shop located on Miccosukee Road," she reported as she referenced her notebook. "Do you know the area?"

"Miccosukee Road?" Marguerite repeated slowly. "Yeah. I know it well," she answered with confidence.

"Great," Marty said as she flashed a quick smile at Howard before continuing. Her pen quit writing as she was talking, and Howard came to her rescue with another one. "I need you to find out what you can about Rory Phillips. He's the owner of the tractor trailer repair shop, and we're pretty sure he was the victim, too." Marty finished her mouthful with relief.

By now Marguerite was sitting comfortably on the customized overstuffed forest-green sofa. She seldom allowed herself breaks when she was working. She much preferred to get the job done thoroughly and expeditiously so that she could schedule the day to her liking.

Marguerite shook her head and clicked her tongue before answering. "I'll see what I can find out. Do you have a home address or know if they had a housekeeper?"

"Uh, do we have a home address?" Marty repeated, as she questioned Howard with her eyes. He jumped to his feet and shuffled papers inside the van for the original media statements the crew received that morning. He found it underneath his special 'good luck' travel ashtray his wife gave him nearly 29 years ago, before they got married. Quickly, he scanned it for an address. "Bingo. Try 129 Buck Lake Road," he coached.

Marty continued after providing the address, "I should be here most of the day. I'm at the repair shop now waiting for an update before we go live at nine o'clock."

She glanced at her watch: 8:38 a.m. Marty hurried the conversation to a close. "I have to go now. It's getting close to airtime. I can't thank you enough for all your help, Marguerite. Take care and we'll talk soon."

"Sounds good. I should have something for you right away." Marguerite ended the call and began dialing her friends.

It's common knowledge that there's no faster form of communications than gossip. After 29 years in domestic engineering and nanny businesses, Marguerite had established an extensive network of reliable 'gossipers.' If there was a connection anywhere in the cleaning or au pair industry, either domestic or commercial, Marguerite would know about it within the next twenty minutes.

"Can't believe I didn't do that first thing this morning," Marty grumbled to herself and Howard.

"Well, it's done now," Howard consoled her and inhaled the first drag from a fresh cig. It was right about then when all the commotion started. It was time for the second media release.

Howard and Marty snatched their equipment and sprinted for their spot in the crowd of reporters. Marty was shoving her way to the front of the line as if her microphone were a guidance missile. Sam was suddenly behind her with his camera, bopping, and weaving his way through the throng like her shadow.

Max was in the van with his ears on connecting the uplink. Howard had joined him after Sam relieved him from camera duty. It was 8:59 a.m. and the media statement would begin with a shocking but anticipated announcement. It was at exactly nine o'clock when the press received confirmation of the identity of the victim.

"Reports now confirm that at approximately 7:30 p.m. last night, Rory Phillips, the owner of Rory's Tractor Trailer and Repair Shop, was killed in what appears to be a freak accident," stated Frank Henry, the media relations officer for the Tallahassee Police Department. He continued his statement.

"The victim was positively identified almost an hour ago. Complete details will be released at the conclusion of that investigation. We have no further comments at this time." Frank Henry delivered the verification of the victim's identity and the few details they were willing to share with the public. Henry braced himself for the dreaded barrage of questions from the reporters who thought they could get more on the story than what they'd been told.

Marty ejected herself from the group and dashed back to the van. Max was ready as usual. All systems were a go at CNB headquarters in New York City. They used a shot of the building's exterior as their background, and Marty delivered the remainder of her report on cue.

She added a personal touch to her report, but with so little to go on, she felt it left a lot to be desired. "We are live in front of Rory's Tractor Trailer Repair Shop," she began. Marty could hear herself saying the words but wishing Marguerite had called before the nine o'clock go-live. She felt herself rush the report. She was tired from the earlier-than-normal start of her day and frustrated from the immense lack of information.

She was still live on camera, but her thoughts were wandering. By the time she began her last comment, she resolved to land the exclusive interview with the widow. There was a story here of real human interest, and she was going to honor the victim's memory by telling it the way his widow wanted it told. As a final note to this sad affair ..." she was on the homestretch, "this is Marty Saunders reporting live from Tallahassee for CNB."

It was over. Marty disengaged her microphone and earpiece. The time was now 9:07 a.m. and Marty was thirsty for another cup of coffee. As she approached the van, Max extended his arm and handed her a cardboard tray filled with her usual convenience store snacks.

"Oh, yes. Thanks, Max," she said with an eagerness in her voice. Marty swallowed hard as she devoured her blueberry muffin and dug into a raspberry yogurt between gulps of coffee. Things were quiet for a moment. Then the ringing of a cell phone sent the group rushing for its source. It was Marty's phone. "Yes? Hello?" Marty inquired with enthusiasm.

Chapter Five

Information Highway

"Hey, Marty," Marguerite was speaking with quiet excitement. "I've got your scoop.

"Yeah, go ahead. Are Mrs. Phillips and the baby okay?" Marty questioned.

"They're doing as well as possible. Her doctor saw her this morning and gave her a mild sedative that won't hurt the baby. She has a nurse with her now and some family too," Marguerite informed.

Marguerite took a breath. "She is resting most of the time but wants to stay awake for more news from police and funeral arrangements." It was as though she couldn't get the words out fast enough.

"Isn't her family doing most of that for her?" Marty asked.

"As much as possible. But her housekeeper, Maria, told me that his wife, Beth Phillips, wants to do as much as possible on her own. Maria cleans for them every week. She cleans their home on Friday's and the shop on Thursday's. Apparently, she was talking with her husband on the cell just before he died, and she swears he had his gun with him," Marguerite gulped into the phone.

Marty returned her enthusiasm by asking, "You're kidding. Do you know what time the call took place?" Marty's excitement was growing now.

Marguerite continued, "Yeah. Maria said it was about 7:15 p.m. last night. His wife was cooking a special anniversary and Valentine's Day dinner and wanted to know when he'd be home, so she could time the meal with his arrival."

"What else did she say?" Marty coaxed as she took notes. She had all the tech devices to increase her productivity, but she still liked a pen and pad for notes. It was easier to flip through the pages than play back a recording or scroll through her emails.

Marguerite added, "She said her husband heard a noise out in the shop and was on his way to check it out when his phone went dead. Beth begged him to call the police instead of checking on the noise."

Marguerite informed. "There'd been a lot of break-ins in the area, and she wanted him to come home rather than take his chances at encountering an intruder. But he told her he had his gun with him, and the alarm system was on, so he'd be okay... said he'd be right home."

"What kind of gun did he have, Marguerite? Did she say?" Marty could hardly get the questions out fast enough.

"A semi-automatic of some caliber. He kept it hidden in a false bottom in his desk; apparently, Rory was a very cautious fellow. He had a special security system at business and his house. He didn't want her to feel vulnerable or unsafe anymore. She was raped when she was in college. From what Maria told me, I guess it was pretty brutal." Marguerite's voice was infused with sympathy.

"So, that's why Mr. Phillips was so cautious." Marty recalled that Beth didn't seem to be a victim. "From what I remember, she came across as a strong and determined woman."

"Yep. Well, she worked hard to get over it." Marguerite continued. "That's why the fancy security systems in their home and business."

"But why the gun? Was this just a precaution too or did he purchase it recently? Do you know?" Marty's questions were firing faster now.

"No. It wasn't a recent purchase. He was a gun collector and kept most of them in display cases at home." Marguerite was on a roll. "He had five of what he called 'active' guns that he kept for self-defense. He kept two of them at the office, two of them at home and one in his car or on his person. He had a concealed weapons permit." Marguerite drew in a breath and paused for Marty's reaction.

Marty didn't disappoint. Quickly, she shot off more questions Marguerite anticipated. "Why so many guns?" Marty was surprised to learn of the arsenal. She could understand one or two, but five, just for protection? "It seems a bit excessive, don't you think?"

"Yeah. But there's more. He taught her how to fire them and how to handle shotguns so if he wasn't there, she could protect herself. He kept two semi-automatics in their bedroom upstairs and a shotgun in the pantry." Marguerite really knew how to deliver the needed information.

"So, she knows how to handle a gun, then?" Marty repeated.

"Oh, yeah," Marguerite responded. "He taught her how to use them. He grew up on a cattle ranch, so it was status quo to have guns and know how to use them. His father taught him to hunt too. Guns were a big part of his lifestyle and he carried it over into his marriage."

Marty interjected, "Tell me more about the guns he kept at the shop."

Marguerite sucked in a deep breath before answering. "Well, like I said, he kept two at the office. He kept one in a secret compartment under his secretary's desk and one in a false bottom in his desk drawer."

Marty was excited now and it was obvious in her voice. "I see. So how did Maria discover the gun in Mr. Phillips' office?"

Marguerite continued tirelessly. "She was cleaning in his office once when she accidentally knocked some paperclips off his desk, some of them landed under the desk when the phone rang. That's when she bumped her head against the gun case. It was just a fluke that she found it."

Marty quickly followed with her next question. "Did she know about the gun in Mr. Phillips' drawer? The one with the false bottom?" she asked eagerly, wondering if she knew of both guns.

"Oh, yeah," Marguerite assured Marty. He showed it to Maria for her protection since she often cleaned when no one was there. He wanted her to be safe, but ever since the break-ins, she'd been cleaning during the day while the business was open and people were around her."

Marty prodded, "So why is Beth so concerned about the gun? There is no mention of any gun in the press release. Yet, you're saying that she's claiming her husband had one of his guns with him. Is that right?" Marty had to verify her source.

"Absolutely," Marty confirmed.

Marty was filled with more questions than answers. "Do the police know about the gun? Was there anything missing at the shop? Any sign of robbery? Was something out of place or suspicious looking?" Marty sounded excited about this new information.

"No. Nothing was missing, no tools or electronics or anything. However, they did find his wallet and smashed cell phone, but not the gun. They think the thief must have taken it," Marguerite stated.

"So, the police know about the missing gun?" Marty gasped almost breathlessly.

"Yup. They know. That was the first thing out of his wife's mouth." Marguerite was happy she was helping her dear friend.

Marty's heart skipped a beat as she asked for clarification. "What are you saying, Marguerite?" Marty spoke the words slowly as she began to deduce the obvious but totally unexpected. "Does Mrs. Phillips think her husband was shot to death and then crushed? Are we talking murder?" Marty lowered the phone for a moment. She was stunned as she looked at Howard.

"Yeah! She doesn't know the order of events or even if he was shot for sure, but she knows it wasn't an accident," Marguerite answered in equal disbelief.

Marty was shocked. "So, there never was a robbery?"

Marguerite continued as Marty slowly focused on her words. "It is hard to say, but the wife's insisting the police find her husband's missing gun. She knows he had it with him around 7:15 p.m. last night and that it didn't just disappear on its own." Marguerite spoke as if she could feel Beth's pain and suspicion.

Marty's thoughts were running amok. *"And I thought this was a sleeper story!* Sad for sure, but now *murder?"* Marty focused her thoughts and continued pumping information from her friend. "What about the autopsy, has it been done yet?"

"No, not yet. It's unclear when it will be done, but the police insisted on a rush job. Beth is chomping at the bit. She's determined to talk to coroner herself. She doesn't want her family to do it for her." Marguerite had given all the information she had.

Marty ended the exchange expressing gratitude to Marguerite. Marty had her story, but questions remained, and the answers were with the coroner's office and the victim's widow.

Chapter Six

The Coroner

"Beth, the coroner is on the phone. Beth, are you awake? It's the coroner." Janice tried to rouse Beth from a slight doze. She sat down on the bed beside her sister and lightly shook her awake.

She'd been dozing on and off most of the day. She refused to take any more sedatives to protect her baby and because she wanted to be alert for the coroner's call. Finally, it came. She sat up in bed while Janice propped up the pillows behind her. As Janice started to leave, Beth took her hand and squeezed it firmly. "Thank you, for everything," Beth said quietly.

"You're welcome," Janice replied as she returned a gentle squeeze to Beth's hand and smiled at her sweet sister. "Call me if you need anything. We're all waiting for the news too." She left the room and silently closed the door behind her.

"Hello?" Beth spoke as if she wasn't sure there really was a coroner at the other and of the telephone. Naturally, she was still in shock. Her system was working overtime to protect herself and the baby. Nevertheless, she was a woman of exceptionally strong spirit, and her mind was surprisingly clear as the conversation commenced. She'd had a little time to compose herself and was operating on adrenaline.

Beth had been thrown from a horse when she was 14 years old, breaking her collarbone and fracturing her left elbow. She knew physical pain, but it was nothing compared to the pain and anguish she was feeling now. She was heartbroken. She blocked everything from her mind and focused on the conversation ahead of her.

"Mrs. Phillips?" Tony Davis asked, making sure he was talking with Mrs. Phillips and not a member of her household. He'd been talking with her sister all morning.

"Yes. This is Beth Phillips." Beth responses were automatic as she spoke the words into the receiver.

"I'm Tony Davis, the chief deputy coroner of Leon County. I finished the autopsy on your husband this morning," he said.

Beth had a fury of questions, starting with "What did you find? Was he impaired in any way?" That really wasn't what Beth wanted to ask, but she had to build her courage.

She knew Rory hadn't been drinking, but she figured that'd be the first thing the police would rule out. After all, everyone thought she was just overwrought from shock and the suddenness of Rory's death. They assumed being pregnant only added to her stressful and somewhat unpredictable condition. She'd heard the buzz around her implying she was 'misremembering' the facts. She had to take the questions one at a time and slowly to build her nerve.

"Impaired?" Davis clarified the question.

Beth responded, "Yes. Had my husband been drinking or was there any substance in his body that could have altered his judgment in any way? Something that might have caused him to become careless and fall when he was under that thing?" She decided to start with a question to which she already knew the answer.

Dr. Davis assuaged her fear. "I see what you're getting at, Mrs. Phillips. Quite honestly, I have found nothing to indicate any sensory impairment. Your husband's blood-alcohol concentration was .02, which was well within the non-intoxicated range."

"In short, Mrs. Phillips, your husband's body in no way indicated any alcohol or foreign substance in his system. It may take a couple of weeks to get back a full toxicology report, but he seemed stone cold sober," Dr. Davis assured her.

"I see. Well, tell me very candidly, Dr. Davis, is it?" Beth hesitated slightly as she recalled his name. "What else did you find when you examined my husband's body?" Beth asked, realizing that she would never again feel the warmth of his body next to hers.

"I found nothing unusual in your husband's body when I examined him." It was common practice for investigations to withhold evidence details. Per the request of the Tallahassee police, he needed to keep the evidence of a spent bullet to himself and Rory's immediate family for the 24 hours. He had dug it out of the inside of Rory's left femur earlier that morning.

"However, I was puzzled by a few things at the scene," he admitted with hesitation. He didn't want to remind her there was very little of her husband's remains or how hard it was for him to do any real assessment of his state of health since he was crushed to death; but he was puzzled by the position of his body.

"I knew it," Beth said as she breathed relief into the phone. "What did you find, Dr. Davis? I know this wasn't an accident. I know it. There was someone there with him. I heard him," She was hoping to get some answers. "Tell me everything, Dr. Davis, and don't leave out anything." She wanted to focus on his words and not the implication they had in her life.

"Well, the first thing that bothered me about your husband's death was the position of his body. Wasn't he supposed to be checking on some mechanic's work?" he asked.

"Yes, there was a new guy that Rory hired a week or so ago. I think his name was Tim something or other. He bragged about his work a lot, a real hotshot, I guess. It's a common problem." She and Rory encountered this malady often.

"Anyway, he said he had to check his work. I remember the time because Rory and I were talking on the phone around 7:15 p.m. last night and we spoke for about five minutes." Beth remembered.

Beth was squirming in her bed as she recalled their last conversation. Her back was sore and her joints ached. Her heart was numb, and she knew she was still in shock and that the real pain was yet to come.

She swallowed hard, ingested a deep breath and continued. "I wanted to know when he'd be home. We had plans." She closed her eyes to block out the pain of the memory. "Rory said he'd come straight home after he checked things out." Beth spoke as if she were giving bland facts about a TV show she'd just watched.

"Did he say what the noise was? Or what it sounded like?" the coroner prodded.

"He didn't say, but it alarmed him enough to make a point of checking it out and take his gun with him. It was his favorite. Well, his favorite handgun anyway." She tapered off for a moment, then continued.

"He kept it in his office in his desk in a false bottom drawer he had made for it. I remember telling him to call the police. There'd been so many break-ins in that area lately that I figured it was probably our turn. Then I heard the alarm go off." Her voice faded.

"So, you were still talking with your husband up until when, 7:15 p.m. or 7:20 p.m. that evening? Is that right?" Dr. Davis reiterated for clarification.

"Yes. I'd say approximately 7:15, as I distinctly remember agreeing with him that he'd be home around 7:30." Beth was recalling every word they'd spoken. "He was interrupted from his paperwork by the noise in the shop."

Beth kept going. "We were speaking when I heard his phone hit the floor. I heard an unfamiliar voice say something, but I couldn't make out what it was. I tried his cell again, but it dropped the call. That's when I called the police and I guess you know the rest." Her voice trailed off.

"The conversation you had with your husband helps me narrow down the time of death. I knew it was approximately between 7:38 p.m. and 8:00 p.m., but with what you just told me, it had to be between 7:20 p.m. to 7:45 p.m."

"That might help the police when they question possible witnesses who may have seen someone around the shop at that time," he started to explain, but Beth interrupted him.

"Were there witnesses?" she asked hopefully. "Denton thought it was a long shot." She remembered his annoying Southern drawl but knew he was a kind man.

"No witnesses yet, but it's still early in the investigation," he encouraged.

"You suspect something too, don't you, Dr. Davis?" Beth questioned him with anticipation. She was secretly hoping that he'd made a great mistake and the body he'd examined wasn't her husband's. She stayed focused on her questions. "I can hear it in your voice. Now, what were you saying about the position of my husband's body?"

Beth was more composed than she anticipated. Perhaps it was because she knew she had to be if she was going to get to the bottom of things. She forced every thought of loss from her mind and focused on the information as facts, only facts.

Davis did think Rory's death was suspicious, but he masterfully and routinely avoided these kinds of questions.

Denton was in the process of ruling out Beth as a suspect. After all, other than the widow's claim that she heard an intruder, she had no alibi. She claimed to be home cooking dinner, but no one could collaborate her story. She could have driven herself to the shop and made his death appear to be accidental. By her own admission, they knew she was proficient with handguns, rifles and shotguns.

However, they had the lottery winnings, so money couldn't have been the motive. She was newly pregnant with their first child, so why knock him off when they were about to become the family they'd been praying for? He was faithful, if for no other reason than he never had opportunity. The two worked together all day and were together all night. No. There was no motive, but they had to rule her out, no matter how improbable a scenario. But starting with the recovered bullet, evidence supporting an intruder was now irrefutable.

Davis wasn't a homicide detective per se, and the Tallahassee Police Department resented the coroner's office, him specifically, for his heroic sleuthing attempts in the past. His job ended with the completion of the autopsy, or so he was often reminded by the TPD.

Davis continued explaining his findings. "Well, his body was found lying face down and angled sharply to the left and his legs were straight out, as if he tried to lunge out of the way," he explained.

"I'd have to make a more accurate study, of course, but from the way things were when I got there, had it been an accident, it's likely he would have been found lying face up, not face down." He cleared his throat before he continued. He hoped his words wouldn't upset her. He hated dealing with crying women, especially over the phone.

He drew in a deep breath and explained, "You see, it's reflexes to look up when you hear a noise above your head. Now, there is very little chance that your husband could have been checking on someone's work without hearing the casing start to fall. He would try to jump clear, which might explain why his legs were straight out," Davis paused for a breath.

"Please continue, Dr. Davis." Beth was hanging on every word.

"It gets a bit confusing. It appears your husband was trying to jump clear of the housing, indicating that he'd heard the safeties snap. However, if he'd been checking on the wiring system, he would have been squatting, which wouldn't have given him time to try to jump clear. No matter how ya look at it, things just don't add up here." Beth waited patiently with anxiety for Davis to tell her everything.

"So, what are you trying to say, Dr. Davis?" Beth held her breath.

He let his words sink in for a moment. "Please realize," he paused to clear his throat again, "it's entirely possible that this was just an accident. However, semi-tractor truck cabover units have a safety system and safety releases, precisely to avoid these kinds of accidents. But the odds of both safety releases failing at the same time are pretty low."

His words simultaneously devastated and liberated Beth. Obviously, she was right. Rory's death hadn't been an accident, but how could she prove it? Who could have done such a thing? What's the motive? Her mind was sprinting.

She fixated her thoughts on a possible motive, then jerked herself back into the discussion. She heard what she had wanted to hear. Rory's death wasn't an accident. But why would an intruder go to such lengths to make it look like one? Who would want to kill her husband and why? She had to know more.

"Is that it? Is there anything else, Doctor?" Beth questioned after realizing she had forgotten to ask the obvious question. "Have you spoken with the police yet?"

"Yes. But I feel you have a right to know the facts firsthand, and I would rather you ask me your questions than the police. Your situation is hard enough without having to deal with second-hand information," he empathized.

"Thank you so much for your consideration, Dr. Davis. I can't tell you how much I agree with you or how much I'm depending on you to help me convince the police that my husband's death wasn't an accident," Beth stated unemotionally.

"Well, Mrs. Phillips, you do understand that what I just told you is hardly proof of foul play. I'm not a crime scene forensic expert. As a coroner, I deal with medical forensics and facts." He was trying to remind her that he wasn't a detective.

Beth's voice changed. Apprehension and foreboding started to swallow her. She needed someone to believe her, someone she could count on to help her find the truth about Rory's death. She silently wondered if Dr. Davis could help her. Would he take the time? Would he have the time? Why should her case matter more than the dozens of others that he deals with on a daily basis?

"Dr. Davis, will you help me? I mean, can you talk to the police and convince them to take my husband's death more seriously?" she pleaded. "You said yourself there are things that bother you about this case, that don't add up," Beth was holding her breath.

She waited for a reply, but when none came, Beth continued with emotion, "I ... I ... I know the angle of his body isn't enough by itself, but maybe it's enough to make them really investigate. After all, you did find a bullet in Rory's leg, and his gun is missing and with your help, maybe they'll treat his death as a possible homicide." She sounded both frantic and calm at the same time.

"Look, Mrs. Phillips," Davis said. "I'll make my report with all the facts and include my concerns as I voiced them to you. But I can't guarantee you that the police department will treat your husband's death with any more diligence than they already are."

"I'm sure they do take his death seriously, Mrs. Phillips, but you have to give the officers and the lab techs some time to sort things out." Tony tried to extend sympathy and yet set some boundaries as well. She needed to know what to expect and what time frames she should anticipate.

His attempt to combat her apprehension was futile at best, but then he never was adept at comforting women. He just wasn't a ladies man or the emotional type. Typically, he kept people at a distance. Occasionally, he let someone in, but it was far and few between.

He couldn't stand the feeling of being vulnerable and hated even more feeling out-of-control. He did, however, suspect something more than just an accident in relation to her husband's death and would make that fact crystal clear to Tallahassee's public servants. But from previous experience, he doubted it would make much difference.

Chapter Seven

It Was No Accident

"Oh. There is one more thing you should know, Mrs. Phillips," Tony Davis said. "We did find some hairs at the scene that didn't belong to your husband. They appear to be human. Also, there were some oily and bloody footprints found between the truck where your husband was killed. They could have been made by anyone."

Before she could interrupt him, he explained, "Now, understand that none of this is unusual evidence at this point. It's extremely common to find lots of human hairs at a crime scene. And due to the nature of your husband's business, it's quite common to expect oily footprints. They're probably nothing. Rest assured, Mrs. Phillips, we are going to follow up on all these leads, including the bloody footprints. If anything, out of the ordinary develops, I will call you. You have my word on that." He was trying to end the call.

"Thank you very much for all that you've done, Dr. Davis," Beth responded. "I'm especially thankful you called me directly. What will you do with the evidence? How is it processed and how long does it normally take before there are more answers?"

"The processing time varies considerably," he explained again. "Maybe give it a couple of weeks anyway. We'll match the hairs and shoe prints from all the employees and regular customers. Police will track the traffic in and out of your shop."

"We're looking to eliminate as many people as possible. You might say we're looking for the odd man out. We'll match clues with possible suspects, anyone that visited the shop recently that wasn't a regular. Things like that. Come on. Have a little faith in the system, Mrs. Phillips." He was hoping to encourage her.

"May I visit with you in person some time, Dr. Davis? Perhaps at your office?" Beth asked. He shook his head in surprise. He thought he'd been dutifully patient and explanatory with her. Nevertheless, he obliged.

"Sure, Mrs. Phillips," he responded with a sigh. "I don't know what more you hope to accomplish or what you're looking to find out, but I'm a public servant and I'm always available during normal working hours."

"You don't have normal working hours, Dr. Davis," Beth replied.

"That's true, Mrs. Phillips. But that's not my point. I'm available Monday through Friday from 9:00 a.m. to 5:00 p.m. I'd appreciate it if you'd respect my hours." By this time, Davis was tired of explaining and needed to get back to work.

"Very well, Doctor. I'll be in touch." Beth canceled the call just as Janice knocked on the door. "Come in," she called.

"How was it?" Janice hedged, not fully aware of Beth's emotional state.

"I was right. Rory *was* murdered," Beth blurted out. "The coroner thinks so, and so do I." Beth heard what she wanted to hear, and she wanted to believe his death wasn't by accident.

Beth continued while getting up, "But right now, I want to know how the funeral arrangements are going and then I want to talk with Captain Denton." She threw back the blankets and deposited her feet on the floor. She was getting out of bed whether anyone thought she should or not. "They think Rory was murdered," she repeated.

"Murdered? Murdered? Beth, are you sure?" Janice was in pure shock. "Who thinks he was murdered? Janice stumbled with her words. "How can it be murder when he was found like he was? I don't understand." Janice was utterly bewildered.

Beth answered her questions quickly. "The coroner thinks it was murder and it's my job to convince the police. After all, there have been a lot of break-ins in that area and it's not unreasonable to think things could have escalated to murder if the intruder or intruders were surprised by Rory."

Beth recited her information logically. A quiet calmness seemed to settle over her. The thought of Rory being murdered gave her a mission. She now had a purpose other than delivering a healthy baby which was job one. She knew she had to find Rory's murderer.

"What do you mean the coroner thinks it is murder, too?" Janice asked, dazed. "I understand your reasoning about the police, but what does the coroner know that the police don't? Are you really sure this was murder? It looks like an accident, Beth," Janice insisted.

"Yes. 'Murder.' I'm sure of it," Beth stated matter-of-factly. Her voice was low and deliberate. She finished tugging on her leggings and quickly shoved on a pair of slippers. "I'll tell you all about it later. I'll go over all the details as soon as I have them, but for now you need to keep this between us. Promise me you won't tell anyone. Not a word," Beth begged.

Janice shook her head back and forth in dismay and disbelief. She was digesting the magnitude of the information. Then she nodded her head yes and stated, "You have my word. I won't tell a soul but promise me you'll take care of yourself and the baby and keep me in the loop." Janice was now more worried than ever about her sister's well-being.

However, Janice had news of her own, "Right now, there are reporters on the lawn and on the phone, all clamoring for an interview with you. I've told them all to just get lost, except for one. I think you might want to talk with her. She's waiting for you downstairs."

Beth cut in, "Are you nuts? You know I don't want to talk with any reporters, for God's sake, Janice. What's wrong with you?" Beth was almost shouting.

Janice responded with equal volume, "No. I am not nuts. Believe me, you'll want to talk with her."

Beth was frantic as she spewed, "Why is she so different? Give me one good reason why I should want to air my tragedy to any reporter?"

Janice responded in a single sentence. "Because *she* knows about Rory's gun." Beth bounded down the stairs to confront the reporter. The public statement didn't include anything about Rory having a gun with him at the time of the accident, so Beth's interest was piqued. They purposely withheld that information pending the investigation.

"What do you know about my husband's gun?" Beth asked accusingly to the woman standing in front of her. She entered the recently remodeled basement which was now a combination trophy-recreation room and den. The den was physically separated from the other two rooms by a large wet bar.

The den was everything you'd expect it to be. It had built-in bookcases, two large mahogany desks, burgundy and green leather wing-backed chairs, and neat piles of paperwork everywhere. Dotted around the room were snapshots and portraits of Beth and Rory, some family members, and friends. Several scenes of Rory's kills were scattered among the family photos. It was obvious that Rory was an accomplished hunter.

Two large custom-framed pictures from different hunts were proudly displayed on the east wall. He had made a Boone and Crockett twice, once for a record mule deer killed in Colorado in 2003 and again for the record elk bagged in Montana in 2005. Achieving one Boone and Crockett was considered by most to be a lifetime achievement. But getting it twice in a lifetime was a real feat. These trophies adorned the walls.

Marty was admiring pictures when Beth's question startled her. She spun around to face her. Even newly widowed, she was lovelier in person than her pictures depicted.

Beth's hair was golden blonde and fine. She wore it short in a carefree bob style. She appeared very athletic both in person and in her photos. Her body was lean with defined muscles, and even while pregnant, she was obviously healthy and well disciplined.

Marty looked directly at her when she answered her first question. She knew this woman would tolerate nothing from anyone at this moment and she gladly yielded her respect. "I know it's missing," Marty stated with confidence. She wondered if Beth would remember her.

"How do you know this?" Beth asked straightaway.

"I can't tell you that. I can't divulge my sources," Marty replied.

"Of course, you can't," Beth retorted with ludicrous sarcasm. She wanted desperately to throw this reporter out of her home but remained as calm and reticent as possible. At this point, Beth was ready to extort information from anyone. She opened her mouth, ready to fire her next question when Marty beat her to the punch.

"Look, Mrs. Phillips, I want you to know how sorry I am about the loss of your husband. I sincerely mean that," Marty spoke with kindness.

Beth amputated her sentiments. "Spare me your condolences. What's your name? I can see you're with CNB. You look familiar. Who are you?" Beth asked, anxiously waiting for answers.

"I'm Marty Saunders. I do a lot of field reporting. That's probably why I look familiar to you," Marty said, extending her hand with her introduction.

"I interviewed you and your husband a couple of years ago when you won part of the state lottery, Marty tried to jog her memory. I did a human-interest piece regarding your desire to use some of the money to open a shelter for women and children." Beth accepted her handshake reluctantly and bought it back as she nodded her head yes, indicating recognition.

"Why is CNB interested in my husband's death? Aren't there more clamorous goings-on in the world right now?" Beth quipped. She was sizing up the woman standing in front of her, deciding whether she would be forthcoming with her information or hold back as much a she could. She was trying to remember the previous interview. They had done several and she wanted to recall their interaction as much as possible.

Marty caught Beth's eyes directly. "There are, I'm sure. But my boss sent me here to gather your story. I can only imagine how hard this must be for you," Marty stated. She moved closer to Beth. "I am so sorry for your loss. You must be devastated." Marty's concern was sincere.

Marty continued her explanation. "There is national interest in this story. It's a devastating twist of fate. People mourn with you when something like this happens, just as they were happy with you when your husband won the Mega Millions lottery a couple of years ago. People live vicariously, Mrs. Phillips." Marty trailed off as she realized how empty her words sounded.

Beth thought about that last statement for a moment. She had almost a million responses for it but decided to let it go. Come to think of it, she did kind of recognize her and remembered their previous interview. Maybe that's why Marty looked so familiar. Nevertheless, she had to stay in control of her emotions, so she fell back on etiquette. "Would you like something to drink?" Beth asked.

Marty responded, "No. Thank you. I'd rather talk if you don't mind. We have more in common than you might think." Marty was more empathetic to the situation than Beth knew. "I buried my fiancé when he was killed in the Boston Marathon bombing. It's been years but I still miss him dearly, and in many ways, it seems just like it was yesterday." Her voice went quiet.

Marty opened up before she could stop herself and explained her loss. "He was a real estate investor and was getting ready to run his first marathon." She paused to collect her thoughts again as she remembered waiting for him at home. While watching TV that day she witnessed his demise along with several others and knew too well how hard a tragic loss can be. "I understand your need for answers, Mrs. Phillips," Marty eased. "I really do."

"Beth," she corrected. "If we're going to play in the sandbox together, we should at least be on a first-name basis with each other. Please call me Beth."

"Marty," she returned the courtesy.

The way Beth looked at it, the story was going to hit the tabloids and the news, no matter what she said or didn't say. If she wanted any control, she should make friends with this reporter standing in front of her who already knew more about her husband's death than her own family.

Marty interrupted her thoughts, "I understand the results of the preliminary autopsy are due sometime this morning. Have you heard from the coroner's office yet?" Marty asked.

"Yes. I just finished speaking with him before I agreed to meet with you. His name is Dr. Tony Davis. He's the medical examiner assigned to my husband's case. He has his suspicions about my Rory's death, and so do I. How did you learn so much about me and my husband's death?" Beth questioned.

"My former nanny helps me out on occasion. I called early this morning for her help. She gave the information that led me to you." Marty wasn't sure how Beth would respond to the gossip mill, but she knew she had to be candid if she was going to win her trust.

"There. I just revealed my source, a code we reporters are imprisoned for sometimes. I trust you'll keep it between us. Yes?" Marty wondered if she'd made an egregious mistake, trusting this vulnerable woman.

Beth indicated for Marty to sit down while she took a seat across from her. "Yes. I'll keep your source between us." She mulled that over for a long minute. "So, your former nanny knows our maid, Maria. I'll have to have a word with her later."

Marty felt horrible. "Oh, please. I didn't mean to cause anyone problems. My nanny is always discreet. Please don't fire ..." Marty started to ask.

Beth cut her off, "I won't be firing her. But I must have a talk with her, especially now that all this has happened. I'll need to be able to count on her discretion now more than ever with reporters camping all about."

"But back to the coroner's report. He has suspicions about my husband's death. He thinks it might be murder." Beth wanted to move things along as quickly as possible. She knew her energy was limited.

Beth was wondering if she'd already said too much. "Look, if I'm going to talk with you about this, I want some assurances that you'll get the story straight and not sensationalize it for glory headlines and news ratings," Beth insisted.

"What kind of assurances can I give you, Mrs. Phillips, excuse me, Beth? I don't blame you for wanting reassurance that the story's going to get told correctly the first time. But I promise you, if you give me this exclusive, it will be told exactly the way you want it and, on *your* terms," Marty assured her.

"I guess I don't have that much to bargain with, now do I?" Beth asked rhetorically. "All I have is your word and hope that you will get it right, *if* I give you an exclusive. Not really a fair exchange, is it?" Beth reasoned as she spoke.

Marty gave her the only answer she had, "You have my word."

Beth sat quietly for a moment, biting her lip. She was reviewing her options. She could give an exclusive to this woman in her basement or risk the tabloids and the news media getting the story wrong.

"All right. I'll trust you for now. We'll see how you do with what I'm telling for now and go from there. As I was saying, the coroner thinks it was murder." Beth assured her.

"Murder?" Marty tried to act surprised; after all, if Beth were aware that she already knew about this too, she might throw her out on her ear. "What does the coroner think happened?" Marty inched forward.

Beth gave a deep sigh and began, "He thinks Rory was trying to jump clear of the housing before it fell on him. He said that Rory's body was face down in a sprawled fashion." Beth was back on her feet. "Would you like some juice?" she questioned as she poured herself a glass of cranberry juice from the fully stocked bar in the den.

"No, thank you," Marty responded, wanting to resume the interview.

Beth continued where she left off without missing a beat. "He said it was inconsistent with a normal accident. He told me that if he was truly checking on the wiring down front of the engine, that when he heard the casing start to fall, he would have been found face up with his legs beneath him in a squatting position. You can talk to him if you need more details."

Beth was excited and drained at the same time. She wanted to find her husband's killer, but she was exhausted with the baby, this interview, the funeral arrangements, and the shock of losing her husband on their eighth anniversary.

"Oh, I will." Marty paused, wondering if she should press the issue, but knowing she had to if she were to report accurately. "Beth, you did say your husband had a gun. Did the coroner mention any gunshot wound or wounds?" Marty asked.

Beth nearly dropped her glass. "Is there nothing you don't already know?" she asked in utter disbelief. "Yes. He was shot on the inside of his right thigh. But you're wondering if Rory was shot to death and then crushed, aren't you, Ms. Saunders, I mean, Marty," Beth corrected, remembering to use her first name.

"Yes. I am. What caliber was the bullet that was found in your husband's leg? Did the coroner say? What caliber was your husband's missing gun?" Marty inquired.

"It was a collector's gun. It wasn't his most valuable gun by any means, but it was definitely his favorite. It shoots a .45 caliber bullet and I forgot to ask the coroner the caliber of bullet in Rory's thigh. I'll find that out when I visit him later today. But let me show you something." They exited the den and entered the trophy-recreation room.

She went straight to an isolated glass showcase, similar to what you'd expect to see in a museum or jewelry store. The conversation continued at an accelerated pace as Beth led Marty on the tour.

"It was a 1911 Switch and Signal handgun. It is a collector's gun," Beth relayed.

"That's the kind of gun he used to check out a noise in a shop?" Marty was dumbfounded. "Who uses the collector's piece for everyday self-defense?" she asked.

Beth laughed, recalling memories of Rory and his eternal lack of practicality. "You had to know Rory. He wasn't what most people would consider pragmatic when it came to guns," she mused. "He felt guns needed to be used to be appreciated. That's why every gun he owned was fired and cleaned at least once a month with only one exception. It was his idea of good maintenance."

By now Beth was busy turning off the special alarm system that was used to secure the antique gun in the glass casement. She proceeded to select the key needed to unlock it. None of his activity seemed to slow her thoughts. "God, he loved that Switch and Signal. Believe it or not, that was his first gun." She smiled as she recalled his love for guns and felt a pang of pain remembering her loss.

Beth jerked herself back into the moment and continued her explanation. "When he was only 6, his great uncle gave it to him, telling him stories of how he had used it during WWI. Can you believe that? His great uncle told him a few war stories and it became his favorite and mostprized possession," Beth paused briefly to catch her breath.

"He told of how it had saved his life on four separate occasions, so I guess as an impressionable 6-year-old kid, Rory thought of the gun as a good luck charm. Guess that's why it was his favorite," Beth explained.

As she reminisced, it hit her again. Her husband was dead. He wasn't going to walk through the door at any moment and tell her this was all a big mistake. He wasn't' going to tell her he wasn't really dead, and things were going to be all right. Beth went blank for a moment as Marty examined the gun in the case.

As Beth got a second wind, she continued. "He comes from a long line of hunters and collectors. You may have noticed." Beth nodded her head, indicating Rory's accomplishments surrounding the room. She was suddenly out of words as her mind was flooded with memories of her husband.

Marty jolted her into the now. "What do you think the gun was worth and was the gun your husband used just like this one?" she asked, feeling overwhelmed for her new friend.

Beth met Marty's eyes and said, "In Rory's eyes it was priceless. But market value, I guess it would be somewhere in the neighborhood of five thousand bucks. Here," she instructed. "Put these on." Beth handed Marty a pair of white cotton gloves like the ones that she had donned shortly before unlocking the glass case.

Marty's eyes were fixed on the gun before her. She was stunned by its impeccable condition. She'd never seen anything like it. "What kind of gun is this? Is that the original box too?" she asked.

"Yes, it is. As a matter of fact, possession of that original box raises the total value of this gun by at least twenty percent," Beth answered.

Marty watched in silence as Beth spread a large, red dust cloth over Marty's open hands. Then she carefully placed the gun into her hands as if it were a premature infant. Beth used a second red dust cloth, plus her gloves, as she carefully began to explain the significance of the gun in Marty's hands.

Beth drew in a deep breath and began to narrate the history of the gun. "This is one of the rarest American-made guns in the world. It's a Singer M1911 Colt. It's an A1, Automatic Colt Pistol. It was modified to prevent hammer bite." She clarified herself when prompted by Marty's facial commands.

"It began production in 1911 and served as the standard-issue sidearm for the U.S. Armed Forces from 1911 to 1986 when it was largely replaced by the Beretta M9 as standard issue. This is a single-action, semi-automatic mag-fed pistol," Beth explained. She heard Rory describe it to visitors so many times that she had the spiels down by heart. She flinched at that thought.

"The one you're holding was designed by John Browning and has a short recoil," Beth noted. "It was made by the Singer Sewing Machine Company during WWII. They began production in 1942 and only made five hundred of them. See?" She pointed at the serial number, S800,169. "We had it authenticated with x-ray testing to determine its originality and insurance value."

Marty responded with curiosity, "You said Singer, as in Singer Sewing Machine? Like sewing machines? I don't make the connection. I never knew they manufactured guns."

"Oh yeah. And dozens of other textile manufacturers did as well, including the railroads. In fact, the gun that's missing was manufactured by Union Switch and Signal, but it's not the same gun as the one you're holding." Beth was unexpectedly happy for a moment as she showed the gun and explained it in a manner that would make Rory proud.

Beth elaborated when she saw the knit in Marty's eyebrows. "As you probably recall from your American history, during WWII our government was scrambling for firearms. So, they commissioned an almost countless variety of our American factories to produce the modified A-1 series."

Beth almost glowed as she relived the times Rory would tell the stories to many other collectors. "As I mentioned a moment ago, the Singer model is highly valued due to its limited number and the original box. It makes this worth nearly mint condition or a total value upwards of four hundred thousand dollars, which is among the few handguns to ever garner that much money at auction." She was on a roll and continued.

"Like I said before, Singer only produced five hundred of these," she said proudly, thinking of how her Rory loved his collection. Marty nearly dropped it when she heard that. Beth just snickered as though it were a common reaction. "Don't worry, it's insured," she said.

"God, I hope so," Marty exclaimed.

"It is," Beth further assured her. "You see, this gun looks almost identical to Rory's missing gun. However, the primary difference is right here," Beth pointed to the arched grip handle. "See." She almost glowed as she pointed out the handle. "Hold the gun in your hand as if you were going to fire it. Go ahead. It's not loaded," Beth instructed as Marty obeyed. "Can you feel the arch of the handle in your hand?" Beth asked.

"Yes. Why?" Marty was puzzled.

"That, my dear, is what makes this gun so valuable. Most of the Colts manufactured during WWI were made with a flat main spring housing, but this series was modified into the 1911 A1 model during WWII." Beth enjoyed explaining the value of each gun and why each has its own value.

Beth felt proud telling Marty the history of the guns. "That's when they installed the arched mainspring housing, like you see here at the back of the grip," Beth pin-pointed the mainspring. "Supposedly, it made for a more comfortable grip and eliminated *hammer bite*. In fact, it's still a hotly debated issue today. Kinda funny, that all this gun's value hinges mostly on its ergonomics, don't you think?" Beth mused.

"It's amazing," Marty handed the gun back to Beth somewhat eager to get rid of it. She felt uncomfortable holding an artifact that represented so much monetary and emotional value to her host. Then her questions resumed. "A gun like this should be fairly easy to trace, wouldn't you think?" Marty asked.

"I should think so. I should say I'm hoping so. I told the police I want that gun found no matter what they have to do. Because, you see, if Rory's gun doesn't turn up at the shop, it proves that someone else was there at the time of his accident or I should say, his 'murder.' It proves I didn't imagine the intruder like the police are starting to think." Beth spoke with rising anger in her voice, knowing that someone had to believe her.

Chapter Eight

Winning the Lottery

Marty eased Beth's nerves with a quick squeeze of her hand. It was a comforting gesture from an almost stranger. Beth looked up and caught Marty's eyes and the empathy they held for her. For some reason, her gut just trusted her almost without question and certainly without real reason.

Beth continued where she'd left off, "I truly believe it wasn't an accident, but I don't understand who or why. I mean, we have money now from winning the lottery and all, but that's only a modest amount dispensed yearly. It's not like we are millionaires or anything. Well, not in the traditional sense of the word. It's owed to us, but we get the distributions over our lifetime." Beth spoke with questions in her voice. She had no idea who would want to kill her husband or why.

"Maybe someone thought you could use the winnings as a ransom or something. Have you had any prank calls or peculiar incidents lately?" Marty quizzed.

"No. That's just it. I've been racking my brain trying to figure out why us? Why Rory? We're not politically active, other than voting in the presidential elections every four years. We don't mess with anything locally or mid-terms. We have our own lives and plenty of interests for both of us," Beth whispered.

"Did you dramatically change your lifestyle after you won this lottery?" Marty queried.

"No. Don't get me wrong, we had every Tom, Dick, and Harry on our doorstep or telephone for weeks. We changed and unlisted our phone number.

But people still contacted Rory at the shop. Finally, he let his secretary, Annette Gibson, screen all his calls and visitors for him. Eventually things died down," Beth could tell she was getting tired and could use a nap.

"Exactly how long ago did you win the prize money?" Marty nudged.

"It's been almost two years now," Beth stated softly. "Rory was notified in December that his winning status had been verified one year ago, but our last installment was made January 3rd of this year," she continued unabated with details no one outside of the family knew.

"I remember Rory and I debated long and hard as to whether we should take a lump sum or opt for the annual installments. In the end, Rory thought the installments would give us more financial security if we were to be hurt or lost our jobs," Beth explained.

"They told us we could either have a lump sum, less taxes owed, or we could get annual payments for life," Beth explained. For some inexplicable reason, she was opening up to this woman without holding back. She felt a sense of trust and sisterhood between them. She couldn't rationalize it, but she felt cautiously safe with her.

She went on, "Like I said, we took the annual installments for practical reasons, and it wasn't such a tax bite either. Rory couldn't stand the amount of money the government takes from you whenever you have a windfall. It's like a combination of rape and extortion wrapped into one." Beth was angry now, remembering their choice wasn't so much a choice as it was a way to keep the government from picking their pockets.

"At any rate, we had a steady income source to fall back on no matter what curve ball life threw our way, and that was what Rory wanted. I never dreamed I'd be a widow at 28," she added. "He wanted our financial security, and now I have it." She sat down on the couch and curled into a small ball and tears began flowing.

Marty soothed her as she offered to get her something to drink. Meanwhile, she handed her a box of tissues from a nearby end table.

She spoke softly as she comforted and empathized with Beth. She was there for her and she wanted Beth to know she could really trust her. She wasn't there to exploit her pain; she was there for a story, but not sensationalism.

After Beth stopped crying, Marty pressed for more details, as she knew they had a mystery to solve and the more details she got, the more they'd have to work with. "I thought these kinds of payment were made either monthly or annually on exact dates and such," Marty stated.

Beth sniffed, "They are. Our next annual payment is due on January third of next year. It's an automatic deposit into our account," Beth clarified. "I don't know how all lotteries are handled, but it's in some kind of insurance annuity, I think."

"It's supposed to be really safe and guaranteed for life. I don't remember all the specifics about it right now, but I'm sure I'll be talking with them later this week. Perhaps after the funeral." Beth was getting very tired of questions. It seemed the more she answered, more remained.

"When is the funeral? Do you know yet?" Marty queried softly.

"Not sure yet. I have some personal things I want attend to before I release that information to you or anyone else. The last thing I want at my husband's funeral is a bunch of reporters and vultures trying to get a story or their hand in the pie one last time. No offense intended," Beth added.

"None taken," Marty replied. "I see your point. Look, if you don't want me to go live with this, I won't. You have my word." Marty swallowed hard. She knew this was a great story, but she also felt Beth's sense of loss.

"Normally, I wouldn't have let you within a million miles of me since we all know how reliable a reporter's word can be," Beth stated unremarkably. "But I'm trusting you with this information, with what's left of my life now." Beth was looking straight into Marty's eyes for confirmation that she could really trust her with this.

"Beth, I'm not lying to you. My boss doesn't even know I'm in here. I didn't tell him yet. And I won't tell him if you don't want me to. I don't even have my camera crew with me. They're outside with the other reporters. I'm not an insensitive bitch that cares only about my career." Marty just shared valuable and verifiable information with Beth.

Beth trusted Marty as much as she could trust any reporter in this situation, maybe more. She was hesitant but felt a connection with this woman. Beth gave her full attention to Marty and looked her directly in the eyes.

"Why should I believe you?" she asked.

"Why did you agree to talk with me?" Marty countered. The tension was suddenly fixed. The two women stared at each other as if in a stronghold. Then Marty broke the silence.

"As I mentioned earlier," Marty said, "my fiancé was killed in the Boston Marathon bombing attack. I know first-hand how intrusive and unreliable some reporters can be. For weeks, they badgered me for my 'feelings' on the matter. They wanted details of when we spoke last. What our plans were. They were vultures feeding on my suffering and that of everyone else who was maimed or lost a loved one that day."

Marty could feel her cheeks flush as she relived the ordeal. "They said they wanted to get individual stories of personal losses. They wanted pictures of us and the wedding dress I would never wear, thanks to some maniacs' random acts of violence." She almost spat the words as her feelings were still raw whenever she thought about it.

The pitch in Marty's voice was high and escalated. She spoke rapidly with exasperation as she keenly recalled the rage she felt from some of the reporters, some of whom were now her colleagues.

As Marty's words soaked in, Beth softened toward her. She was convinced she was trusting the right person, the right reporter. Beth knew she had to trust someone sometime and it might as well be someone who shared empathy regarding the loss of a loved one.

"Okay. You can go live with what I've told you, but only after I've had a chance to talk with my family and get an update from the police," Beth said. "Maybe you could accompany me to the coroner's office. I need to speak with Dr. Tony Davis, the chief deputy coroner who did the autopsy on my husband this morning," she shared as she extended the invitation for later that afternoon.

"Didn't you just talk with him over the phone before you saw me?" Marty quizzed.

Beth smiled and said, "Yes, I did."

Chapter Nine

Captain Denton

"Mind ya, it was purely by accident that we found the slug. I mean, it wasn't like we expected to find a bullet. It was just routine evidence collection. The coroner found it during his autopsy." Captain Gene Denton exhaled the last puff of smoke from his cigarette and crushed the butt into a generic glass ashtray. He took a sip of cold black coffee before speaking into the receiver again.

Beth didn't reveal that she already knew about the slug from the coroner. She wanted to hear what Denton and his men had uncovered and didn't want to show all her cards at this time. Chances were good that the coroner had already told them that he'd talked with her, so she didn't feel a need to bring it up. She remained glued to the phone while Denton continued.

"As I was sayin', because this is now a high-profile case, we've accelerated the collection and procedures of the evidence. Ballistics did a stellar job of turnin' round the evidence and the coroner did yer husband's autopsy in the middle of the night. It helped that they knew the missin' handgun was a 1911 Switch and Signal and knowin' what they were lookin' fer simplified his job." Denton was peering over the crime scene photos as he spoke.

Beth could tell the authorities were doing a great job, but she was tired, distraught, and in shock. At times, she struggled to be rational. His phone call came at a low point for her. But she was bolstered by the fact that they were now admitting to knowing about the bullet too. She knew they had to take her seriously about an intruder being at the scene and that she wasn't 'misremembering' her facts. Denton put her on the speaker phone while he continued to examine the crime photos.

"What was the caliber of the bullet, Captain?" Beth questioned.

He searched through the stacks of paper that cluttered his desk. "If I recall right, Mrs. Phillips, I believe it was a .45 caliber,' They're mighty 'popalur' and easy enough to come by," Denton said. He had been on the force all his adult life.

He had a slow manner, and his drawl put a person at ease. He was 5'9'"and thanks to his affinity for southern cooking, he weighed in around 270 pounds. His 59th birthday was less than a month away and he was planning on early retirement at age 62. Just three more years to go.

He found the ballistics report. "Yep. That's right. It was indeed a .45 caliber bullet. Funny thing though, it bein' a collector's gun and all. It seems odd that he'd have an antique gun for self-defense. And didn't you say he had the gun with him?" Denton asked.

"Yes. That's Rory's gun. It must be. That's the exact gun I told you was missing when I gave you my report last night. It was his favorite, an A1911 Switch and Signal. Where did you find it?" She was hopeful and assuming they had found Rory's gun.

"Well now, hold on there, Mrs. Phillips. I never said nothin' about findin' the actual gun. I said we found a bullet that had been fired from a gun simil'r to yer husband's," Denton clarified. "Mrs. Phillips, let me be very clear with you, we haven't found any gun, as yet." He could see he was going to have his hands full with this one.

"Be reasonable for a moment, Captain," Beth replied. "Do you have any idea what the odds are of that slug being from someone else's gun? I know for a fact that not even one out of every 200-gun owners will own an A1911 Colt," she stated with certainty.

"As a matter of fact, there's over six-hundred variations of that particular model and I'd love nothing more than to jaw this over with you, Captain Denton, but I have a husband to bury and I firmly believe, a murderer to find." Beth's fatigue and frustration were escalating. "Now do you think we can get down to discussing some solid leads about my husband's case?" she asked in desperation.

Denton shifted in his chair. He was uncomfortable because of his bulk and the amount of time she was taking from him. "Now don't go getten yer feathers all ruffled up on me, Mrs. Phillips," he said. "I can assur' you that we are doin' everyth'ng possibl' to investigate yer husband's untim'ly passin' and that includes treatin' it as a suspicious death." He lit up another cigarette and puffed once before he continued.

"Evidence is mount'n, Mrs. Phillips, that yer husband definit'ly encountered an intruder. We have yer statement that ya heard an intruder and evidence of a fired bullet. We just need to tie up a coupl' loose ends." He took a long drag and finished his sentence. Denton was already treating the case as a homicide; he just didn't want Mrs. Phillips to know that she was their prime suspect.

He would have to verify the call Beth made to her sister last night and it would take a bit of time to get the information from her cell phone carrier. Due to the proximity of the shop and their home, he needed to triangulate the cell phone towers to prove she wasn't in the area at the time of the murder. It was a long shot that she committed his murder, but he still had to check it out. He had to do some digging into their personal life to eradicate a motive for her. This would take a bit of time too.

He continued and emphasized, "And, please, bear in mind, Mrs. Phillips, that it's our job to do the investigin' of yer husband's death, not yers." Denton was setting boundaries. "It'd be a whole lot easier for everyone concerned if you'd just let us conduct the investigation and ya just worry about takin' care of yerself and that baby of yers," he said, hoping she would do exactly that.

Denton was trying to do his job, but he could tell she was gonna get in the way of the investigation on every front. He hoped showing concern for her baby would refocus her efforts, but his strategy didn't have much effect.

"Don't patronize me, Captain Denton," Beth retorted. "I'm fully aware of my responsibilities to myself, my unborn child and my husband's memory. Rest assured, you can expect my full cooperation, just as I expect you to keep me informed promptly of all new developments." *Click*. Beth hung up before Denton could lavish anymore of his Southern charm on her.

It had only been about twenty-six hours since Beth and her family got the news about Rory's death. Beth was in a haze but couldn't stop herself. She'd seen and read enough to know the first 72 hours of an investigation are the most crucial. She pushed herself to be in the moment as events unfolded around her. She could rest later.

It was noon when Beth and Marty arrived at the coroner's office. They used the CNB van to transport Beth without drawing any attention from the droves of other reporters. Their senses were heightened as personnel escorted them down the hallway. When they passed the exam room, their noses were slapped with the pungent stench of formaldehyde and decay. It was a smell that would haunt Beth whenever she recalled the death of her husband.

As they entered the office of Dr. Davis, he showed them in and suggested they be seated in a couple of chairs in front of his desk. They dutifully complied. His office was stark white with sparse furnishings. His certificates and licenses were the only decorations on his walls. His desk was older and made of heavy solid oak. It sported a desk calendar and an old Rolodex. He was clearly old school, yet his computers were cutting edge and he seemed to be somewhere in his thirties.

Beth spoke first as she leaned forward in her chair. "Can we get right to the point, Dr. Davis?" She wanted to hear everything he had to say. When they were on the phone earlier, she was so overwhelmed, she'd forgotten to ask him if her husband had suffered. She needed to ask that question in person so she could read his body language and get the truth.

"Did my husband suffer, Mr. Davis?" Beth asked. It took all she had to wait for the answer. He must have suffered some from the bullet in his leg, but she wondered if he had time to feel anything else. She knew the answer was no, but she needed to hear it from him.

"Other than the bullet in his leg, I don't believe he did. And considering the amount of adrenaline activated by his circumstances, I seriously doubt he felt much pain in any part of the encounter." Tony was being as gentle as he could, given the situation.

"I see. Thank you for your candor. It eases my mind to know he didn't suffer much," Beth said. "Is there anything else, Dr. Davis?" Beth was relieved with this information, but with the relief came a wave of exhaustion that she tried to ignore as she pressed on for as much information as she could get.

"The findings I have so far aren't much different from what I told you earlier this morning. My biggest concern is the position in which I found the body. As I said previously, your husband was found face down with his body at an angle and his legs straight out. This indicates he was trying to jump clear, so he must have had some warning that it was about to fall. I'm sorry to be so graphic, Mrs. Phillips," he stated with empathy.

"I understand. Please, go on, Dr. Davis," Beth encouraged, as she swallowed hard.

Marty was taking copious notes and neither Beth nor Davis seemed to mind. All the information was in his autopsy report, so he saw no need for alarm, and Beth wanted Marty to get the exclusive story correct. With permission from both, she was recording the conversation on her cell phone too. It's much easier to flip through pages to find something rather than hunting for it on a recording. Yet, a recording's important for capturing the mood and tone of what was being said.

"As I was saying," Davis continued, "for whatever reason, your husband had enough warning that the cabover was about to fall that he attempted to jump free. Maybe he was cornered by the burglar who tried to make it look like an accident." Then he asked abruptly, "What about any surveillance footage?"

Beth shifted forward in her chair, knowing she had another ally in her camp. "There wasn't any. It was one of the first questions I asked Capt. Denton. The video cameras malfunctioned." Marty wanted to ask some of her own questions but remembered that her place was as a guest of Beth's, even though the reporter in her was urging her own questions.

"Was there any sign of a struggle? What clues did you find?" Beth questioned.

"I was unable to discern defensive wounds on his hands. However, I found a bullet lodged in his left thigh." He spared her the detail that given his manner of death, there was virtually no way to determine defensive wounds. "Strange thing though, the bullet entered the inner thigh and that's unusual. I only found it because it lodged in the bone."

Beth was livid, "Why didn't you mention this before?"

"I couldn't mention it until Denton contacted you." He continued before she could get off another question. "As I was saying, the bullet indicates that your husband might have been trying to get away from his assailant. I really can't think of any other plausible explanation for a bullet in that location. It caught him on the inner thigh of his left leg and entered from a crazy angle which trajectory indicates came from behind him." Davis waited for Beth's next questions.

She wanted to take the facts as they were presented to her, now that she knew they were withholding information from her, she knew she couldn't trust them.

"Then that must be the bullet Denton told me about," Beth deduced. "Were there any other bullets?"

Davis looked directly into her eyes. "No. I only found the one. You should check in with Denton to clarify if there were any other bullets recovered at the scene."

Beth's voice pitched upward as she asked her next questions. Marty turned the sheet in her notebook.

"Back up a minute, please," Beth said almost gleefully. "Let me get this clear." She cleared her throat before spelling it out for herself and Davis. "The bullet evidence combined with the surveillance cameras malfunctioning, and my having heard Rory talking with someone proves that Rory did encounter someone and tried to defend himself. Would you agree with that, Dr. Davis?" Beth was trying to form a clear picture of events.

She continued undaunted, "And the fact that he was shot in the back of the leg indicates an intruder as well. Also, we know that Rory was found trying to jump clear of the casing, so it follows that my husband was murdered. How much more proof do you need?"

Before Davis could answer, Beth exchanged looks with Marty and then back to Davis and followed with more questions. "Did you find anything else? Was there any other evidence that tells you that this was not just an accident?" She sat back with her hands facing up in her lap.

"No, there's nothing else, Mrs. Phillips." He was starting to lose his limited patience.

"Call me Beth," she insisted. "I hate all the formalities that come with funerals. I don't want to go through any more than I have to; so, if you don't mind, please call me Beth."

"No problem, Beth," Davis said.

"Initially my findings showed the probable cause of death as 'catastrophic bodily trauma.' However, considering the evidence, I'm inclined to officially change the cause of death to homicide." He knew that would calm her momentarily, but in the end would trigger more tenacity.

Beth and Marty looked at each other and simultaneously sighed with relief. Finally, they had a solid official in their camp.

"There's just one problem. I may be overstepping my bounds, Beth, but this still doesn't get us any closer to a murderer unless we have a gun for comparison. I wish there was more that I could do for you," he said with real remorse for this widow. Tony meant what he was saying. For some reason, she had gotten under his skin. He wasn't sure why or how, but he genuinely felt compassion for this woman.

"I understand," Beth said. She went numb as the reality that her husband was murdered smothered her. Everything seemed surreal.

"The rest is up to the police now," Tony said with a finality in his voice. He needed to wrap things up as he was tired from staying up all night doing her husband's autopsy. "I recommend you give them time to do their jobs. But I can assure you that with my amended report and the ballistics evidence I gave them, this will elevate your husband's case to a homicide investigation. I think everyone's convinced that this was not an accident, Mrs. Phillips."

He added, "If it's any consolation, I believe your husband put up a real fight to save his life." Tony leaned forward and planted his foot on the floor beneath his desk while he closed the folder on his desk. Both Beth and Marty took his cue to end the meeting.

"Thank you so much for all your help. You've helped immensely, and I won't forget your kindness." Beth stood up, extended her hand and thanked him again for his help. Marty followed suit and they were soon back inside the CNB van headed back to Beth's home.

Chapter Ten

The Funeral

Back at home trying desperately to relax, she joined Janice and John in the kitchen. She filled them in on the latest information from both the coroner and Capt. Denton. Shortly afterward Janice scheduled a meeting with the funeral director for six o'clock that evening. It was 2:30 p.m., so Beth would have time to take a quick rest and freshen up before they met with the funeral director.

Janice and John drove her to the funeral home. She couldn't believe the barrage of questions and decisions she was being asked to make on the spot. What kind of funeral did she want? Did she want to have a memorial service at a later date, or did she want to cremate his remains now? Did she want to bury his remains in a memorial garden, or did she want to scatter his ashes? The list went on for better than half an hour.

She had no idea what she wanted to do with his ashes, but she did want a small ceremony right away. She needed some closure for now and she would give some thought to having a memorial service after the baby came. That way family and friends could plan for the event instead of having to make costly last-minute arrangements to attend the funeral.

After she selected an urn and paid for the services, she chose to have a portrait of him on display. She wanted him to be remembered as he was in life, not for the gruesome death he suffered. The funeral would be in two days. Tomorrow night would be the wake, and the service would be the following morning at 10:00 a.m. She would keep his ashes for now.

"Beth, you've been going full speed since all this has happened and you've got to let someone else do some things for you. You have to let us help you," Janice was insisting. "You haven't given yourself any time to grieve, let alone rest for you and the baby."

Beth looked into her sister's face for a moment before responding. "I know you're right, sis, but I feel like if I stop, I won't be able to handle all of the pain and fear, let alone get up again and tend to things as I should."

"I'm Rory's widow now and it's ultimately up to me to get to the bottom of everything. I just don't understand it, Janice." She cried as she buried her face into Janice's open arms for a hug. "I just don't understand, why? Why Rory?" she asked, determined to one day know the answer.

"But you're not in this alone, Beth. We're here to help you," Janice soothed as she pulled back from the hug, looked into her sister's eyes and tucked a shock of hair behind her ear. "John and I will help you through this, I promise. And you have the baby to look forward to," She tried to lift her spirits a bit.

"I know. But it's not the same without Rory. He never even knew we were pregnant. Now, I'll always remember our eighth anniversary with his death." Beth was almost hysterical as the thoughts of her loss washed over her. She finally slept. It was a light sleep, but she felt a bit refreshed and she definitely had her second wind.

It had been two days since Rory's funeral. Capt. Denton was on the phone. "I have some good news fer ya, Mrs. Phillips," Denton stated matter-of-factly. "The bullet taken out of yer husband's body proves there was definitely an intruder there with yer husband. Now that we have evidence, we're official'y investigatin' the death of yer husband as a homicide. But ya probl'y already knew that based on yer conversations with the coroner." He implied he didn't care for her demanding demeanor.

Time was both standing still and racing forward for Beth. It became a dizzy existence from one day to the next. She struggled separating the days. Rory's funeral left her hollow, and she was finding out how slowly the wheels of justice turn.

Beth knew Rory was murdered almost from the beginning. So, it came as no surprise that the police were just now concluding the same. She thought they should have deduced it much sooner, but at least they knew now. She tried to get out of their way and let them do their job, but she didn't know how to spend her time. She felt simultaneously frantic and comatose.

She knew there had been an intruder when she was on the phone with Rory. And she knew Rory was too good of a shot to miss, if he saw it coming. She turned her attention back to Denton. "I'm so relieved," she said. "Do you have any suspects yet?" She briefly let her mind wander, trying to think of anyone who may have wanted to hurt Rory.

Denton's voice brought her back into the conversation. "Not a one yet," he said. "We're puttin' together a possibl' list of persons of interest, but, Mrs. Phillips, do you know of anyone who mighta' wanted to harm yer husband for any reason?" he asked hopefully as he continued. "Did you notice any change in his manner of behavi'r lately?" Denton hoped the answer was yes, so he'd have a place to start. He lit a fresh cigarette and continued the phone call.

"We believe whoever killed yer husband staged it to look like an accident. Since we've recovered a bullet, it means this ain't no accident, so it musta' been business or personal. According to you, there weren't any missin' tools or anything else of value taken, so we have to figur' out why yer husband was targeted," Denton recapped.

Beth answered emphatically, "No. He wasn't acting unusual in any way. Things for us were going so great. I was going to tell him that I was six weeks pregnant when he came home that night. It was our anniversary and we were finally pregnant."

Beth's voice caught in her throat as she remembered the night. Hot and stinging tears welled in her eyes. Her lip quivered despite her best efforts to control them. She hated when her emotions got best of her. She didn't want to appear weak.

Denton proceeded, "Well, what about his business life? Was there any change there? I know ya'll just won that Mega Millions lottery. Was he plannin' any major changes b'cause of it?" Denton questioned like the detective he was.

Beth shook her head 'no' even though she was on the phone. "We decided to just take the annual installments rather than the lump sum. It saved us a bundle on taxes and Rory said it provided financial security for us in case we had a rainy day."

Beth trailed off as her eyes welled again with tears and memories. "So, to answer your question for the second time, Capt., Denton. No."

"He wasn't acting differently or peculiar in any way," Beth was a bit surly. She had been through this questioning with nearly everyone since Rory died and she was getting quite tired of it.

"I'm sorry to keep badgerin' ya, Mrs. Phillips, but since it's been official'y classified now as a homicide, we have to start all over, official'y speakin'," Denton explained.

"Did our secretary give you all of the invoices and customer lists yet?" Beth asked. "Well, yes, ma'am. We are doin' all of that and followin' up on some shoe prints and hairs we found at the scene. We're tryin' to rule out all the employees first, then take it from there. But all that will tell us is the type of shoe, his height, weight, and gait. Unless we have a suspect for comparison, it's useless information."

"I understand, Capt. Denton. You're doing all you can with very little to go on," she eased. Then she was suddenly struck by the obvious. "Did you check the security footage from all *three* cameras, Captain Denton?" Beth hoped that it had been overlooked and would now reveal the man who took her husband from her and their unborn child.

"Why yes, ma'am, we did that first thing. R'member? We talked 'bout it the first day we met? The cameras weren't workin' properly, so that puts us back to square one," Capt. Denton reminded her.

Beth was impatient, "I know you did. But there was an obscure third camera. Maybe you overlooked it somehow. It could easily have been missed." Beth was unrealistically hopeful.

Denton cut her off. "We checked all three cameras and none of 'em were workin,' Mrs. Phillips." Denton wasn't trying to be mean, but he had to get through to her. Having to explain every detail of the investigation twice was wearing on him and costing precious time.

Beth was maddened with that bit of information. "Then you knew all along that there was an intruder, from the very beginning, but you didn't believe me when I told you so." Beth's anger was growing.

He pushed back, "Well, ma'am, that's why it's called investigatin.' It yielded nothin' new, till we found the .45 calib'r slug. Then we knew for sure there was an intruder on the night in question… till we had the slug, we only suspected foul play. The bullet is evidence. And now we're lookin' for a person of interest, a suspect, Mrs. Phillips."

"Who could have done this and why? Why? It just doesn't make any sense. What possible motive could anyone have to kill my husband?" Beth begged with rhetorical questions.

"That's what we're goin' to find out, Mrs. Phillips," Denton vowed. With that promise, the phone called ended.

Janice brought the mail in and laid it on the kitchen counter with a pile of others. She sorted the personal mail from the shop's mail. Beth stumbled into to the kitchen and watched Janice sorting it. Janice stopped when she saw an envelope from Alliance Life and Investments.

"They handle and oversee our payments from the lottery winnings," Beth shared with Janice. "They send us our annual automatic proof of payment receipt. The insurance company directly deposits our annual check into our savings account. Open it." Beth sipped some pear nectar as she encouraged her to hurry.

"Umm, Beth, I don't think this is what you're expecting," Janice said after reading it briefly. "It appears to be a cease and desist order for future payments from your lottery winnings. Due to Rory's death, the lottery winnings are stopped." She handed it to Beth, who had a worried look on her face.

Beth reached for the letter. "Stopped? What if I just take the rest in a lump sum? Is that what they want me to do?" Beth queried out loud as she handed the letter back to Janice.

"No. Not according to this letter," Janice stated while looking it over again. "Per this letter, you don't get any more money. Period." Beth was agitated as Janice continued to read. "Wait. That can't be right. This must be a big mistake," Janice insisted. "It says because Rory died, you're no longer entitled to any more payouts of any kind." Janice went silent for a moment.

"I can't believe this," Beth exploded. "We won all that money. And now we don't get any more of it because Rory died? This can't be true." Beth snatched the letter from Janice. "There has to be some mistake. We won the money, Janice." Her voice was high-pitched by now. "The whole world knows we won that money. They can't do this. Tell me they can't do this to me, Janice. What about the women and children's shelter? What about my future and my baby?" Beth was no-holds-barred hysterical as the full impact of losing the lottery winnings hit her.

Janice took the paper back from Beth's hands and laid it on the table while she read the words again. "I'm sure this is just a big mistake, hon. They can't just up and take all your winnings because Rory died. We'll get to the bottom of all of this Monday morning when everyone's back to work from the weekend."

"In the meantime, it's not good for you or the baby to be this upset," Janice continued as she got a low-dose lorazepam for her sister. "Here, take this. You haven't been quite this upset in a while and you really need to relax and get some sleep."

She pressed the pill in her sister's hand and gave her a drink of water. "There now. Let's walk you upstairs and get you into bed. You and the baby need your rest," she said as she guided her up the stairs.

"There's nothing more we can do about this today. So, just watch some TV or read a book and chill for a while," Janice soothed her sister as she clicked on the remote and started thumbing through the channels. She couldn't find anything so she handed it to Beth, hoping she would find something to distract them.

Beth grabbed Janice's hand and asked, "Will you stay with me until I fall asleep?"

"Sure thing. I was planning on hanging out with you anyway, but let's talk about the baby, your Bambi. What names are you considering and when can they know the sex of the baby?" She questioned to get Beth's mind on more happier events.

"Well, boy or girl, their first name is going to be Rory with a 'y' for a boy, and Rori with an 'i' if it's a girl. I kinda like Rori Elizabeth after both of us if it's a girl. And maybe Rory Michael if it's a boy after his father," Beth mused.

"Ummm, what about Michael Rory for a bit of a change?" Janice suggested. "That way it will give the baby some sense of individuality rather the whole 'junior' or 'the second' thing that most kids have to deal with." She was trying to keep her sister talking so she wouldn't have time to think of anything else before the pill kicked in. She didn't have to wait long. When she looked over at her sister for a response to her suggestion, Beth was quietly sleeping.

Janice crept out of bedroom and went back downstairs to re-read the letter and prepare some questions for the good company of Alliance Life and Investments. After reading the letter a second time, Janice started to do some internet research regarding the payout methods of lottery winnings.

She discovered that most are funded by an insurance annuity of some kind and that there were plenty to choose from, and each annuity had a different payout option. However, the vast majority of lottery winnings are funded by a straight life annuity which yields the greatest payment amount over the lifetime of the annuitant.

She wanted to know what kind of annuity Beth and Rory had selected and what rules governed it. Why does the death of one person end the payout for the widow of a lottery winner? These were all good starting point questions and Janice couldn't wait to get the answers.

She rubbed her eyes and dragged her hands down over her face as if to close out the worries of the day and the challenges of tomorrow. She picked up her cell phone and called her husband, John, as she poured herself a glass of red wine.

They discussed the letter as she read it to him over the phone. "This letter is to request proof of death of Rory Michael Phillips via death certificate," Janice read. "Hitherto, this letter is to inform you that after we receive proof of death all lottery payments will immediately cease and desist. There will be no further payments per your chosen payout option."

"How can they know to send a letter like this so fast?" John asked, puzzled at the speed in which the lottery had heard of and processed such a letter.

"That's what I'd like to know," Janice exclaimed. "I mean it has been all over the TV and every magazine and newspaper and don't forget the gossip rags. But still? That's awful fast. It's only been 20 days now, 21 days since you sent them a copy of his death certificate." Janice was speaking almost at the top of her lungs. She was obviously livid by this new turn of events.

"Calm down now, honey. Getting loud isn't going to change anything. We have to keep a cool head if we're going to sort this out," John cautioned. "Why don't you just put it down, get a glass of wine and take a nice whirlpool bath. That always relaxes you, and you've been going full blast since all of this has happened."

"I already have the glass of wine, but the whirlpool does sound good," she agreed.

"You're doing an amazing job taking care of your sister, but don't forget to take care of yourself in the process. I love you, honey, and I'm proud of the way you're taking care of things and getting all the legal stuff done for her. Go relax and I'll see you in about an hour." He then hung up before she could get herself worked up again.

John was a former SEAL with three tours under his belt. He now worked in sales for a medical supply company, and Janice worked in the traffic division at a local radio station. She brought home the steady paycheck while John brought in the gravy, and there was a lot of gravy.

Medical supplies are always in demand and John was aggressive with his territory. By the time he got home, Janice was fast asleep lying diagonally across their bed. He gently kissed her forehead, left her sleeping and went back downstairs. He poured himself a cocktail and sat down in his recliner to read the letter.

It made no more sense to him now than it did when Janice read it to him over the phone. He got up and collected Beth's legal file of lottery winnings paperwork from the kitchen table. He sat down for a second time to read the letter and with a second drink.

It took a lot of diligence and digging but buried in a tiny little box was an 'X' beside the words *straight life annuity*. Using the internet, he started digging into what a straight life annuity is, how it works and why it would stop paying after Rory died when there was still all that money left.

He got lots of 'hits' for 800 numbers that offer a lump-sum cash settlement for annuities, but after clamoring through all of that, he found only one definition for a straight life annuity. They are also referred to as a 'pure' annuity or a 'no death benefit' annuity. In short, it's a payout option that offers payments for the life of the one person or the 'annuitant,' and that's it.

Some people choose the straight life annuity because it yields the largest amount of money in regular payments since there's no way to know exactly how long the annuitant will live. But it's very likely they won't live long enough to exhaust all the monies in the fund. In other words, no matter how much is put into this annuity or, in Rory's case, no matter how much money he won, he only got payments for as long as he was alive. *There are no beneficiaries with a straight life annuity.*

John rubbed his eyes and refocused them on the screen. It further read that the straight life annuity is usually meant for employee pensions, retirements, and for those who have no one to leave their money. The information begs the obvious question, what happens to all that money?

John searched and searched for the answer. In the end he discovered that with a straight life annuity, the insurance companies legally retain every dime of the remaining monies, even if a person dies after only receiving one payment. Actually, if an annuitant has already chosen the straight life payout plan and dies before the first payment has been made, then no payments will be made. The critical factor is that once you've selected a Straight Life Immediate Annuity purchased with a lump sum as it is with lottery winnings, you must begin drawing from it immediately. It is also considered a Single Premium Immediate Annuity, SPIA. Once you've selected this choice, the contract cannot be altered or changed in any way.

When purchasing a straight life annuity, some people pay into it thinking they'll have that money for retirement and something to leave to their heirs, even though their financial advisor is required to disclose how it works. In the end, there are frequently surplus funds because the annuitant usually dies before the money in the fund is exhausted and anything remaining becomes the sole property of the insurance companies. Obviously, it's a dirty little secret the insurance companies don't want people to know.

All other annuities offer a 'joint with rights of survivorship' rider clause that covers the lives of both the husband and wife, or any two people who want to jointly invest in an annuity other than the straight life.

John read on. The Securities and Exchange Commission laws dictate that insurance companies are self-regulated from state to state. The SEC regulates only the variable insurance and investment products. Insurance companies and their representatives inform the annuitant of the pros and cons of all their insurance products prior to any sale.

Most insurance agents go out of their way to thoroughly explain all the details of investment choices and make recommendations based on the clients' specific goals, working years, and several other important factors.

The vast majority of insurance agents offer a variety of investment choices and do right by their clients. The straight life annuity is almost solely used to fund windfalls, such as lottery winnings, settlements, and pensions in which one person is paid for life. It is not a mainstream option.

He continued reading. Most agents do practice full disclosure, but often people are focused on the positives of their investments and how much money they'll receive, and don't catch the consequences of their actions. The bottom line is 'caveat emptor, 'let the buyer beware.'

Chapter Eleven

Lotteries

Marty was on a new assignment, this time covering another school shooting in Oregon. These shootings were starting to feel like mainstream America. She had covered three in the last two months. She was thinking they were far too common when her phone rang. She saw it was Beth. They had exchanged contact information so Marty could follow the story. They had become fast friends.

"Hello, Beth. How are you and the baby doing?" Marty asked.

"We're doing fine right now. Thanks for asking," Beth answered. "But I need your help again."

"What's up?" Marty questioned.

"I got a letter from our attorneys that handle our lottery winnings stating the insurance company wants proof of Rory's death and that all payments are going to stop as soon as they get the death certificate." Beth was choking back her tears.

She continued, "John did some research online and found out that we may have something called a straight life annuity and that it's legal to do what they're doing." Beth's anxiety continued to grow as she spoke.

"Beth, breathe," Marty encouraged. "Email me copies of the documents and let me take a look at them. I'll get back with you later when I'm through here. If this is true, we can go public with it and maybe pressure them to pay out."

Beth hedged, "It's a lot of money in my world. It's almost a hundredand-forty-nine-thousand dollars a year, and that was pretty life-changing money for us. It takes care of our mortgage and monthly bills and gives us a comfortable lifestyle and savings account. We have a healthy emergency fund and were counting on that money to build a women and children's shelter. Without Rory's income, I don't know what I'm going to do. I was really counting on the money to help us through this time." Beth was embarrassed to disclose her financial woes.

"I only earn about three thousand gross per month at my job and Rory and I didn't have much life insurance. It was only for a hundred-fifty thousand. It was a whole life policy," she said with disdain. "Whole life insurance," Beth whimpered. "I never thought Rory's whole life would end at age 32." Beth was crying now, weeping softly into the phone. "I've got to go now, Marty. I appreciate any help you can give us," she said as she hung up the phone.

Beth was vomiting into the toilet. She wasn't sure if it was due to her nerves or the pregnancy. Either way, she felt like hell. Janice wouldn't be home for hours and she was looking forward to seeing her. She needed to talk with her sister because she could always make things seem better than the really were.

In the meantime, she knew she should lie down and take it easy. She had her regular check-up tomorrow morning at 10:00 a.m. She was hoping they would be able to tell the baby's sex this time. She was only about twelve weeks, but she was hopeful.

Beth finally felt like the vomiting would stop for a while, so she headed to her bed. She snuggled down inside the covers. She felt cold all over. She grabbed the remote and flipped through her options. She put on a familiar movie so that if she dozed off, she wouldn't miss anything.

Janice accidentally woke up Beth as she came into her bedroom to check on her. Beth lazily sat up and wiped her eyes before she focused on her sister. "I missed you today," Beth told her. "I'm so upset about this whole lottery mess and thinking about my baby that it still hasn't hit me, that Rory is really gone. I keep expecting him to walk through the door and tell me it's all been a horrible nightmare."

"I know what you mean. I think the same thing," Janice cooed as she wrapped her arms around her sister. Beth cried softly for several moments, then gathered herself, dried her tears, and blew her nose.

"So how was your day?" Beth teased.

Janice laughed and answered, "It was fine. Same old, same old. "You know product placement issues, spots missed, too many spots, wrong times, and my personal favorite, the real estate shows listings aren't updated before airtime. Yeah." She spoke sarcastically with a mock cheer movement.

"They get their ads to us a day before airtime and because they're one of our biggest clients and sponsors, we're supposed to move heaven and earth to get them uploaded overnight." Janice's delivery of the day made Beth laugh out loud.

"I'll start dinner. What do you feel like tonight?" Janice asked.

"Something mild. I still don't have much of an appetite. Soup sounds good," Beth answered.

"You got it, sis. How's potato soup sound?" she asked.

"Sounds really good," Beth looked forward to it already. "I'll come down with you. I'm feeling much better now," she said as she got up.

Beth changed gears. "I put in a call to Marty and I emailed her all the docs she needs to review our situation," Beth shared. "She's covering another school shooting in Oregon and as soon as she's done with that, she'll review it for us." She paused. "Can't believe all the school shootings anymore." Beth shook her head, thinking of all the pain these needless deaths were causing.

Janice steered the subject to the lottery winnings. "John said he was gonna make some calls today too. As soon as he gets home, he'll catch us up with the latest, so let's just hang till then, Hon. With John's help, we'll quickly get us to the bottom of things," Janice promised.

Marty flopped down on the bed to read the emails. She was in another hotel room. So much of her life on the road was a 'same song, different verse' kind of existence. After a short while, all the hotel rooms, airplanes, and cabs looked and smelled the same. The stories were the only real challenge, and school shootings were the worst because nothing compares to the loss of human life. The news was starting to sound like trite reruns and sometimes it didn't even make the lead story.

Marty finished her day, grabbed a drink, and sat down in front of her laptop. After reviewing everything, she concluded that what Beth told her was right. However, she knew the mainstream public probably wasn't aware of how the straight life annuities work and that it had to become public knowledge. She smelled an exclusive story if she handled things right.

Her story wasn't uncovering anything new. Straight life annuities were set up long ago and worked a lot like term life insurance. They were created to cover the life of only one person. Period. At that time, they were designed to fund pensions, families of their employees be damned. The insurance companies kept the rest of the monies, if any, that were left in the employee's coffer.

Marty had a hunch the information presented in a real-life situation such as Beth's would wake up the general public to the injustice of letting the insurance companies keep all that money. There just shouldn't be an insurance policy or investment that doesn't allow for any beneficiaries.

Marty picked up the phone as she grabbed her Coke. Beth answered and Marty got right to the point. "You were right, Beth," Marty hated to be the bearer of bad news. "Since it appears your winnings were funded with a straight life annuity, I don't see a way around it. The only hope we have is to go public and try to humiliate them into paying out or at least get you some kind of settlement." Marty felt deflated having to confirm Beth's fears.

Beth was silent for a long moment then sighed deeply before she spoke. "I don't know what to think anymore. First, I lose Rory and now I lose our income, too. I almost don't want to get up in the mornings. I'm scared. I'm scared for myself and I'm scared for our baby. I don't want to lose our home. I don't want to lose anything else," Beth sobbed.

"I know you don't, Beth," Marty said, trying to ease her fears. "I'm not done on my end yet, but it might take me a couple of days. Is that okay with you?"

"Yes, Marty. Take all the time you need if you can fix this," Beth said with some small hope. "I'll be waiting to hear from you. Do you know when we'll be able to see each other again?"

Their friendship had grown during the ordeal and Marty had kept her promise to Beth about her story being told from her truth. "I'm not sure when or where my next assignment will take me, but I have some time coming, so I'll look into it and get back with you soon." Marty hung up the phone with a feeling she'd given Beth a ray of hope.

John arrived home a little earlier than usual. He had a lot of information to share and none of it was good. Normally, he'd procrastinate but knew Beth had to know as soon as possible. "It's complicated," he began as he endeavored to explain the news he had learned earlier that day.

"I called the attorney general's office today," he said. "Apparently, the lottery commission makes sure all the lottery rules are followed during the playing of the lottery and the distribution of tickets. They police the vendors to make sure nothing is rigged or altered. They set up and monitor the games much like a watchdog. But they don't handle how the monies are paid out; that's handled by selected insurance companies."

"As I understand it, with the lottery you won, Beth, you had a choice of either a one-time lump sum of cash, or an installment plan over the entire life of the annuitant. With the installment plan, you wait longer to receive the money you've won and, again, it pays more money than annuities that have beneficiaries. Of course, the taxes are withheld on both options, in which case the money you receive is much less than the original amount of money that you actually won.

"For example, if you won a million dollars, depending upon which tax bracket you're in, your take would be approximately seven-hundred thousand in a 30% tax bracket." John spoke as gently as he could. He paused to sip his beer and let his news settle before continuing.

"From what I have gleaned, you don't get any of the interest earned on the money while it's invested in the straight life annuity. That interest money belongs to the insurance company as well." John and Janice were both maddened and sickened by this.

Beth nearly doubled over. The news was devastating to say the least. She didn't know what emotion was the strongest, disbelief, rage, or sadness? "This can't be true," she exclaimed. "This just can't be happening to me right now. It's so unfair. How is this even legal?" Beth was exhausted from the legal rhetoric.

Beth wanted more answers and she wasn't sure where to find them. It was a good thing she had Marty and her family to lean on. They were a long way from a solution. After tiring of talking about it and becoming overwhelmed, all three of them went to bed early, but sleep evaded them.

Chapter Twelve

The Scam

"Everything looks great, Mrs. Phillips. Your baby is healthy," Dr. Heidle advised. Beth was at her checkup. She was almost twelve weeks. "Would you like to know the sex of your baby?" he added.

"Yes! Of course, I want to know. Which is it?" Beth asked eagerly, knowing in her heart that it was a girl. Dr. Heidle confirmed her instincts. "It's a girl," the doctor said with a broad smile. Janice and Beth exchanged looks of happiness.

"A little girl!" Janice smiled at her sister with a tear of joy in her eye.

"A girl. I'm having a daughter," Beth exclaimed, totally happy for the first time since Rory's death. But it was bittersweet when she realized her husband wasn't going to share the news or enjoy being a father. His life was cut short, too short.

Janice drove Beth home and engaged her with talk of the nursery and a baby shower. She wanted to keep her occupied with as many happy thoughts as possible. She needed to keep her interested in everyday functions if they were going to get her through this ordeal.

Marty had done some digging on her own and had put her assistant on research detail to find out how lotteries are run. She bunched herself into a comfy recliner and read through the report. For once, Marty was at home and between assignments, and it felt good. The email in Marty's inbox was lengthy. It read: "The following is the information, regarding lotteries that you asked me to gather for you. If you need anything else, please advise."

"There are several kinds of lotteries and they are operated from state to state. The purpose of lotteries is to raise monies for projects such as schools and scholarships, to funds for municipal infrastructure, for example, roads, bridges, and buildings.

"They can be used to fund almost anything in lieu of increasing taxes. There is a big payout to the winner or winners, and the remaining funds are used for commercial projects while a portion of the monies go to the vendor or vendors whose store or stores sold the winning ticket or tickets.

"As tickets are sold, a portion of the monies collected go into the 'jackpot' while the remaining funds are ear-marked for pre-determined state projects. On average, about sixty cents of each lottery ticket go into the 'jackpot' while the remaining forty cents gets divided among the state or states as the case may be.

"For example, it could be assigned to an education fund for twenty years to boost the salaries for teachers, repair, build, or renovate schools, their equipment, fund a new bridge, or road repairs. A state or mutual states' lottery can pay out a specific amount of annual income for a specified period of time and a specific project.

"Retailers jump at the chance to sell lottery tickets. It generates a lot more foot traffic, additional sales of goods or services, and is easy advertising. On the face of things, it seems like a win all the way around. But just like the 'house' always wins in Vegas, the insurance company is the 'house' in the insurance game. It wins the big money where lotteries are concerned.

"The insurance companies reinvest the interest earned from these annuities into anything on the NYSE, the NASDAQ, or other national and international trading options. Sometimes they choose to keep it liquid by opening a new account, earning interest and dividends, and reinvesting the monies in a new or existing financial portfolio." The report ended there.

Marty felt sick. Sick for herself and her dear friend Beth. She also knew she had a story to tell and tell it she would. She picked up her cell phone and called her boss, Joel. She briefed him on the information and emailed him the memo from her assistant.

She'd meet with him in two days to discuss the matter in person. Now she had the daunting task of telling Beth. She had waited until morning to call her. Things sometimes seem less frightening in the light of day, but she doubted that it would make much difference.

"Hi, Beth. I did some more digging on the lottery issue. I've sent you an email with an attachment you need to read. I've copied my boss on it and we're meeting in a couple of days to talk about what our next steps are in exposing this charade." Marty briefly recapped the email for her. She anticipated her reaction.

"It's nothing but a huge racket," Beth exclaimed and continued to pour out her heart.

Marty was outraged when she hung up. She could hardly wait to talk with Joel and break the story.

After meeting with Joel, he didn't hesitate to have Marty do a follow-up interview with Beth. Marty phoned Beth with the good news and planned the follow-up. The interview went off without a hitch. She broke the story and it was garnering momentum and public support. The insurance industry wanted to shut the story down, but it was too late. The facts were beginning to emerge.

Beth's phone rang and she eagerly answered it when she saw the caller I.D. on her cell phone. "Hi, Marty. What have you heard?" she asked.

"I can tell you that we have a much larger story than just what's happened to you," Marty replied. "This goes far beyond the individual in these cases. I still have more research to do, but with what I have, I think I can rattle a few cages of the big-wigs," she stated with confidence.

Three months had now passed since Rory's accident. Beth hadn't heard from Capt. Denton and she wasn't hopeful that anything new would turn up. She'd talked with the medical examiner a couple of times in the past two weeks and he said pretty much the same thing. Her hopes were dwindling fast.

Denton was right about the widow Beth. She was going to hound him until he found some answers. She was stuck to him like a tick on a dog. But he knew she was right about this being a murder. He just didn't know where to go. He needed to catch a break in the case.

Beth and Janice were meeting Marty at the airport. Beth couldn't wait another minute to hear what Marty had uncovered. They met her at the gate and the drive home was all about catching up on the baby and the day-to-day motions that finalize a person's life.

Death certificates had to be sent out. Documents had to be signed and accounts had to be transferred into Beth's name. Arriving at Beth's house, they sat down with coffee and cookies, and Marty spread out her research files on the kitchen table.

Beth spoke first, "Are there any other annuities that don't allow any beneficiaries?"

"Good question," Marty went on. "No. As far as my research has turned up, the straight life annuity is only financial instrument that doesn't allow a beneficiary."

Beth continued, "Research says they were among the first annuities formed and they operated much like a life insurance policy does. It was set up to insure one life, much like a term life insurance policy. This annuity was set up to pay out to one annuitant."

"The fact that Alliance Life and Investments and thousands of other insurance companies thought it fair to keep all the remaining funds, including all generated interest, should be criminal and is nothing short of pure extortion." Marty waited for Beth to respond.

"But we have insurance that paid us on Rory's death, and it covers me to age 100. It's called whole life insurance and we were each other's beneficiaries. And they've already paid me, so again, why is the straight life annuity allowed to keep my money?" Understandably, Beth was confused.

"That's the trillion-dollar question and that's what my reporting is exposing. It's gaining momentum and people are riled up about it. They want to see an industry-wide policy change. We'll have to see how this plays out, but I think we're making progress. Have you been following my story in the news? Also, have you heard anything from the attorneys of Alliance Life and Investments?" Marty inquired.

Beth replied, "Of course, I'm following your reporting and I appreciate it like you can't believe. But no. I haven't heard back from Alliance yet. I'm being stonewalled and nothing seems to move them from their position. All the pressure from the press is concentrated on the industry and not so much on Alliance Life and Investments. We need to target them specifically," Beth urged.

"I'll start that this week," Marty said with conviction and a new path to follow. Something had to be done for Beth and her baby. She needed that money and was counting on it for her livelihood, and Marty was determined to do everything in her power to make that happen.

Denton was still working on Beth's case. He knew there were a couple of hairs found at that site, they hadn't gotten a hit on them yet but were still trying. Unlike the movies portray, it can take quite a long time to run things through all the databases.

But who murdered Rory? That question kept eating at Denton. In the beginning of the investigation, he was all for putting this to bed as an accident, but that was short-lived. His brother, Don, was a big wheel driver and when he brought up the subject to him, Denton was left with more questions than answers.

"Well, first of all, those housing don't slip," Don explained at a dinner table. "They're held in place with hydraulic safety releases. It ain't like yer cars and pickup trucks that you prop up the hood with a stick. These are cabovers and they make them strong for just that reason. They don't want anyone getting crushed to death if the hood moved the wrong way or that little stick snaps."

Don continued, "So, what yer lookin' at, lil' brother, ain't no accident. Someone had to force that hood down on him after defeatin' the hydraulic system. Even if he was gettin' ready to dismount, whether he was a jumpin,' or using the ladder, he couldn't have been smashed the way you say or in that position without someone doin' him in."

Denton was digging into everything about Rory's personal life. That included his marriage, his business affairs, and his community involvement. Turns out, he really had broken ground on a home for battered women and abused children, just like he said he'd do when he won the lottery.

He found out about Beth's rape that happened years prior and knew that was the reason for the women and children's shelter. Rory made good on his promise, and Beth was going to see it through if she could get the money from their lottery winnings.

He knew the money was bogged down by an insurance issue or something to that end. It was all over the news about how straight life annuities operate, and he figured that was the place to start. Follow the money and he'd find the answers. Just what does happen to *all* that money? These were his thoughts, and this was his plan to continue the Phillips' investigation.

Chapter Thirteen

Mark Stein

"Please sit down, Ms. Saunders. Would you like something to drink, coffee, tea, water?" Mark Stein, the attorney general for the state of Florida, asked politely.

"No, thank you. I'm fine," Marty responded.

Mark Stein was a businessman and full-time politician. He'd been in politics since he was in his early twenties. He started out slowly and at the bottom of the food chain. He won small elections, such as city councilman in Gainesville, and worked his way up to state attorney general. He was well-educated and known for being able to talk his way out of tight spots.

Stein wasted no time with idle banter and got straight to the point. "I've read your email, Ms. Saunders, and I'm not sure how I can help you. But I'm here to listen."

"As you know, Mr. Stein, I'm here to learn more about what happens to all the monies insurance companies are keeping and reinvesting from straight life annuities," Marty said.

"Well, Ms. Saunders, it is perfectly legal for insurance companies to fund lotteries, but I'm sure you already know that," he answered.

"Yes. I know it's legal, but I'm asking *you* what happens to *all that money*? You know as well as I do that if any other industry carried out this practice, they'd be indicted for extortion and fraud." Marty took a deep breath awaiting his response.

"Ms. Saunders let's clarify things. You're questioning just the straight life annuity, aren't you?" he asked.

"Yes. For now, that's the one I'm concerned with because it's mostly used to fund lottery winnings. Why do the insurance companies get to keep all the money, plus interest? Why doesn't it go to the spouse or heirs? That's what I specifically want to know." Marty rapidly fired her questions.

"Well, hold on there, Ms. Saunders." Stein said, trying to calm her down. "You know the insurance companies keep the monies for their own interests. But they also contribute to a number of charities and community causes, such as national and world-wide disasters and selected projects." Stein danced around the questions with the ease of a true politician.

Marty clenched her teeth. "I'm sure they can, and perhaps do use a portion of the money for such charitable contributions, no doubt to their advantage as another tax deduction. I'm sure they need all the money they can get," she pushed back. "But can't you just admit that the fat cats are lining their pockets with billions of dollars and flamboyant luxuries while essentially *stealing* the inheritance of unsuspecting public and investors?" she volleyed.

Stein sat straight back in his chair and put his feet flat on the floor as he leaned forward to speak. "I think you're just upset that insurance companies make a lot of money and do well for themselves. I believe it's called free enterprise. Welcome to capitalism, Ms. Saunders. Look it up," he barked back.

Marty countered with a tone to match his own. "Don't patronize me. I'm here questioning the methods of insurance companies who are fleecing money from everyday citizens." She was sweating. She could feel her heart hammering in her chest as she grew more enraged with Stein sitting there with righteous indignation and condescending lies.

Stein ignored her last comment and bulldozed her with his response. "Unless you have a plan to rewrite insurance laws, Ms. Saunders, I think we're done here. I've answered all your questions and I'm sure you can show yourself out." He pushed back from his desk and picked up the phone to make a call to no one in particular, or so it seemed.

"I plan to do just that. Rewrite the insurance laws. Mark my words, Mr. Stein," With that Marty left without slamming the door while fighting all her impulses to do so. Marty later detailed the outcome of her meeting to Beth and her family. "He was no help, but he's made me more determined than ever to rewrite the insurance laws." Marty paused to catch her breath.

Marty was livid. "You should have seen how smug he was about the whole thing. He was patronizing the entire time. Almost sneering at me. It made me physically ill in my stomach." Marty remembered Beth's condition before she had time to filter her comment.

"So now what?" Beth questioned as she poured herself a glass of orange juice. "What's your itinerary look like?" she asked, hoping Marty could stay a bit longer.

"I have to be in D.C. tomorrow morning. My flight gets in at nine. Why? What do you have in mind?" Marty asked. They made plans for later, after Marty ran a few errands. Then they enjoyed catching up the rest of the evening.

Meanwhile, Denton had news. "This is Capt. Denton. I'm calling for Beth Phillips, please," he said as he crushed a cigarette butt into his ashtray. He'd finally caught a break in the case.

Janice answered the phone. She was taking a second sick day as she had come down with a severe cold that was being passed around her office. "She's not here right now, but I can give you her number or take a message," she half coughed into the phone.

"I've got her number and I left her a message to call me as soon as possible," Denton said. "Just tell her I've got news fer her and she should call me immediately." He thanked her and hung up.

Janice wiped her nose and wondered about the news. She was eager to tell Beth about the phone call. Things really couldn't get worse since they'd been at a standstill for months. She wondered how the news would change the investigation.

Janice called Beth first and then John. She left a voice mail for Beth and talked with John about Denton's call. He didn't know where she was either. As it turned out, Beth had driven Marty to the airport and was headed back home.

About an hour went by before Beth called Denton. He answered the phone in his Southern drawl. "Gotta new lead that just might crack the case wide open on yer husband's murder," he told her with real happiness in his voice.

"What is it?" Beth questioned breathlessly.

"Do ya remember that hairs we found at the crime scene? Well, turns out we traced one of them to a known hit man, name of Jason White, goes by Whit." Denton was trying to explain this as gently as he could.

"A hit man?" Beth almost dropped the phone. "Like, a mob man kind of hit man? One that contacts to kill people … kind of hit man? Like in the movies kind of hit man?" Beth was puzzled and more than stunned by the news.

"Ahh, yes, ma'am, that's the kind," Denton answered. "There's no purdy way to sugar coat it, Mrs. Phillips. There was a contract put out on yer husband."

"But why? Why would anyone want to kill my husband, much less hire a hit man to do the job?" She was almost crying now. "This whole thing is like a reel from a bad movie."

"Well now, ya can look at it like that, or you can be happy that we have a lot more to work with now," Denton encouraged. "There's only a handful of people we know who could afford to hire Whit. And that narrows down the list of reasons why yer husband was bein' targeted." Denton lit another cigarette.

"Whit? Who is this Whit, and do you have a list of people who could afford him?" Beth questioned. Before he could answer, Beth was onto her next question. "How does this change the investigation?" she asked, already drained by this disturbing development. She was almost afraid of what he might say next. Denton drew a big drag and then exhaled slowly into the phone as he spoke.

"I mean that whoever hired him had a lot of money and that yer husband was more than likely killed because of his newly found wealth. That there lottery ya'll won may have been his undoin'." He blew out another puff.

Beth continued, her mind reeling from the news. "But we didn't take the lump sum. We just took the annual installments. We aren't millionaires in the sense that people may think." She was becoming exhausted trying to take in all this information and explain her wealth, and now the lack thereof.

Denton sensed that she was overwhelmed with this news. "Perhaps we can continue this in my office tomorrow, Mrs. Phillips. What time works for ya'll?" he asked, trying to accommodate her as much as possible.

"Perhaps you're right, Captain. How about nine? Will that work for you? Can I bring my sister or my brother-in-law with me?" she asked in case John could get off work if Janice wasn't feeling better.

"Sure thing, Mrs. Phillips. Ya bring whoever ya want. I'll see you then." Denton hung up the phone and got up to pour himself another cup of bitter black coffee.

After Beth talked with Denton, she called Janice and shared his news. They made plans to see Denton the next morning. Beth was more than happy that Janice was feeling well enough to go with her.

Denton was away from his desk when they arrived, but his assistant seated them in his office per his instructions. He had a few more documents to get. "Welcome, ladies," he said as he walked in with a cup of his usual black coffee. He took a seat as he slapped a file down on his desk.

Janice and Beth exchanged pleasantries with simultaneous hellos. "What news do you have for us today, Captain Denton?" Beth inquired as she looked at her sister and then back to Denton.

"Well, like I was tellin' ya yesterday, Mrs. Phillips, we're pretty sure we now know who killed yer husband. Denton repeated, As I said, it was this feller goes by the name of Whit."

"This is big. Really big. What we found out on him this mornin' could choke a horse. He's been responsible for seven recent deaths that we know of, and he's suspected in who knows how many more." He swallowed a sip of coffee.

"How is he still on the streets?" Beth shrieked while Janice looked equally horrified. "Shouldn't he have been locked away for life for at least some of these murders?" she twisted her wedding ring for something to distract her while she struggled with the additional news about her husband's untimely death.

"He has slick lawyers and a few judges workin' for him and his whole outfit. He's not the head of the snake, but he's been rumored to be his top gun," he informed them. "The head of the snake is a man by the name of Donovan Black. Goes by 'Black Jack.' He's the command." Denton drained the last drops of his coffee.

"FBI's been tryin' to bring both of 'em in for the last two decades. Whit, the feller who killed yer husband, is on America's top ten most wanted list." Denton reached for a smoke and the women shook their heads as they both looked at Beth's small budding belly. He nodded in understanding, set the unopened pack back down on his desk and proceeded to turn it on its corners as he talked.

"So, what's the plan to catch this man?" Beth stumbled with his name again. "You said his name is Whit, is that right?" She was wringing her hands in her lap. Now she was one step closer to justice of Rory. "Who are these people and why did they kill my husband? What did Rory do to warrant a hit man?" She started to sweat and felt clammy all over.

Denton explained the situation as he helped himself to another black coffee. "We're gonna trap 'em. Donovan is the mastermind of various illegal dealinz. He hires top talent to do his wet work. He never gets his hands dirty and just squeaks by within the framework of the law."

He continued, "This is big, Mrs. Phillips. He has a bunch of shell companies for launderin' money. But no one's ever been able to make anything stick. The FBI's been after 'em for years. So have we. But neither one of us have been able to lock 'em up." Denton paused with a sip of fresh coffee.

"So fer, every time Whit has killed, it's been either fer money or to shut someone up." Denton explained as he fumbled through the file and continued before he was interrupted.

"Recently we've noticed a pattern in the people he seems to be targetin'. We think his last seven victims have been lottery winners." Denton leaned forward and looked Beth straight in the eye. "But here's the kicker. All seven of the prize winnin'rs had their money in those straight life annuities." He finished with a nod and a glint in his eye.

Denton knew all too well that Beth knew exactly what he was talking about, since she had informed him of this with phone calls and emails. He held her eyes for a moment, letting the information sink in before he continued. "All the winners chose the installment payout program. There has to be a connection here." He got up to pour himself to a third cup of coffee and sat back down.

Moving on, he said, "We cross-checked the insurance companies that invested their lottery winnin's into straight life annuities." Denton could see the women were busy absorbing his words. "Turns out every one of those companies's strugglin' financially. They're all in the red. Times being what they are, insurance companies are lookin' for solid investors and have coerced the winners into optin' for straight life annuities because their payout is so large." He hoped she wouldn't take offense to that broad statement.

Denton rocked back in his chair with a half-smile on his face. "Like I said, Mrs. Phillips, this reaches far beyond yer situation and the murder of yer husband. It's big. It's affecting, at minimum, seven other families that we know of. Hell, probably many more. I think we can catch 'em, Mrs. Phillips, if we follow the money." Denton smiled.

Beth and Janice looked like wide-eyed children drinking in a bedtime story with rapt attention as Denton continued.

"We think Whit's killin' off lottery winners who choose the installment payout plan. Ya see, the insurance companies get to keep the influx of those new lottery winnin's and if they kill off the annuitants before they have to pay out the installments to 'em, then that there's how they're remain' solvent in these unsettlin' economic times. This keeps them obligated for years to come and they have more going out than they do coming in. It's simple economics." He nodded his head and flashed a smile again.

"I don't understand. Why wouldn't they kill the those who chose the lump sum? It would keep them from having to payout all that money. Why aren't they killing them? I thought the whole purpose of these murders was to keep the monies from the lotteries." Beth asked as she tried to reason with this information.

Denton anticipated that question and was at the ready with an explanation. "Because if a bunch of lottery winners who took the lump sum started droppin' dead from accidents or mysterious circumstance, they'd run a great risk of bein' discovered. However, if'in folks go missin' from these means after takin' a lifetime installment plan, no one's gonna notice as much."

"Unbelievable! I can't believe my ears," Beth said as she drop-jawed. She and Janice looked at each other and back to Denton.

"That can't be true, can it?" Janice asked in disbelief. For a brief moment you could hear a pin drop in Denton's office.

"But how do we catch them?" Beth asked with bewilderment. "No one else has been able to do so for years. You said so yourself. What can we possibly do that will catch them?" She had little hope their efforts would yield success since Donovan and Whit had eluded authorities for so long.

"We smoke 'em out, Mrs. Phillips. We smoke 'em out! How do we go about it, yer a wonderin'? We set a trap and all we need's the bait, and the FBI have the bait. Don't worry. This is gonna work out." He smiled as he watched their expressions change from perplexed to hopeful, and a broad grin lounged across his face and lingered.

"Back up here just for a moment, Capt. Denton." Beth halted despite being nearly at a loss for words. "You're telling me that he's killed seven people or, more precisely, murdered seven people for failing insurance companies, just so they wouldn't have to pay out on the lottery winnings and he still hasn't been brought to justice? How does he keep getting by with this?" she queried in disbelief.

"I was gettin' to that, Mrs. Phillips. And that's a good question and I have just the answer fer ya." Denton paused for the effect. "They have hot shot attorneys, and more than a few friends in high places. These were not overt murders per se, all their deaths seemed to be from natural causes or accidents, like yer poor husband, Mrs. Phillips." Denton suspected more but knew he'd have trouble just proving the seven murders.

Denton was forthcoming. "Some were killed in automobile accidents or by anaphylactic shock. Some died from heart attacks or strokes. One was killed with a vaccination shot and one died from sleep apnea. She just never woke up. I think you get my drift, Mrs. Phillips." As Denton concluded he closed the file on his desk. Beth and Janice were speechless. They were in total shock by this news. What had they gotten themselves into?

Chapter Fourteen

Katie Lestler, the Bait

"Hi, Beth. It's so good to hear from you. How's everything?" Marty asked as she was putting on her blouse. She was getting ready for another live report this morning at a ribbon-cutting ceremony at the Smithsonian. It was the first stop for a new Egyptian exhibit touring the United States.

"Things are getting better, I think. But I need some time to update you on all the latest news. You'll want this story," Beth told her, knowing she was as dedicated to getting to the truth as much as she was.

"Well, can you give it to me in a nutshell for now?" Marty suggested as she put on a fancy, white, oversized T-shirt to go with her black leather mini skirt. She looked around the room to make sure she had everything. When she was a rookie traveler, she often forgot things, but after logging thirty-thousand miles, she had a rhythm and routine which eliminated forgotten items.

"In a nutshell, Rory was killed by a hit man named Jason White," Beth began to explain. "Goes by the nickname 'Whit' and he works for 'Black Jack.' His real name is Donovan Black." Beth took a breath.

She went on before Marty could get a word in edgewise. "I know this sounds like I'm making it up, but I'm not. He's killed at least seven people, but he made all the deaths appear to be from natural causes or accidents, just like Rory's death was made to look like an accident."

Whit may have gotten away with Rory's death too, if I hadn't heard them talking when I was on the phone with him or if they hadn't found the bullet in Rory's thigh." Beth couldn't get her words out fast enough.

She continued with pain in her voice. Beth explained all the details that Denton had just given her.

Marty jumped in, "The forensics showed a malfunction in the safety system. I remember seeing that in the CSI reports. So, in short, you're saying you know who murdered Rory, but we can't prove it yet. Just who exactly is 'Whit' and Donovan Black again?" Marty asked as she finished brushing her hair.

Beth walked to the refrigerator and got out the milk. "Donovan Black. He's the head of the snake, as Denton puts it. He's the man the authorities are really after. He supposedly concocted this whole nightmare, and he's been ordering all the hits on the unsuspecting lottery winners. I'd be thrilled if they just got this Whit guy. He's the one who murdered my husband." Beth poured herself a glass of milk.

"We've got him, Beth," Marty assured her. "The hair places him at the scene of the crime," Marty breathed excitedly. They were truly working together with each other's information.

"All we have to do is set up a national manhunt with his picture everywhere. We'll find him with the public's help, that is if he's in the country. Do you have any recent pictures of him or something we can do an age progression?" Marty asked while slipping her shoes on and giving a last glance in the mirror to make sure she looked her best.

"I don't know if the authorities have a current picture of him, but I'll find out," Beth responded. "According to Denton, pictures of Whit are non-existent. He's adept at avoiding cameras and alters his appearance with plastic surgeries."

"He's managed to dodge the authorities for years," Beth took a quick breath. "What makes you think going public with this is the smartest course we can take?" Beth asked as she dipped a chocolate almond biscotti in her milk. She'd been craving them for the past two weeks.

Marty encouraged her, "You'd be amazed how the media can flush out people who are living underground. Media coverage effects change. Just ask the politicians and athletes. Media influences people." Marty closed the door behind her and changing focus, she shifted the conversation to the authorities. "What are Denton's ideas?"

Beth jumped in, "He says we're going to follow the money trail. He thinks that's the fastest way to find both of them. The FBI's planning to stage a fake lottery winner as 'new bait' to draw out Whit. They're concentrating on finding him first, so they can stop the murders."

Marty slung her handbag over her shoulder and pulled her carry-on behind her. Their conversation ended with unanswered questions, but the using 'new bait' idea intrigued her, and she was excited about knowing the identities of the murderers. This story kept evolving.

A month passed as the FBI assembled a lottery sting operation with a rigged winner. The bait was Katie Lestler, a seasoned FBI agent. Katie had a lot of experience in undercover work. She was known for her ability to quickly adapt to changing dynamics in sting ops. So now everything was in place. Katie was the co-winner of a large lottery.

If things went according to plan, Katie would be the next mark. Like Beth and Rory, she chose the installment payout option to expedite the inevitable attempt on her life. The pressure was on the FBI and Katie to draw an attempt on her life as soon as possible.

They didn't have to wait long. One evening while Katie was driving home from her undercover temp job, the car's wheel, gas and brake pedal were seized simultaneously. Someone else had remotely accessed her car. No matter what she did, nothing changed. The car's computer had been hacked and she was at their mercy.

Katie didn't remember a time when she had been so frightened, and that entailed quite a bit from her experience as a federal agent. She quickly called 911. Her team had eyes and ears on her vehicle, so they knew she was in danger.

"911. What's your emergency?" the operator answered.

"I've lost complete control of my car and I don't know what to do before I have a wreck," she said as real panic set in. Her only hope was with her team being able to hack into her car's computer and return control to her before she crashed. Little did she know they weren't able to override the hack.

"Can you put the car in neutral?" the dispatcher asked.

"I can try. I can't. It won't go in. It won't budge. Now what?" she asked in a calm tone. Her FBI training was kicking in and she knew she had to remain calm.

"How fast are you going and are you on a public street or highway?" the dispatcher questioned.

"I … I'm on a public street in the downtown area," Katie answered. The calm voice of the dispatcher helped quiet her nerves.

"How fast are you driving?" the operator asked.

Katie looked down at the speedometer, "It says 33 mph and I'm in the middle of town. It won't be long before I run into someone or vice versa. I'd try to jump out, but my doors and windows are locked, and I can't unlock them. It's as if the car has a mind of its own," Katie said, knowing that was exactly what was happening. It had the mind of a killer driving her car.

"Are there any small trees, barrels or trash dumpsters that you are moving toward that could absorb the shock of impact?" the dispatcher asked.

Before Katie could respond, a black SUV with blackened windows came from a side street and T-boned her on the driver's side of her car. It was driven by a man. The air bags exploded, and Katie lay still in her seat with her head slumped backwards against the head rest.

Her body had been pushed slightly into the console. Her legs were twisted beneath her and the blood drained from the left side of her head. She was still wearing her seat belt and she felt pain in the lower parts of her abdomen. It came in waves as she flickered in and out of consciousness.

Emergency vehicles were on the scene almost immediately. Her team had followed her via GPS and had a standby ambulance ready for dispatch near the downtown area. Police crews were next to arrive as the fireman trucks quickly rolled up.

It took the jaws-of-life to extract Katie from the car. They back boarded her into the ambulance that rushed her to the hospital. She was in the trauma one unit for assessment. They ran a battery of tests, starting with a chest x-ray and an ultrasound of her abdomen. She was still fading in and out of consciousness as they worked on her.

It appeared she was bleeding internally, so Katie was rushed into emergency surgery. It was a matter of time now. The sacrifice from agent Lestler was great, but only time would tell if she would recover fully, or at all.

Back at the scene of the accident, the officers couldn't find either a driver or passenger of the black SUV. There were a couple of eyewitnesses, not always considered reliable sources in matters such as these. Police took their statements and asked if they could come down to the precinct to help with a sketch artist. They both agreed.

One witness did see a driver. He described a tattoo of a snake on one of his arms. Both witnesses described the driver as a tall man, around one-hundred and eighty pounds. He wore a black T-shirt, black jeans, and black sneakers.

Per one of the witnesses, the tattoo on his left arm was of a coiled snake ready to strike. It had piercing green and red eyes. Both eyewitnesses said they saw him running from the scene in a southwest direction toward the train station. How original. A professional hit man that catches a train.

Katie's sting team fell back and let the Tallahassee Police Department do their jobs while her team kept eyes and ears on her with the help of another FBI agent. His name was Drake Sommers, who had recently finished working a three-year undercover task. He checked out the train station for leads. The crime scene unit was still at the crash site, getting pictures and collecting evidence from both vehicles. The black SUV had a few fibers but no fingerprints.

Katie woke up with her head feeling like someone had taken a jack hammer to it. She had a ruptured appendix, a deep cut over her left eye, bruised ribs, and a bowel obstruction which rushed her into surgery, but she would make a full recovery. She was lucky to be alive and that the impact didn't permanently damage her spine or legs. She was expected to remain in the hospital for six to ten days.

They FBI authorized a press release that she had survived, hoping that would draw Whit in for a second attempt on her life. After all, she was confined to the hospital and it would be an easy place to finish the job.

For Katie's protection, the FBI alternated plain clothes officers in the waiting room of the hospital. Also, they covertly staffed a nurse to work the night shift and let the waiting room members take turns visiting her throughout the day.

It was the Friday after her accident when Whit made his second attempt to finish the job he'd started. He was dressed in blue scrubs and had the appearance of belonging in the environment, but he had the mission of a soldier.

As an experienced hit man, he was onto the FBI plain clothed officers. They were so predictable. Idiots, he thought to himself. However, he didn't expect anyone on the medical staff of being an undercover agent.

He didn't think they'd go that far in their attempt to keep her safe. He wasn't sure how much they knew about him. He'd heard all about the 'lottery murders' story. Some rumors referred to them as 'dead giveaways.'

It was all over the place, but he didn't know if they were on to him as the assassin.

Marty delivered the news. She was following the story of the lottery murders and the outcome of the 'lucky winners' lives. Her updates were covered as a human-interest series called '*Lottery Murders.*' *The Other Side of Winning It Big!*

The media storm brought unwanted attention to the covert operations and overall role of the insurance companies. So, the fact that Whit had failed to kill Katie in the accident didn't find him any favor in the eyes of his boss, 'Black Jack,' Donovan Black. The pressure was on to kill her as quickly as possible and make it seem like complications from her accident.

Whit entered Katie's hospital room. She was between awake and sleep; she was groggy from all the medication. She could barely hold her eyes open. She didn't recognize him, so she pretended to be asleep. But even dazed from sleep and drugs, Katie knew something was up.

She had a gun under her bed sheets for her protection. As the killer approached her bed, he told her it was time for another dose of intravenous Ativan. Her senses were vigilant. Since she had a morphine pump for pain and anxiety, she knew he had to be Whit.

Still she feigned sleep, just peeking through her eyelashes while he was crossing the room toward her. She recognized the snake tattoo on his left arm, and he fit the vague description the eyewitnesses had given. She slipped her hand underneath the covers as if she were trying to get more comfortable. She gripped her pistol.

The gun made her feel safe. She quietly flipped off the safety and wrapped her hand around it in a ready-to-fire fashion. The stranger advanced to her chart and then to the side of her bed, ready to administer the syringe.

It was filled with succinylcholine, which paralyzes its victims. However, they're still cognizant of what's happening around them. Just as he started to insert the needle into the IV port line, Katie shot him through the covers. She hit him in the chest near his heart, not bad for her condition and close range.

Immediately, the regular hospital staff and her team were in her room. Whit was crumpled on top of her. He attempted a second time to inject his venom straight into her veins, but she got off a second shot that lodged in his shoulder. He slumped to the floor. Blood was everywhere. Whit was still alive but not by much.

Chapter Fifteen

Jason 'Whit' White

Marty, Beth, Janice, and John were in a meeting with Capt. Denton. He took a deep breath while speaking. "Whit survived his injuries and cut a deal with the FBI. He rolled on his partners and turned state's evidence. He gave up Donovan, Mark Stein and everything he had on them. It doesn't matter if we get Donovan on one murder or dozens, we still get him," Denton declared.

He took a drag from his newly lit cig, then turned to Beth. "Whit's entered the Federal Witness Protection Program, meanin' it'll be harder for him to resume his murder-for-hire career. However, he's slippree'enough that if he got the right offer, he'd be back in business. But that's highly unlikely since Donovan now has a price on his head for rollin' on him and his sloppy work when he failed to kill Ms. Lestler." He lit another cigarette without realizing it. Denton had been a chain smoker since he was 15. He's tried several times and as many products to quit, but they all failed. He made his peace with it years ago.

"Whit knows he'll always be lookin' over his shoulder fer the rest of his life," Denton stated with confidence. "The only option he had left was to turn state's evidence. If he goes to prison, he's dead on the first day by the hands of Donovan's men.

"Hell, Whit'l be lucky if he stays alive to testify against him." Denton paused as he took another long pull on his new cigarette before he remembered Beth was pregnant. He put it out and twirled it in his fingers, obviously needing his next smoke.

Denton continued, "Given all this new information and names Whit's given up, the FBI has a case against Donovan that's growin' by the minute.

There's enough to upend the insurance world too." Denton smiled a deep satisfied smile as he looked at them.

Marty interrupted. "Is it true that so far, there are seven insurance companies involved in this conspiracy? That's what we've verified. Has that information changed?"

"So fer it's just the seven. Our ultimate goal is to bring Donovan and his henchmen to justice. But this is really outta our hands. It's the FBI's investigation now. Has been ever since they baited the trap," Denton said with satisfaction.

Marty responded while avidly taking notes. "But we don't know anyone in the FBI, so can we continue to get our information from you?"

"Sure," Denton responded. "As long as we know somethin', I'll be passin' it on to ya'll. But like I said, it's the FBI's investigation now."

"Thank you so much, Captain Denton," Beth leaned back a bit, to reduce the smell emitting from Denton's ashtray.

Marty jumped back in, "Seven. You said so far there are seven insurance companies involved in the conspiracy." She jotted it down for accuracy in her next report. "Considering the power of big insurance, it makes the battle of David and Goliath seem like a picnic compared to a plethora of lottery winners trying to topple the insurance companies," Marty finished as she sipped her latte.

Denton pointed out, "On the other hand, the public is enraged. People are realizin' the truth behind these straight life annuities and they're beginnin' to revolt. But on the other hand, like you said, Ms. Saunders, we're goin' up against big insurance and that's a fight that'll meet with some serious opposition and repercussions." Denton was fidgeting and jonesin' for a cig.

"Most people want the lump-sum payout," Beth said in an all-too-familiar voice, "but some want the security of annual or monthly income, like we did because the lump sum takes such a hefty tax toll."

"Didn't you say you've received two payments so far?" Marty asked Beth as she referred to her notes.

"That's right. We just got our second payment in January. Our next payment was supposed to be in January of next year. But given the letter, I won't see another penny of our winnings. Given Whit's pattern for knocking off winners, I guess we were lucky to have gotten two payments. It kept Rory with me for an extra year." She looked up at Marty as she realized again how uncertain her future was now that Rory was gone.

Marty chimed in, "My research revealed that currently, insurance companies are scrambling to get legislature to help them limit their lifetime payouts on guaranteed annuities, specifically, from the Lifetime Income Builders annuities. These annuities have beneficiaries. However, these particular annuities promised a guaranteed specific rate of return on annuity products sold mostly during 2006 to 2008 during the housing bubble."

Marty continued undaunted, "In short, most insurance companies are desperate to stay alive. Between these and some variable annuities they sold in the nineties, their solvency is teetering. Some of the annuities based their payouts on five to 6% 'over' the original investment amount. They can't possibly cover those rates of return in this economic environment. They're looking for a way out." She waited for a response.

Denton was on his next cup of cold coffee. It was more like swill. "We have to stop 'em and seek industry-wide reform. But that's up to the politicians. It has nothin' to do with our police work." Denton stood up and thanked them for coming in and promised to stay in touch.

They left Denton's office in bewilderment. They were glad to be one step closer to capturing Donovan but were deflated knowing Whit would never serve a day behind bars or face the death penalty now that he was protected in the Federal Witness Protection Program. WITSEC.

Marty reported the outcome of her meeting with Florida State Attorney General, Mark Stein, from the steps of his office building. She had a knot in her stomach from the disgust with him. Her nerves were frayed and dangling like a bungee cord.

Dinner was from a popular national pub-style restaurant. It was easy, good and as close to homemade as anyone was willing to attempt. Conversation, on the other hand, was bountiful and fully charged with the events of the day.

Beth started. "I still can't believe any of this is legal."

Marty broke in. "We need to fight to get the laws changed."

"How do you propose we go about it?" Janice chimed in.

"We have to do this one case at a time, in court. I imagine in civil court," Marty responded. "I believe it will take multiple wins of civil suits before there's any real reform."

They're going to try to slap a Band-Aide on this mess and call it fixed. We have to lobby for reform. But the question now is, can Whit stay alive long enough to testify?" Marty looked from face to face, seeing if they were with her on this.

"Isn't that the FBI's job? Didn't he get the witness protection program in exchange for everything he knows about Donovan?" Janice asked.

"That's the deal," Beth stated with pain in her voice. So, whose case do we start with?" Beth asked. She desperately wanted to give some meaning to the senseless loss of Rory.

Marty answered sympathetically, "First, we start with Mark Stein's case. His guilty verdict will be the closest we get to justice for Rory, *if* he lives to testify. We have Whit's and Stein's recorded confessions and dirt on Donovan, but the defense will argue they were made under duress, so we need them on the stand. But first things first. For now, everything hinges on Stein's trial." Marty hoped this would give them all some hope.

Chapter Sixteen

Donavan Black and Drake Sommers

Katie had fully recovered from her physical injuries but not from the emotional pain. At the FBI Academy in Quantico, Virginia, she was taught how to deal with mental and emotional stress, so she didn't understand why she was experiencing so much emotional pain.

She applied all the tactics she had learned, but she couldn't eliminate the feeling of vulnerability that she had felt while lying in that hospital bed. She knew she had a target on her back. In fact, she was at the top of the list now that she had survived two attempts on her life. She should have been dead by now. Donovan Black wanted her dead and she knew the clock was ticking. It was personal now.

Every time she got in a car, she worried about a bomb and the incident that landed her in the hospital, completely injured physically, emotionally, and mentally. Katie would be looking over her shoulder until Donovan was apprehended or dead. He'd really gotten inside her head. It felt as though she had little control over her circumstances.

What bothered her most was the countless life-threatening situations she'd been in before and she had always landed on her feet. She was known for her quick thinking in tricky situations. But during those times, she had a sense of control that got her through the challenges of the daily life as an FBI agent.

Those experiences paled in comparison to her current ordeal with Donovan. No one really knew what he looked like. He went to extreme lengths to conceal his identity. There were no current pictures of him, so doing an aged composite was guesswork at best. With all the plastic surgery done on his face, pictures were moot.

Katie's survival caused a real conundrum for the FBI. They knew she was the star witness if the case came to trial. If for some reason Whit didn't survive, Katie's testimony would sway the jury to a guilty verdict. However, she had to be kept close under wraps so that she too would live to see the trial and testify. The FBI had its hands full.

Katie was 27 and single. This fact played to her advantage because the fewer ties she had, the less leverage Donovan had over her. The fact that she didn't have a husband, boyfriend, or any children to kidnap or murder gave her a leg up in her career. Personal lives really weren't an option for those who chose to protect and serve. It made for a lonely life, but she didn't plan on doing this forever.

She wanted to put in her time at the bureau and then try her hand as a wife and mother. She often pondered what type of new career could challenge her mentally and physically. It was a tall order for a would-be ex-FBI agent to find a secular career that offered the excitement and pace she was used to as an agent. But for now, only the-here-and-now mattered, and that's where she focused her attention.

How would the FBI protect Katie and still draw out Donovan? That was the million-dollar question. They decided to bring her in from field ops and put her on administrative duty for an undetermined amount of time. By putting Katie on admin, she'd have regular nine-to-five hours and engage a daily routine. The FBI expected Donovan would be planning his next attempt on her life, and they knew he was out for the kill this time.

Katie figuratively went kicking and screaming into desk duty. After she graduated from Quantico, she was immediately put into field service. She'd never served a day behind the desk and she hated the idea that she had to go through this rouse. She wouldn't start until next Monday, but she was already sick of it and it was only Friday.

Katie was staged as living alone in a one-bedroom apartment. At first, the FBI toyed with the idea to temporarily moving her in with some other agents. But Katie convinced them it would put more lives at risk.

They conceded to her way of thinking but with the quid quo pro that an undercover agent would protect her twenty-four-seven. They had carefully selected an apartment complex that had two vacant but adjacent apartments.

The agent chosen for her bodyguard and 'neighbor' was Drake Sommers. He was 6'3" and weighed in at 187 seven pounds. He had dark hair and green eyes. He was disciplined and kept himself in peak condition for his career. He had been on the force for 11 years; five were undercover and the past six had been in the witness protection program. He'd seen his share of situations.

He was divorced with a 7-year-old son, Stephen, who lived with his mother. His ex-wife, Emily, had sole custody of their son due to the inherent dangers of Drake's job. He seldom had the opportunity to see his son other than via video chats. It was a real challenge to line up schedules for a visitation.

Emily worked as a nurse on the day shift so she could spend her evenings and some weekends with her son. During the day he was in school, and his grandparents watched him after school and on weekends and when Emily had to put in overtime.

Stephen was having a normal and happy childhood since his parents didn't hate each other after their divorce, instead they respected each other's career choices. They realized that their work left little time for each other, let alone for dual parenting.

Drake was assigned to Katie because of his overall experience as an agent and his recent familiarity with the witness protection program. Katie would never admit it, but she was comforted by his presence next door. However, she realized it put one more agent's life in danger. Donovan's men were expert excursioners and she knew if someone were willing to trade his life for hers, she would most likely die.

Now that Katie had a regular schedule, her evenings were free for a social life. She started spending more time with Janice, John, and Beth. Since John was an ex-Navy SEAL his skills were equal to, or better than Donovan's men.

Because Katie was assigned the task of bait during the length of this ordeal, she had gotten close to all three of them and worried for their welfare due to their close relationship with her. Sometimes Katie would spend the night at Janice and John's house for added protection. Those were the nights that Katie didn't have to sleep with one eye open.

It was the day of the arraignment for Mark Stein. He sat in court stone-faced while the charges against him were read. To look at him, it was obvious he was devoid of any human emotions such as guilt or remorse. He was a true sociopath.

The court clerk read out loud every name of his alleged murder victims and Katie's name as an attempted murder. Their names were important to the victims' families. The utter upheaval of the victims' families could not be overemphasized.

"Mr. Stein, how do you plead?" the judge questioned after every name that was read. Stein replied the same every time. "Not guilty, your Honor," he said with sarcasm and a smug smirk.

The judge's docket was full. But due to the nature of the trial and all the publicity the case was garnering, he set the trial date as soon as possible. He rearranged his calendar just to accommodate an early trial and set the court date for November 7, 2022. That was the best he could do. It was five months away.

As Stein was paraded out of the court, a sea of news cameras greeted him. Microphones were immediately thrust in the faces of the defense and prosecution attorneys. The case, like most high-profile cases had already been tried by mass media and public opinion. The public verdict was guilty and let him hang.

As expected, Stein's bail was denied, citing a flight risk. His attorneys tried their best to get him released on a five-million-dollar bond and his own recognizance, but the judge wouldn't consider it. His attorneys argued, where could he go? His face had been splashed worldwide for several months. Attempting to flee would be pointless.

By now there was a bounty on Donovan for a million dollars to the lucky chap who cared to turn him in. The price was right, but the possibility of living long enough to enjoy the reward called for consideration. All roads led to Donovan as the mastermind of this whole conspiracy and everyone wanted him brought to justice, but only a handful of people knew what he looked like, and they weren't talking.

Whit was put in isolation for his protection and suicide watch for fear he may try to kill himself rather than accept his fate in the witness protection program or have to rat on Donovan. They figured Donovan would have him assassinated while being held over for trial. Whit felt like a caged racehorse standing at the starting gate, waiting to spring loose at a full out run. All Whit hoped for was a chance to escape. He wanted to get very lost somewhere on the planet where he hoped Donovan couldn't find him.

Katie was becoming familiar with her new routine. She didn't like it, but it was the fastest way to draw out Donovan and his men. By the third week after Whit's arrest, Donovan sent the kill order. It was about 10:30 p.m. on a Tuesday evening after Katie got home from visiting Beth, Janice, and John. They shared a home-cooked meal and watched a new movie they all wanted to see.

Katie had just walked into her apartment and set down her purse and keys. She went to the fridge to grab a cold bottle of water. It was July and there was a heat wave covering half the nation. She bought a case of bottled water over the weekend, and she already downed most of it. There were just a few bottles left. She had taken one to the gym earlier that day, but she had a smoothie instead, so she put it back in the fridge for later.

'Later' became now, as she yanked the top open and started to drink it. Almost immediately she could feel her throat close and her breathing became labored. She knew she had to get help fast. The pain in her stomach and esophagus was excruciating.

Her body was starting to seize, and she didn't have long to get help. She reached for the cell phone in her purse and just got 911 dialed when she felt her body immobilize. She had ingested succinylcholine, or sux. It was the same drug Whit attempted to use when she was in the hospital.

The Sux temporarily immobilized her, but she was still aware of what was happening to her and around her. She could hear the 911 operator asking if anyone was there and the nature of the emergency, but she couldn't move or speak. Her system was shutting down.

Drake was next door and aware that Katie had just arrived home. She was supposed to check in with him by text, giving the all-clear that the apartment was safe. However, this night he heard a noise that sounded suspicious. He got to her in time to start CPR. He kept up the life-saving procedure until the paramedics arrived about two minutes later.

Fortunately, the drug wears off quickly when given in prescribed dosages for specific protocols, such as surgery. However, an overdose can suffocate a person when the lungs become paralyzed. It can also cause a surge of potassium, which can lead to cardiac arrest.

It's a perfect kill drug that breaks down almost immediately into natural substances found in the body. So, it's hard to detect unless technicians know what to look for, and even then, it can be too late to find it in the body quick enough to save a life.

The paramedics followed normal protocol for respiratory failure. They had no idea that there was a bigger issue of possible cardiac arrest lingering in the shadows of Katie's sudden illness.

She was in the ER when Drake was questioned six ways to Sunday about Katie's condition when he found her. What was his relationship with her, and did he know how long she was in this condition? Did he know what she had ingested and how did she get it?

Drake had few words for them. He covered the basics of how he found her and why he had been the one to call the paramedics, but he too had no idea why or how she was in this condition.

"I heard her fall and that's why I was the first person on the scene," Drake explained. He knew in his heart that this was a direct assault from one of Donovan's men. He didn't know if Katie would make it through this third attempt on her life.

Drake called Beth, who notified John and Janice and they met him at the hospital for the vigil. They waited anxiously for what seemed like hours before Dr. Patel came out to see them.

"Are any of you direct family members to her?" he asked.

"No," they all responded in chorus.

"Well, without any immediate family members present, I can't go into detail other than to say she seems to be out of the woods for now," Patel informed them.

Drake pulled the good doctor aside and flashed his FBI badge. Dr. Patel elaborated as little as possible, knowing he had the right to ask for a warrant. But the lateness of the hour and the fact that she seemed to be doing well factored into his decision to cooperate with the FBI.

"As I said, she seems to be doing okay for now, but we'll keep her overnight for observation. Do you know if she might be allergic to anything?" Dr. Patel wanted to give him good news, as well as find out more information if possible.

"I don't know of any allergies. Is that what you think happened, Dr. Patel?" Drake asked. "Do you think this was a reaction to some allergy we don't know about?"

"I'm not sure what to think at this point." Some of her symptoms seemed like they could be an allergic reaction because of the respiratory failure." He was tired from a thirty-six-hour shift. There had been a massive car pile-up on the interstate causing the overtime.

Dr. Patel stated, "At one point, she couldn't move her legs, so that presents a bit of a puzzle. We're doing follow-up tests to rule out other issues." He became vague as he trailed off.

"So, she's awake?" Janice asked as she approached them.

"Yes. She's awake and you can see her for a few minutes until they have to take her for more tests," Dr. Patel replied. "She's in ER, bay three." Then he took Drake aside and asked him a few more questions while the rest went one at a time to see Katie.

"So, you said you found her on the floor not breathing, but conscious. Is that right, Agent Sommers?" Patel asked.

"Yes. That's exactly how I found her," Drake replied.

"Did you notice if she'd been eating or drinking anything?" Dr. Patel questioned.

"Yes, I did. She was drinking a bottle of water. I brought it with me for you to analyze. It doesn't have any unusual odor to it, but maybe you can run some trace on it?" Drake asked hopefully.

"I'd think that would be more up your alley, Agent Sommers, but sure, we'll have our lab take a look at it. Based on your suspicions, should we run some heavy metal tests for poisons? Anything in particular we should be looking for?" Patel inquired.

"Nothing comes to mind, Dr. Patel, but please search for poisons or paralyzing agents," Drake answered, wishing he had better intel.

"Thank you, Agent Sommers," Dr. Patel said.

"Given the circumstances, it'd probably be much faster if your lab ran it for trace elements," Drake suggested.

"Well, thank you for narrowing it down for us, Agent Sommers." Dr. Patel nodded with sarcasm. His fatigue was getting the better of him.

Chapter Seventeen

Katie Awakens

Katie was awake and breathing on her own. She was glad to see everyone around her. Then Drake walked in and she perked up. She wanted to talk with him about the incident. She knew she owed her life to him. If he hadn't been next door, it's unlikely the paramedics would have made it in time to save her.

"How are you doing, Katie?" Drake asked as he took her hand in his.

"Much better, thanks to you," she answered as she squeezed his hand.

"What happened?" Drake asked, eager to know more.

"I'm not sure, but I think there was something in my water bottle," she answered. "I came home and grabbed a bottle of water and barely had some when I felt my throat start to close."

"We're having it tested as we speak, hon," he said. "Where did you get it?"

"It was in my refrigerator," she explained. "I took it with me to the gym earlier today and was about to drink it there when I decided to have a smoothie instead. So, I brought it home and put it in the fridge for later."

"So, one of Donovan's men got to it while you were working out. Did you notice anything or anyone out of the ordinary?" Drake asked.

"No. I didn't see anyone, and I kept my bottle with me most of the time. The only time I wasn't watching it was when I had the smoothie. I got to talking with another member. We chatted for a while, but even then, I had it right next to me. It must have happened while I was paying for the smoothie." She spoke with dismay as she realized she'd been set up.

"Had you ever met this member before today?" Drake asked, wondering if she had been the culprit. "Did you get a good look at her?"

"No. She was friendly, but we only exchanged pleasantries. Nothing to remember, just which smoothies are the best and that kinda thing. Nothing more than a few words." Katie admitted.

Katie realized she was speaking to her assailant. She wished she'd paid more attention to her appearance. "She was rather unremarkable. She was quite ordinary, other than her dark red hair." She gave an exact description, but it was so generic it could have been anyone.

"So, what's our next step, Drake?" Katie asked, mortified that she'd almost been assassinated once again by the bidding of Donovan.

"I'm not sure, yet," he said. "I imagine we'll keep things as they are. You did nothing wrong, Katie," Drake soothed her. "We all get played at some point in our careers and given what you've been through, it's a wonder you're still able to function as an agent."

Beth chimed in, "Katie, we're just relieved you're okay." Beth and Janice arrived to see how she was doing.

"Yeah. You're still with us and that's the most important thing right now," Janice announced, finishing the thoughts of everyone. No one slept well that night, as they were on edge with worry for their friend, Katie.

"He's not going to give up until he kills me," Katie insisted. "You'd think he'd be running out of ideas and hit men by now, wouldn't you?" she asked rhetorically. She hated to lose it in front of them, but with each attempt she grew more and more despondent.

"Don't worry about it," Beth asserted. "Just get better fast."

"No worries, Katie. We're going to get you to trial," Drake said emphatically.

"We'll see," Katie muttered as she started to wind down. It was clear to all that she needed some rest, so they said their goodbyes and left the room.

They decided to meet at Beth's house and discuss their options regarding her safety. Drake knew there were FBI agents surrounding her room, and one agent posing as a nurse was put on duty for her constant safety. The FBI nurse was embedded in the ER and Katie's room for the overnight observation.

Back at Janice and John's house, Beth asked the obvious question to Drake and everyone in the room. "What else can we do?"

"It's hard to say at this point," Drake said as he was thinking over their options. "We can't really step up surveillance without overtly tipping our hand. I suppose I could move in with her, posing as her boyfriend. It would carry some risk, but it may be our only option. I'll have to talk to our handler, Dave, first thing in the morning. I'll call him after speaking with Dr. Patel."

"What if she moved in with me for a while? Why can't that work?" Beth wondered out loud.

"That wouldn't solve anything," John interjected without waiting for a response from Drake. "You don't have the skills to protect her, and then both of your lives would be at risk."

"John's right," Drake pointed out. "I really don't see a lot of options here. Katie is a field- trained and experienced agent. I'm confident she can fight them if she sees them coming. But right now, that's the big concern. We can't fight what we can't see. Katie was on her game today and she still had no idea she had been drugged."

"How long before you know if you're going to pretend to be her boyfriend and move in with her?" Beth asked anxiously.

"I'm sure I'll know something in the morning," Drake assured them.

Katie was watching the ceiling tiles and lights go by as she was wheeled down the hospital hallway on her way for a CT scan. Because of the FBI's involvement, they were leaving no stone unturned. They checked and double-checked her room and the hospital staff. They felt confident in her safety, knowing they had embedded one of their own near her room.

Katie could feel the cool breeze from the gurney as she was passing by the open doors to other hospital rooms. She'd never been sick a day in her life, so this was all a new experience for her, and she didn't like any of it.

She arrived in the CT room and was shifted from the gurney to the CT machine. They inserted the pillow under her legs and asked if she wanted a warm blanket, to which she gave a hearty 'yes.' The room was cold. CT and MRI rooms are kept cold due to the amount of heat generated from the big machines."

After she was positioned correctly, she waited for the machine to move her body through its tunnel and be told by a machine voice when to hold her breath and when to breathe. It was a painless procedure and it went by rather quickly. She was grateful for both.

She was returned to her gurney and taken back to an ER while waiting for a room. They had already taken several vials of blood and done an ultrasound on her upper and lower abdomen. They took x-rays of her chest to check for blood or edema in her lungs. That was all they needed for now. It was just a matter of time for the test results to come back.

Katie was awake at 1:17 a.m. per her cell phone. They'd given her a light sedative, but it had no effect on her. After the heavy dose of succinylcholine, she received earlier that evening, she wanted to stay awake to fend off any further attempts on her life.

Once again, she felt vulnerable. This was getting to be an old habit. She could remember, not so long ago, when she was in control of her life.

She went to work. She caught the bad guys and life was good. Being an agent wasn't a career choice; for now, it was a life choice.

Up until now she was happy living this life, but recent events, including the one earlier today, made her yearn for a quieter one. In the still hours of the morning, she decided if she lived through this, she was going to retire from the Bureau.

She was high-spirited and loved a fast-paced lifestyle, but there had to be other career choices that would make her just as happy, or at least almost as happy, as being an agent for the FBI. She was hungry for high energy and good stress. She worked well under pressure but wanted to fully live her life without having to look over her shoulder.

The nurse came in to check on her. Katie was wide awake, and they exchanged pleasantries. She remembered not long ago she was in this very hospital she shot Whit, who was about to kill her. She feigned sleep then, so she made sure she was as awake when her nurse came in.

"How are we doing tonight?" the nurse asked.

"I'm doing well, thanks, how about you?" Katie offered.

"I'm doing great. It's not too busy tonight, so it gives us more time to spend with our patients if they need us. Can I get you anything, water, another blanket, or pillow?" the nurse queried.

"Water would be nice, thanks," Katie responded. Then she remembered the last time she drank water that day and vowed not to drink it, just to be on the safe side of things.

She was suddenly groggy, halfway between sleep and barely awake. "Do you know if the doctor has determined what happened to me?" she asked with anxiety in her voice.

"Oh, I don't know, dear." The nurse stayed busy with filling her water and getting her ice. She kept her face from Katie's view. "I'm sure the doctor will be around early in the morning to check on you and he'll update you then." She spoke like she was on polite autopilot. Then she silently slipped out of the room. The hardest thing for Katie was waiting for dawn.

She stirred lightly as the day nurse opened the blinds. It was early morning around six o'clock and raining outside. Drake arrived right before the nurse walked in. Katie opened her eyes and smiled. He pulled up a chair and began talking with her.

"How did you sleep? Are you feeling better?" He shot off questions faster than she could answer them.

"I … I … I'm all right." She struggled with her words for a moment as she sat up in bed. She was mad at herself for falling asleep. It could have killed her. She found her tongue again and said, "I'm feeling much better. Thanks for being there for me yesterday. I wouldn't be here without you," She said it with genuine appreciation.

"Not a problem," he said as he sensed her uneasiness. "What's going on with you, kid?" he probed.

"I'm not myself. I'm making all these stupid rookie mistakes and I'm jeopardizing lives, not just my own but yours and the others as well," she stated with anxiety. Drake was about to say something when Katie cut him off. She knew if she didn't get it out now, it might go unsaid forever if Donovan got to her again.

"I'm going to leave the force when this *thing* … is over," Katie stressed. "*If* I live through this. I've made up my mind. I don't want to live like this anymore, always wondering if today will be my last," she sighed with relief.

Drake could tell from the look on her face that she was serious about this decision. "Kid, I think you're just spooked. Anyone would be. But don't make any hasty decisions," he counseled. "Let's get you through this first. Then take a sabbatical and see if you really want to leave."

Katie thought about it for a moment, after all, it was coming from Drake and she cared what he thought. "Maybe you're right. I don't know what I think these days. I've never wanted anything to be over so badly in my life." Her voice was starting to shake. "Do they know what I was poisoned with yet?" she asked, hopeful they had some answers by now.

"Not yet. But it's early and we'll know soon. Dr. Patel knows I'm with the FBI and has agreed to cooperate with us, without the aid of a warrant. He doesn't know what your connection is with us though," Drake explained.

"Well, that's something. Who is the nurse we have embedded?" Katie quizzed.

"It's the same one we always use. In her line of work, she's always busy. Why do you ask?" Drake asked.

"I had a nurse come in around one this morning and she made me a little jumpy. It wasn't what she said, but it was the way she moved around the room that bothered me. She made me uneasy. Of course, it could just be my imagination too. Anything is possible at this point," Katie replied and continued without missing a beat.

"I didn't get her name, but there was just something about her that made me think she had more business here than just nursing. I've never met her, so I don't know if it was her." Katie was starting to shiver, partly from the temperature in the room and partly because her nerves were on edge.

Drake filled her in. "I've never met her. She's fluent in five languages and was recruited because she really is a nurse, not an agent. I'll look into it for you," he promised.

Katie smiled, offered her hand to his and gave it a squeeze. "I really am grateful to you, Drake," she said softly.

He smiled back at her and returned the squeeze. "I know you are, kiddo. Now get some sleep so you can get out of here. I'll stay here, so get some sleep. That's an order. I'll handle everything," he insisted.

Dr. Patel arrived around 6:30 a.m. and started with some good news. "We know what she ingested yesterday. It was succinylcholine," he said. "It's a good thing you asked us to test for heavy metals as soon as you did. Any longer and it probably wouldn't have been detectable." He paused briefly, then explained how it works.

"Sux is a neuromuscular blocker. It's used a lot in the ER for short-term immobility and in operating rooms as an anesthesia component. It breaks down very fast in the body and is naturally present in our systems." He continued his explanation as simply as he could. "If you weren't looking for it, you wouldn't find it. For those reasons it's often the murder drug of choice."

"Where would one get their hands on this?" Drake asked.

"Well, you can get it off the internet but no guarantees of the quality or potency, or you could steal it from a pharmacy or any medical clinic," he stated firmly, as if an FBI agent should already know this.

Drake did know and was merely double-checking his facts. "Or a hospital," he said as he nodded his head yes and raised his eyebrows for affirmation.

"Or a hospital," Dr. Patel confirmed, mimicking Drake's gestures but taking offense to his implication.

Drake gave the information to his boss and the other agents on the case. Then he called John and shared it with him. Drake trusted John and knew he'd have his back if things got messy. It was a real boon that John was around to take care of the girls for the course of this case.

He went back into Katie's room to fill her in. Katie was sitting up next to her bed and talking with Beth about her baby. Beth enjoyed talking about her baby. It kept her looking forward to the future instead of thinking about her recent loss.

"I'm surprised to see you're back so soon," Katie said as Drake entered the room.

"I was in the neighborhood," he quipped. "So, are you ready to get out of here yet?" he asked and half-stated.

"I am. I'm absolutely ready to ditch," Katie affirmed.

Drake looked at Beth. "Aren't you due in September or is it October?" Drake questioned with an unsure look on his face. His memory wasn't what it should be on things he considered less than life-threatening.

"September 19th, so it could easily be October if I'm late," she answered with enthusiasm.

"September. That's what I thought. So, I got it right then," he said, surprised he was in ballpark. "I have some news for you," he said, changing topics.

"Good or bad?" Katie asked with eagerness in her voice. She wanted to know what almost killed her and she wanted to get on with her life. Whatever life she had left.

She was sure she was going to die by Donovan's hand if he kept coming after her like he was. If nothing else, yesterday's attack convinced her that she was in the fight of her life and she wasn't going down easy. As soon as this was over, she was taking that sabbatical like Drake suggested. She secretly hoped he'd go with her.

"Depends on how you look at it, I guess," Drake replied. "We know what you ingested. It was sux. He knew she was familiar with the drug. That's why you were having so much trouble breathing yesterday, Katie. Your lungs and heart were shutting down. It's a miracle you survived," he explained with genuine gladness she was still among the living. Katie and Beth exchanged looks and then looked back at Drake.

"The man is ruthless," Drake continued. "He'll stop at nothing, but neither will we. We're looking for Donovan, but also for whoever's doing this to you. We're getting closer, Katie, and that's why his attempts on your life are getting more sinister."

"We have to get Whit to tell us who is most likely trying to kill you. We have a prison meeting with him today at three, before he enters the witness protection program. Part of his deal includes giving up everyone involved in this conspiracy. It's bigger than we anticipated." Drake insisted as he polished off his coffee. He'd have brought her one, but knew her nurse wouldn't let him give it to her.

Katie drew in a deep and long breath before she spoke. She thought for a moment and then inquired, "When am I getting out of here, so I can do my job with you and the rest of the team?"

"It should be within the hour," Drake replied, comforting her. "They're getting your discharge papers ready right now." He was glad to see that she was eager to get back to the job at hand.

"Good," She nearly shouted. "Beth, will you please hand me my clothes? I'm not waiting around for his next attempt. I want to go with you to see Whit," she said with closure in her voice. Arguing with her would be useless. She was going with Drake. Period.

Drake and Katie went back to their apartments so they could freshen up before their three o'clock meeting with Whit. Katie was finally home, and the first thing she did was take a long, warm shower. The water seemed to wash off the cobwebs of her fear and steel in her a new resolve to fight off Donovan at every turn. She blow-dried her hair and put on her makeup. Then she selected a monotone blue top with pants.

She wanted to play down her femininity as much as possible. She didn't want to draw any more attention to herself than she had to. She hated visiting prisons almost as much as she despised hospitals.

Drake knocked on her door. "You ready?" he asked as she let him in.

"Yes," she replied. "More than you may think. I've been mulling yesterday's events over and over in my head and the more I think about it, the more I want to investigate that nurse."

"Don't know it, but I'll call Dave and find out." He volunteered to make the call. Dave was their handler and head of their task force. With a flip of a button on the steering wheel, he said, "Call Dave."

Dave saw Drake's name on the caller ID and answered, "What's up?"

"We need the full name of the nurse that we have embedded at the hospital," Drake requested.

"We?" Dave questioned before Katie chimed in. "I'm here, too."

"Hi, Katie, how are you doing today?" he asked, regarding her health.

"All better, sir," she answered. "Ready for some answers about Teresa and what we can find out from Whit today."

"Glad to hear it," Dave replied. "The last name is Santos. Teresa Santos. She's worked for us for about six years. She's got a clean slate. Why? What do you have on her?" he asked, wondering if she could be a mole.

Dave continued as he pulled up her profile on the FBI's secure website. "Says here that she's from Seattle and nothing else of interest other than the normal background stuff. She checks out on our end. What don't I know?" he asked with some concern in his voice.

"Nothing specific," Katie responded. "It's just that last night I had a nurse come in to check on me and she seemed a bit familiar. I could be imagining the whole thing, but she made me uneasy. The way she moved around the room made me jumpy." She noticed the paranoia in her own voice.

She continued anyway, "Since I was poisoned and there's easy access to the drug they found in my system, it makes me think that two and two go together," she said with more conviction in her voice now. "I didn't get a good look at her, but she could be the same woman I met yesterday at the gym."

"It makes sense," Dave responded. "I'll do some snooping on our end and get back to you. If it was Teresa, she's likely to try some type of medical event again, so keep your eyes and ears open," he cautioned.

Chapter Eighteen

Hector 'Diamond' De Soto

Drake and Katie made their way inside the prison. It was always an uncomfortable visiting any prison, but this was a maximum-security house and it made the red tape a bit longer.

They were finally ushered into a private visitors' room and awaited Whit's arrival. Suddenly the door opened, and he was brought in wearing wrist and ankle chains. He sat down slowly. His appearance wasn't off-putting, but his odor and disposition made up for it. Katie couldn't shake the rancid smell.

The conversation began with Katie, who spoke with authority. "Tell me everything you know about Teresa Santos."

"She's a nurse that works for us," he answered, unsurprised they knew of her. "She's responsible for more than a dozen deaths. All of them in a hospital or as a home health care worker." Katie and Drake glanced at each other, confirming their suspicions.

"How long has she worked for Donovan?" Drake asked.

"Don't know for sure, about five years. We use her a lot. She's good at what she does and so far, no one has suspected her of anything. Why? Did you catch her?" Whit probed.

"Not yet, but I think she made an attempt on my life yesterday," Katie responded. "Tell me, why did you try to kill me in the hospital when you could have just as easily used Teresa?"

"Simple. Two reasons, really. One, it was my job to take you out and I take a lot of pride in my work. I wanted to finish the job myself," he oozed. "Two. Teresa was on another assignment."

He continued with a warning, "If they are using Teresa, she'll take you out one way or another. She'll wait until the coast is clear before she'll make her move, then she'll kill you right under your noses." He beamed with arrogance.

It stuck in Katie and Drake's craw that this creep was going to skate and enter the witness protection and relocation program. Agents would be risking their lives to protect this bastard. Actually, agents were already risking their lives to keep him safe.

Two agents were embedded in prison until Whit could be integrated into the federal program. One agent was a guard and the other in general population. However, Whit was kept in isolation and allowed exercise one hour a day in the yard. The agents were there to protect him during his exercise when he was at risk.

"What methods does she use to kill?" Katie asked with daggers in her eyes.

"Whatever the situation calls for," Whit stated matter-of-factly. "If you're in the hospital, it depends on how serious your injury is. It may take only a nudge to check you out, but if it's non-life-threatening, she has to get more creative." He shifted in his seat and belched out his next words, wafting another surge of stench in the small room.

He continued. "For example, she might hang the wrong IV or try using sux. That's her favorite drug because it flies under the radar. No one ever thinks to look for it and if they do, it's usually passed through the body. It's a great kill drug," He smiled disturbingly.

"Sux," Katie said as she looked at Drake and then back to Whit. "That's what I ingested yesterday. She laced my water with it."

"Then you're lucky to be alive. I've never known Teresa to miss on a hit before," Whit said unemotionally.

"Never mind that," Drake said. "Tell us who is most likely to take over your job now that you're in here?"

"That's hard to say, but maybe Hector. Hector De Soto goes by 'Diamond,' because he's a 'diamond' in the rough. I gave him that name. I was grooming him to replace me one day," he said with smugness. "I mean they could have chosen someone else, but I don't know anyone good enough to follow me other than Diamond."

"So, where and how do we find this Hector 'Diamond' guy? Are there any pictures of him or can you describe him to us?" Drake questioned.

Whit leaned back in his chair and shuffled his feet underneath the table. "Beats me. Could be anywhere. And there's an old mug shot of him, but I don't know what year it was taken." He shrugged.

Whit turned his attention to Katie. He leaned forward into Katie's face and growled, "He goes wherever the job takes him. If he's after you," he held Katie's eyes for a moment, "then he's probably close by. Let's just say there's a lot of people who do this job. Could be anyone, anywhere. Ya never know," he mocked.

"Look, you're an informant. Now inform," Drake spat at him.

"Hey, I told you what I know," Whit defended himself. "It's probably Diamond, but there's a lot of us. There's a lot of lottery winners to be taken out. The job is regional."

"So how many of you are there?" Katie asked with curiosity.

Whit hesitated as he counted in his head. "There's roughly half a dozen of us. Donovan tries to keep us from knowing exactly how many there are," Whit confessed. "We work better alone, no back up and all. Besides, loose lips sink big ships and the fewer there are the less Donovan has to handle."

"So basically, we're looking for this guy 'Diamond' and the nurse, Teresa Santos," Katie recapped. "I'm guessing the hospital is a good place to start looking for Santos," she stated rather than asked.

"You're right. I'm sure you can find her if she just tried to kill you yesterday. She doesn't suspect that you're on to her, does she?" Whit asked.

"I don't think so. I think she was in my room early this morning, but she didn't try anything. Any ideas why she passed on me?" Katie queried.

"Were you awake?" Whit asked with a smirk on his face and condescension in his voice.

"Yes, I was," Katie responded, remembering Whit's attempt on her life while she pretended to be sleeping.

"Well, she probably didn't want to risk an encounter with you. You're lucky, she usually doesn't back off so easily," Whit hypothesized. "I'm sure the holes you put in me were more than fair warning to her. She wants to get you when you least expect it."

"Where is Donovan?" Drake insisted. "Where do we find him? You must know, you and Stein were his right-hand men. Where does he live?" Drake pushed harder. He was tired of being in the presence of this asshole. Everything about the deal Whit had cut made him want to puke. He secretly hoped that Donovan did get to him, but only after the trial.

Whit leaned forward and locked eyes with Drake. Then he spoke, "He lives where he wants to live when he wants to live there. He owns houses all over the country and the rest of the world for that matter. He's a powerful person with lots of wealth," he said as he danced around the question. Whit continued undaunted. "He spends a lot of time in Florida when he's in the States."

"He owns a club in Miami and a house in Naples. I can give you a few addresses, but I don't know where he is. He's probably planning my death as we speak. Who knows, it'll probably be Diamond who takes me out." He was proud of his trainee and wanted the chance to engage him and see if he could still take him.

"We know about his places in Florida. Where is he now?" Drake insisted.

"Couldn't tell ya or I would. I tell ya he likes the sun and night life. He pops into his club now and then. It's just he has so many disguises and gets so much plastic done that few recognize him." Whit was being totally honest because he knew identifying Donovan would be a nightmare at best.

Drake was pissed. He knew too well this was true. "We're keeping you safe, at least until after the trial ... no guarantees after it though," Drake said straightforwardly. "A lot of bad things can happen in the program. Who knows, you might make it, you might not. We don't hold a lot of hope for you," Drake confessed with pleasure in his voice at the thought of Whit's death. It'd be one less hit man after Katie.

Drake smirked as he pushed away from the table to leave. Katie followed his lead. They knocked on the door for the guard.

"Lots of luck," Whit mocked as they left the room.

As they walked to the parking lot, Katie made a suggestion. "I'll start with Teresa if you take on Diamond. See if you can get that mug shot," she quipped. She was so upset from their encounter, that she accidently snapped a little at Drake. She regretted it immediately. "I'm sorry. I didn't mean to be short with you. It's just that Whit won't pay for his crimes and I can't stand that."

"It's okay, kid. I know you didn't mean it and I get why you're upset. I am too," he agreed.

"Can you believe the stupid names criminals give each other? It just so laughable. It's downright petulant." Katie shook her head trying to dismiss the images of Whit mocking her.

"Sounds like a plan," Drake answered. "At least now we have more to go on. He already gave up the names of his other victims and has given up how he killed them in detail. But we still don't know where to look for Donovan." They got inside the SUV.

"Whit's last victim was Rory Phillips in Tallahassee," he added as he took a right turn into traffic. "It could just be a coincidence that Rory Phillips lived in Florida, but we'll start looking for Donovan in Miami. We've been sittin' on his properties off and on for years. Never got 'em."

"Maybe we've been looking at this all wrong," Katie mused as she finished her thinking out loud. "We've been waiting for Donovan to keep making attempts on my life, but what if we start watching the other winners of the lottery and draw him out from that point? You heard Whit."

"There are a lot of lottery winners that Donovan's targeting and a lot of hit men going after them. We know Teresa and Diamond are coming after me, so we're on top of that." Her voice was getting higher as she gained control again.

She kept going. "In the meantime, I'm sure he'll keep trying to take me out of this world, but we'll be on the offensive by tracking Teresa and shutting her down. I'm not sure who I'm more afraid of, Teresa or Diamond." As apprehensive as she was, Katie was excited by the new tact they were taking to capture Donovan and Santos. This was just what Katie needed to get her life back on track.

Katie intended to be relentless about catching Teresa Santos. The more she thought about it, the better she felt about herself. She didn't have to be the 'sitting duck' anymore. She was now in hot pursuit of her would-be assassins.

It was July, and the heat was in the triple digits across most of the Midwest and South. Beth was now in her second trimester. She was physically feeling much better now that some time had passed, but her emotions were still raw. Her baby was healthy and developing as she should. She'd decided to name her Rori Elizabeth after her father and herself. It honored Rory and it kept him alive in both their lives.

Beth wanted closure and the only glimmer of hope for any justice was convicting Mark Stein and catching Donovan. After all, he was ordering all the 'hits.' It wasn't the same as making Whit pay for murdering her husband, but she knew it was the best she would ever get.

Beth took consolation in the fact that catching Donovan would put a stop to all these senseless murders once and for all. She wanted to help bring down big insurance and make Donovan pay, and she was willing to do anything she could to make that happen. Her testimony would be a big help.

Now everything hinged on the trial, and it was still four months away on the 7th of November. It was the People vs. Mark Stein in one of the biggest trials since O.J. Simpson's. They were vetting the jury pool. The publicity about Rory's death had dwindled the selection due to daily news and social medias, but as soon as the trial started, it would become another media circus. Right now, it was like the calm before the storm.

Janice was on her way over to Beth's for lunch. After that, they were going to do some shopping for the baby and the nursery. Beth was looking forward to getting out of the house. Most of her first trimester was spent resting due to the trauma of losing Rory and the whole debacle with the lottery winnings. But today was going to be different. She and Janice were only going to think about the baby and the nursery.

Janice arrived shortly before noon. "Hey, are you ready for some lunch and shopping?" she asked her sister. "I am," Beth exclaimed as she grabbed her purse and keys. "Let's get going. Where are we having lunch?" she asked on their way out the door.

"There's a bistro that just opened on Tenth Street downtown. I thought we could give that a try," Janice half asked, half stated. "They're supposed to have awesome salads."

"That sounds perfect, but I'll probably get another craving before we get home again. I'm craving donuts and jerky," Beth countered. "Don't ask me why. But for now, the salad sounds nice and light and we won't be too full to shop."

Over lunch they were discussing the theme for the nursery and decided to do it in a *white jungle motif* when Beth's phone rang. It was Katie. Beth eagerly took the call and covered one ear so she could hear every word. She whispered to Janice that it was Katie. Janice was hanging on every word, trying to fill in the gaps in the conversation.

"I thought you could use an update," Katie began. "We talked with Whit today." She swallowed hard before continuing. "And now we know who is trying to kill me. It's a guy named 'Diamond' and a nurse, Teresa Santos. She likes to use poisons that are all but undetectable. She laced my water with succinylcholine."

"What did Whit have to say, and succinyl... what?" Beth asked.

Katie answered. "It's succinylcholine. It temporarily paralyzes the body. I spent the night in the hospital again. But it doesn't last long in the body, so I'm feeling much better today," she explained before she continued unabated.

"Whit thinks Donovan may be back in the States and if he is, he'll probably show up at one of his places in Florida. He has a club in Miami and a home in Naples. We have agents sitting on both places right now." Katie coughed briefly before continuing. "We have more investigating to do, but I think we have a real chance at catching him." She was so excited to be the one to give Beth the good news.

"That's great. I'll sleep better knowing that creep is behind bars. But are you sure you're all right?" Beth was happy to get the good news but bothered that attempts on Katie's life had increased.

"I'm fine, or at least I will be when this is all over." Katie reassured her, changing gears. "How are you and the baby doing? How are Janice and John?"

"I don't burst into tears as much as I did. So, I guess we're doing well. In fact, Janice and I are shopping for the baby and some nursery items today, after we finish lunch. You'll have to see it when it's done. Maybe by then the trial will have started, and we can be that much closer to getting all of this behind us." Beth wanted this whole thing to be over and she wanted to know her friend, Katie, would be safe.

"It sounds like you two are having fun. I like the theme you picked for the nursery," Katie replied with sincere interest.

Beth answered happily, "a white jungle motif is cute and cheery. It's what I want and it's easily available."

"I wish I could go with you," Katie said as she realized she needed to get back to work. "I'll stay in touch, and you two have fun and take care." Katie ended the call and started tracking Teresa Santos' cell phone calls.

Drake was busy following the money trails of the current Mega Millions lottery winners. Some people waited until the last moment to come forward to collect their money and reveal their identities, especially now that the population knew of the lottery murders.

Chapter Nineteen

The 'Lucky' Winners Are

Drake focused on recent Mega Millions lottery winners. There were six of them. Despite the publicity surrounding the lottery murders, kill orders were still being dispatched. The lucky winners could be in danger. They lived in Florida, Alabama, Georgia, South Carolina, Louisiana, and New Jersey.

The Florida winners were Tommy and Jean Nichols, an elderly couple from Tampa. The Decatur, Alabama, winner was a bachelor, Buddy Finch. Jane Mullins, from Shreveport, Louisiana, was newly divorced with five children and her winnings were a godsend.

Georgia's winners were Robert and Naomi Davidson from Buford. The winner in Mauldin, South Carolina, was Rowena Jarvis, and the New Jersey winners were sisters, Tiffany, and Megan Smith.

Katie began breaking down their risks. "The elderly couple is the most vulnerable because they already have health issues, and it isn't a stretch to see either one of them landing in a hospital if they haven't already. They could be Teresa's next target," Katie stated emphatically.

"They all chose the installment payout option, so they had to be eliminated as quickly and soon as possible. They may not be aware they're in imminent danger." Drake was hanging on Katie's every word. He was so happy that she had changed her attitude and was in fight mode again.

As a health care worker, Teresa was privy to inside knowledge of the specific health issues of Tommy Nichols. He had heart and liver problems. His wife, Jean, had hip issues. They only needed to take out Tommy since he was the annuitant.

Buddy Finch was the Alabama sole winner. He was a playboy and didn't really have strings or anyone to leave the money to other than his mom and little sister. He liked fast cars and was known to be reckless with them. They could easily make his death appear to be an accident.

Jane Mullins was desperate to get her money. Having five children from a once-blended family meant a lot of mouths to feed and children to clothe. She was awarded sole custody of the kids due to the violent nature of her ex-husband. His previous wife was killed in a hit-and-run accident, and they never found the driver. She adopted her former husband's three children and was raising them as her own.

Georgia winners Robert and Naomi Davidson were in their late fifties and wanted to use the money to spoil their friends and family and complete their bucket list. They chose the annual installment plan so they would have a steady income stream during their retirement. Their first installment was due in two months. The annuitant was Naomi.

Rowena Jarvis, the South Carolina winner was a single mother of three. She worked as a loan officer at the Bank of Georgia. She was divorced and her children ranged in age from three to eight years old. She had a working knowledge of annuities, so she decided on the lump sum. She was smart.

As the most recent winner among them she'd been following the lottery murders and knew the installment plan would put her on the hit list. The other winners had won their money prior to the story breaking and had already chosen their payout plan and couldn't change it once they selected it over the lump sum option.

For the lucky Smith sister of Jersey City, Tiffany was going to school to become a veterinarian and Megan was working for a small advertising company. They too chose the installment plan. The winning ticket was in Megan's name. Tiffany was going to use money to pay off student loans and Megan was planning on starting her own ad agency. They needed the steady income to qualify for two small business loans.

Knowing the annuitants could no longer change their choice of their payout plans, they had to act fast. After they reviewed the winners list, Drake decided the priorities were Jean and Tommy Nichols, the retired couple in Florida, Buddy Finch, the bachelor in Alabama, and the sisters, Megan and Tiffany Smith. The FBI had a limited amount of task force for this assignment, and they had to go with the installment payout plan winners first.

Contacting the winners was out of the question. They all watched the news and read the tabloids. All the publicity about the 'lottery murders' had reached them by now. Most kept a low profile and tried to collect their winnings as quietly as possible. The typical fanfare that surrounded lottery winners was temporarily eliminated due to the murders. People were scared, but still wanted to collect their winnings.

Drake gave Katie an update on his progress. "We've got all six of the installment plan winners under surveillance. We haven't told them about us because we don't want them to change their daily routines. Knowing their routines makes it easier to anticipate where they'll be and when they'll be there so we're ready to intervene."

Katie responded, "Sounds good, but we still have to deal with another immediate issue, the press. The lottery murders have them rushing to change their options only to find that under current insurance laws changing their installment option is impossible."

"This story is a media darling. To our advantage they're trying to put enough public pressure on the insurance industry and the national AG's office to force a change. Maybe it'll slow down Donovan," Drake pointed out.

He knew she was right about this being a media circus. They sat down at their favorite coffee shop and continued to exchange information while they enjoyed much-needed caffeine and a quick snack.

When Marty broke the story about Florida's Attorney General, Mark Stein, he was forced to resign shortly before he was indicted. The public wanted someone to blame for these heinous crimes, and he was at the top of the food chain.

Stein's unwilling temporary successor met with public outcry for justice, which had him scrambling to get his arms around the magnitude of the situation. The White House wasn't faring any better. It was an election year and neither candidate had answers, but both vowed reform in the insurance industry.

The interim Florida Attorney General, Adam Charles, cleaned house and staffed his best advisors. The first thing he did was issue indictments against the seven insurance companies and the CEO's in the alleged conspiracy. New heads were taking their places, indictments were flying, and the new guys were stuck mopping up the enormous mess. It just wasn't fixable fast enough.

Marty was covering the story non-stop and nearly every day she had an update on the events taking place and the lawsuits being filed. It merited a class action suit, but it was feared it would be too lengthy. So, motions were filed, and the courts moved forward with suits against all seven companies.

The hospitals were covertly aware and on the lookout for Teresa Santos. Knowing things were heating up, she took home health care assignments. All they had to do now was wait for the precise moment to take her in. They were hoping she would take another run at Katie, so no one else would be put in harm's way.

Santos routinely altered her appearance, changed her name, and made slight cosmetic changes to her face and hair. Occasionally, she'd have a little plastic work done, but that was only for extreme measures when she knew she'd been made. She didn't think Katie could identify her based on their brief encounters.

Teresa was right. Katie didn't get a good look at her, but she took no chances. For this job, she wore a wig in a different color, cut and style from her own and wore her make-up to resemble a hipster. Still, Katie and Drake managed to track her down.

Teresa was embedded in Angels of Mercy traveling health care services. This was the perfect cover for her. No one asked questions about traveling nurses. Due to the high demand for them, their vetting process wasn't as thorough because of a larger staff and bigger budget.

Katie and Drake followed Teresa home one night after her shift ended at an in-home medical visit. Katie disguised herself in a dark wig and some hipster clothes. She figured if she blended into Teresa's world, she wouldn't tip her hand. Most likely Teresa didn't figure Katie would be on her so soon after her last attempt on her life.

Teresa got off at 11:30 p.m. and went to her car. She was driving a Toyota Camry, white with Florida plates. Drake ran them and the car belonged to one Kristy Hennessey. She came up deceased. So now they knew the name of her most recent victim and they could check with the local Tallahassee Police Department to find out what they knew.

Drake immediately placed the call. Hennessy's death must have been within the past 24 hours or less because her name wasn't on his 'hit' list yet, and there wasn't anything on the news.

The police Commander, Robert LaRue, took the call from Drake. Due to his position, he knew of Beth's case and had an intimate knowledge of the 'lottery murders'. LaRue, took a swig of sugared coffee. "Says here that Hennessey died from natural causes. She overdosed on some Ativan."

"She had a bunch of prescriptions and she probably lost count of what she'd taken," LaRue continued. "She had pill boxes to keep her straight, but overdoses happen more often than you think when people are taking a lot of meds."

"According to family and friends, she wasn't depressed. In fact, she was planning to use the money to take her family on a vacation to Hawaii. She'd been planning it for a couple of weeks. On the surface, it appears to be dumb luck," LaRue added, "Initially no one knew about her lottery winnings. Due to all the publicity, she hadn't come forward until the last day. However, in light of recent events, we're treating her passing as a suspicious death."

Drake jumped in with questions, eager to know the details. "Did she die at home? How and where was she found? Was anyone with her when she died?"

"She was at home with her family, asleep in the house," LaRue answered. "She was 22 and living in a basement apartment of her parent's house. She was being treated for bipolar disorder, and that's why there were so many meds."

He continued without prompting, "Her parents assumed she had gotten confused about how many pills she had taken and accidentally overdosed. They found her when she didn't come up for breakfast and rushed her to the ER. As for the lottery murders, we've been looking in that direction."

"Yeah. That's exactly what I'm saying," Drake confirmed. "When can we meet to compare notes? We have reason to believe it wasn't an overdose. We think she was slipped a heavier dosage without her knowledge, which makes this another lottery murder." Drake felt sick inside knowing he didn't have her name on his list. Despite the circumstances, he wished he could have prevented Hennessy's death.

There were too many lotteries and not enough manpower to cover all the winners across the nation. There are 180 lotteries worldwide with 46 of them in the United States which is far more than any other country in the world. Keeping up with all of them is a colossal task, especially with so little manpower.

Drake was impatient to meet with LaRue. For once, they might be able to get ahead of Donovan and they could possibly hang another murder on Teresa. "One last question, do you know if Hennessy took her lottery winnings as a lumpsum or regular installments?" Drake asked.

LaRue responded, "I'm not sure, Drake. Based on the information we got from her parents, I assumed it was the installment plan. I'm following up on it and will get back with you." LaRue wanted to cooperate because he wanted these criminals off the street as much as Drake.

"That'd be great. Thanks, LaRue," Drake said as he hung up. He filled Katie in on his conversation. "I think it's time we both get some sleep so we can tackle this with fresh eyes in the morning."

"Sounds good," she said as she entered the vehicle on the passenger's side. "Let's go already. Take me over to Janice and John's. I'll call 'em and let them know I'm coming. If I'm going to be at my best in the morning, I need to sleep over there where I can actually relax and leave the worrying to John."

"Ask if there's an extra bed for me," he insisted. "You'll have double the protection tonight and we can get an early start." Katie made the call and they both spent the night at Janice and John's. Katie took the spare bedroom and Drake took the couch, each wishing they were in the same bed.

Morning came extra early. Katie was awake at 4:14 a.m. She couldn't sleep so she got up. Lying in bed wasn't her forte. She was restless and needed to pace out her frustration. She didn't want to wake the rest of the house, so she quietly slipped down to the kitchen and made herself a single cup of coffee. Keurig's was so handy for moments like these.

She was opening the refrigerator door to retrieve some milk for her coffee when she noticed the spectacular sunrise through the glass French doors. Softly she opened them and stepped outside onto the veranda to enjoy her coffee. She was warm in her chenille robe. She was thinking about talking with LaRue this morning and how much closer they were getting to an arrest.

Then she started thinking about the list of lottery winners that were still targets. She was most worried for the older couple in South Florida. They were the weakest and most vulnerable, and she was determined to get Teresa before she could get them. She imagined how she'd feel getting Teresa Santos off the streets for good. Florida carries the death penalty and life in prison without parole. She was thinking about the trial ahead of them, when Drake interrupted her thoughts.

"Good morning. I see you couldn't sleep in either," he said as he smiled at her. She returned his greeting.

"What a beautiful view," Katie said as she nodded toward the sunrise. Drake smiled and agreed with her.

"Did you sleep well?" he asked.

"Extremely, thanks. But I'm an early riser. I see you are too. Do you feel rested for the day?" She was interested in his response as they had a big day ahead of them.

"I slept well. I was tired." He yawned and stretched, hoping she believed his white lie.

"Looks like you could use some coffee too. I'll get you a cup," Katie said in soft voice.

"None for me. I'm strictly a Mountain Dew or Coke man. Gotta have all that sugar, I guess," he said, knowing he could really use the jolt.

"Let me look. I know they drink sodas, but since I don't, I wouldn't venture a guess as to what they have on hand." Katie finished her sentence from the kitchen. She was checking the fridge and pantry for soda. There was one cold regular Coke left in the fridge and she handed it to him without mentioning that it was the last one. She figured he needed his caffeine as badly as she did.

"Here," she said. She couldn't get over how handsome he was. There was no denying they had a mutual attraction for each other. Maybe it was heightened because her life was in danger.

"Thanks," Drake answered as he took the can from her hand. He knew she was vulnerable because her life was on the line and after three attempts, she was skittish and didn't know who to lean on. Every time he comforted her, it was all he could do to keep it on a professional level as only a deep friendship.

They both wanted more but didn't know how to ask for it, plus there was the issue of their jobs. How would they be able to maintain professional acuity and a personal relationship? They sat and talked about the case while dancing around their feelings for each other. It was 6:30 a.m. when Janice and John came down for breakfast.

They joined Katie and Drake in the kitchen. Janice went to the coffee pot and brewed a pot for herself, John, and Katie. The Keurig was great for single servings but based on the day ahead, they needed a full pot of coffee.

"Who's hungry?" Janice asked.

"I am," they replied in unison. She and Katie fixed pancakes and eggs. It was a much heavier than normal breakfast for everyone, but given the events the day promised, it was unlikely they'd have time or thought for food again until late that night.

They ate with good appetites and enjoyed easy morning conversation amidst the talk about the possibility of arresting Teresa today. Katie was so stoked she could hardly sit still. After breakfast, Katie asked Drake if they could drop by their apartments for a quick shower and a change of clothes.

He agreed, and it was what they needed to eagerly face the day before them. It was just after 7:00 a.m. and they would take over surveillance of Teresa's house after they checked in with LaRue.

Chapter Twenty

Teresa Santos –
Evil Incarnate

Katie and Drake met with LaRue at the downtown Tallahassee police station at 7:30 a.m. It was an early start to a long-awaited conversation.

"What do you know about Kristy Hennessy?" Drake asked.

"Not any more than I told you last night. It sounded like you have information for me," LaRue answered.

"I do," Drake responded. "We believe that Ms. Hennessy was murdered. We think Alma Sanchez, alias Teresa Santos, killed her. She is a professional assassin, works for Donovan Black. Ya heard of him?"

"Yeah, goes by Black Jack,' right?" LaRue answered.

"Yeah, that's the one," Drake confirmed.

"If he's involved, then you're in the deep end of the pool, son," LaRue countered. "So, who's this Alma Sanchez?" He paused to recall her name. "Is that what you said?"

"Goes by Teresa Santos now," Katie said. "She's an actual nurse he recruited five years ago."

"She is currently a traveling nurse and embeds wherever she's needed. She tried to kill me a couple of days ago by lacing my water with succinylcholine." Katie took a deep breath, allowing some time to collect her thoughts again.

"I'm sorry to hear that, but glad you're okay. So how does she play into our body in the morgue?" LaRue asked.

"She could have slipped into the basement apartment and switched the strength of her dosage," Drake chimed in. "She does work for Donovan and we all know he only hires the best."

"I'm willing to bet that the Ativan in her system was more than enough to kill her," Katie paused briefly. "Currently, Santos is embedded with Angels of Mercy traveling nurses. You said she was rushed to the ER after her overdose. Santos could have inserted herself inside the ER long enough to execute her. She could have easily injected her IV bag or given oral medication with the extra Ativan."

Katie paused as she finished stirring cream in her coffee and having a sip. "If she gave her an extended release, she could have ingested a higher dose from her home medication. Either way, she would have just stopped breathing. Can you …" Katie couldn't finish her statement before LaRue cut her off.

"Already on it. You wanna know what hospital Hennessy was in, don't you?" LaRue continued without waiting for an answer. "She was taken to the ER at Tallahassee Memorial. So, you're right, it could have been before or after, but according to the autopsy report, she had more than twice the lethal amount of Ativan in her system."

Due to our conversation yesterday, we rushed the autopsy in order to determine cause of death. It was ingested approximately three hours before she was pronounced dead." There was a knock on the LaRue's door. A young man handed him a piece of paper. LaRue was surprised and pleased police investigators were already onto Santos.

"We ran Santos' address from her HR file. Doesn't exist," LaRue stated. "None of her information checks out. She gave an address to nowhere in Miami. Seems like all roads here are leading to Miami and Santos. Guess that means you two are up for a road trip," he said as he looked from one to the other.

LaRue continued, "Like the FBI, we've just issued an arrest warrant for Santos. We're working with the Miami precinct. We'll have our men check with the Angels of Mercy right now. By the look of things, you two need to get down there as fast as yesterday. If she's spooked, we have a limited window to catch her before she's out of the country and in the wind." LaRue wanted her caught as badly as Drake and Katie.

"You're right," Drake said as he stood up to leave. Katie joined him.

"Thank you for your time," LaRue said.

Drake and Katie thanked him for his help while shaking hands with LaRue, and Katie pushed her chair closer to his desk.

"If you need anything else, don't hesitate. Good luck to ya," LaRue said with little optimism in his voice. "I don't need to remind you that this whole thing is a media hot button, and all eyes are on us to end the bloodshed," There was frustration in his voice.

On the way back to their apartments, Drake said, "You heard the man. Are you up for a road trip to Miami?"

"I'm up for anything that will get us there the fastest," she agreed and was already making arrangements. "I've been checking flights as we've talked. There's a Delta 417 leaving at 10:00 a.m., gets us in around noon-thirty. I booked us. We just have time to pack a few things and get to the airport. I booked us a rental car too." Katie was efficient.

Katie quickly gathered her things. She kept a 'go-bag' on hand and only had to add a few personal things. She was ready in five minutes as was Drake. They threw the bags in the back of the SUV and drove to the airport. "If we're lucky, we'll catch Teresa today," Katie said as they pulled away from the curb.

A few hours later, LaRue's men started interviewing all personnel on duty the night Kristy Hennessy was admitted to the ER. They turned over every rock they could find and only one resident had anything to say. He explained how Hennessy coded shortly after a woman loosely matching Teresa's description arrived in the ER.

The resident on duty told them all he remembered. "She was near the IV with a syringe in her hands. They stabilized her and kept her for observation while they prepared the paperwork for her admission. They were going to keep her overnight for observation."

He continued, "I saw her push something into Hennessy's port and a few minutes later she coded. They were trying to stabilize her for the second time and that's when they lost her. She was pronounced dead at 3:16 a.m. after various resuscitation attempts."

They now had an eyewitness that could corroborate the findings of the autopsy. It was one more witness to keep safe. They had to catch Teresa Santos.

Drake got a text from LaRue. It simply read; 'we have an eyewitness that saw Santos with a syringe near Hennessy.' The plane landed a bit sooner than scheduled. They grabbed the rental car and took off.

Katie drove while Drake ran down one of Teresa's former addresses. It was a long shot, but it was a place to start. The third door they knocked on a woman answered. She was obviously a dancer at Donovan's club. She still looked like she had earned her money from last night. Her hair was disheveled but in a sexy way and she wore an orange oversized T-shirt and white short shorts.

"What do you want?" she asked in an exhausted tone.

"We're from the FBI," Drake said as he and Katie flashed their badges. "We'd like to talk about your boss, Donovan Black. May we come in for a minute?"

"We won't take long, I promise," Katie stated, convincing her to let them in.

Her stage name was Tiffany Sweets. Her real name was Michelle Lindy. "What's this about?" she asked as she reluctantly let them in.

"We want to know if you've ever seen this woman at the club?" Drake asked as he and Katie stepped into her living room and showed Santos' picture. "Does she look familiar?"

Michelle looked at the two pictures of Teresa. "Sure, I recognize her but with dark hair and a slightly different nose." She studied the picture more closely.

"She comes around the club sometimes with Donovan. But I've never talked with her or anything. She doesn't come around all that often either. Just once in a while, ya know?" she explained as she took out a cigarette and lit up. "Ya mind?" she asked more out of habit than courtesy.

"Has she been by recently?" Katie inquired.

"Yeah, now that you mention it." She blew out her first drag. "She was in two nights ago." She took in another long drag.

"Was she with anyone at the time?" Katie asked.

"Yeah. Donovan, just like I said. She was draped all over him," she answered with annoyance in her voice.

"Have you seen Donovan since?" Drake pushed.

Michelle thought for a moment and answered stoically, "No." She puffed. "Not since I saw him with her a couple of days ago. They looked like they was in a real deep conversation, real intense, if you know what I mean."

"Did you overhear what they were talking about?" Katie queried.

"No. I never heard what they was talkin' about, ya know, as I was across the room dancin' and all. Look, I've got other things to do today." Michelle's tone was irritated. "So, if ya don't mind," she said as she walked to the door and nodded her head for them to leave. "Is Donovan in some kind of trouble or something?" she asked almost as an afterthought.

"No. We're just following up on some police business," Drake answered.

"But you're the FBI. I thought you guys only worked on serious cases and whatnot," she responded. "Is this about the lottery murders that he's supposed to know something about?" she pried.

"Well, we don't have anything yet, Ms. Lindy, but we thank you for your cooperation. You've been very helpful. We'll contact you again should we need to," Drake assured her.

When they were in their vehicle, they looked at each other with glee and hopefulness. "Donovan's in the country. We've got 'em, Katie," Drake said with obvious relief.

"I know. But that was two days ago, and he may have already fled again," Katie noted, not trying to be skeptical but keeping reality afloat.

Teresa was on the home health care circuit in Valencia Lakes in Tampa. She had been working for home health care services on and off for quite some time. It was her cover for home-bound clients that needed to be eliminated.

She could usually arrange to be assigned to the clients of her choice. Occasionally, she'd work for some elderly folks that weren't on her hit list just to throw off suspicion. She didn't want anyone to pick up on a pattern between her nursing care and the rate of deaths on her shifts. She recently arranged things so that she was assigned to her newest mark, Tommy Nichols. This was a rush job due to all the heat they were taking from the press, and not to mention the upcoming payout. The clock was ticking.

Tommy had heart and lung issues and he was the only one that needed to die. Teresa was going to see him today. The job would be done by mid-morning or earlier, long before the feds would catch up with her.

The FBI toyed with the idea of asking the Nichols if they could put cameras and microphones in their house but decided against it due to his advanced Alzheimer's. They feared he might slip up and give away the clandestine FBI surveillance.

Drake and Katie landed back in Tampa from Miami, shortly after two o'clock. They drove back to TPD to catch up with LaRue. "We just missed her." Drake spoke with obvious frustration in his voice. "Probably by not more than forty-eight hours. She was spotted with Donovan a couple of nights ago." They started exchanging information.

Teresa had a two-day jump on Drake and Katie and she only needed the one early morning to get the job done.

Drake and Katie continued the conversation in LaRue's office. "A stripper saw them a couple of nights ago," Katie said. "She said they were in a real intense conversation about something. Probably planning their escape to wherever there's no extradition or planning the next attempt on my life," she stressed.

"So, who'd be next on the list?" LaRue asked.

"According to our records, other than me, it's an older couple living in Valencia Lakes, a bedroom community of Tampa," Katie answered.

"I'm familiar with Valencia Lakes," LaRue informed them. "It'll be easy to set up a stakeout. Consider it done."

Katie and Drake needed a strong drink but only after they got Santos. Then they'd have something to celebrate… until then, they were running on adrenaline. Little did they know that they were already too late to prevent the latest hit from earlier that morning.

Teresa was a hard woman who took great pride in her work. The fact that she was a hired assassin made no never-mind to her. She was a perfectionist all the way. She arrived at the Nichols residence at precisely seven in the morning. She rang the doorbell twice, so they'd be sure to hear her.

So often the elderly have trouble hearing. After a lengthy pause she rang the doorbell again. Within a few moments a man opened the door. He was still wearing his pajamas. Natural deaths seemed more plausible when folks were still in their pajamas than when they're fully dressed.

Most fatal heart attacks happen in the morning, especially on Monday mornings just as the patient is waking up from a long night's sleep. All this played into Teresa's hand to make it appear that Mr. Nichols died from natural causes.

Tommy Nichols had her identify herself while he did the same. "Hi, I'm Tommy and over here is my wife, Jean."

She smiled. "Hi." She charmed them.

"What did you say your name was again?" Tommy asked due to advancing Alzheimer's.

"It's Teresa. Teresa Santos," she answered as she looked him square in the eyes and shook his hand again. "Now, I understand you've had home health care before. Is, that right?" she queried knowingly.

Teresa noticed pictures of their children and grandchildren dotted all over the house. They made no difference to her. She had a job to do. She was on an assignment and had no room for empathy.

"Oh, that's right, we have had several different gals out here to help us every day," Tommy said. "They even sent out one male nurse once to help us. Do you remember that one time, Mother?" he asked his wife.

"I do. He was quite big," Jean responded.

"My gosh, he sure was strong. And he could really handle my size and all, ya know. I'm awful big for you little gals to handle me," Tommy said with a slight chuckle.

"Oh, I'm sure I can be of help in any situation, Mr. Nichols," Teresa assured him.

"Ah, you can just call me Tommy. Everybody does. You can too," he said lightheartedly.

"Now, let's see how your home is laid out and then show me your meds and which room you prefer to spend most of your time," Teresa stated while following Mr. Nichols throughout the house.

She stopped in the bedroom with him, and he showed her all the medications he was taking. She noticed the digitalis, Exelon, digoxin, hydralazine and alfuzosin, and a daily low-dose aspirin. This was going to be easier than she thought. They were neatly arranged in daily pill boxes for Sunday thorough Saturday with four compartments to manage when to take them.

"Have you eaten breakfast and taken your morning meds yet?" Teresa offered.

"No. Not yet," Tommy answered as he invited her to join them in the kitchen.

"Would you like me to whip up something for the two of you then? It's really no trouble at all," Teresa emphasized.

"Well, if it's not imposing on you, we could go for some scrambled eggs and toast," Tommy suggested with caution.

"Perhaps a bit of coffee too, or is that allowed on your diet, Mr. Nic, I mean Tommy?" She corrected herself to use his first name and asked again. "Can you have coffee on your diet?"

"Yes, he can," Jean spoke up. "Tommy can have a couple of cups in the mornings."

Teresa made a pot of coffee right away. She then excused herself to use the bathroom. She had her choice. She could mix the overdose of digitalis in the egg mixture or put it in his coffee. She opted for the last meal scenario. She brought the deadly dose of digitalis with her so there wouldn't be the nuisance of explaining the different dosage and pill count. She knew the meds he was taking by reviewing his medical chart before arriving.

There was light chatter around the table. Jean and Tommy were sitting at the breakfast table, sipping at their coffee and enjoying each other's familiar companionship. "So, where are you from? How long have you been a nurse?" Jean asked as she watched Teresa making their breakfast.

These were typical questions wherever she went. Sometimes she'd tell the truth if there was only one patient. But in cases such as this, where Jean would still be alive and a viable witness to his manner of death, she never told the truth.

"Jean, would you mind popping in the toast for me?" Jean obliged and now occupied with her own task; Teresa slipped the deadly dose of digitalis into Tommy's egg mixture. She whipped a separate egg mixture for Jean's scrambled eggs. This went unnoticed by both Jean and Tommy. Because the heart attack was going to happen so quickly after ingestion, Teresa would serve Jean first to ward off any suspicion of foul play.

This method had served her well over the years. If anyone did notice she was mixing up two separate bowls of eggs, she had a ready answer that she was trying to control the salt or cholesterol content for heart patients. All her elderly patients required minimal intake of sodium and cholesterol. It was a handy cover.

The toast popped up and Teresa was ready for it. Jean put it on the plate and let Teresa apply the butter and jam, not too much of either. Then she set the plate in front of Tommy.

"Enjoy! After breakfast, we'll give you your meds and get you bathed and comfortable," she soothed, wondering how much longer it would take.

Three bites in, Tommy looked pale. His breathing became labored and he fell on the floor. Jean panicked and Teresa played her part worthy of an

Oscar. She grabbed her emergency bag and began giving Tommy CPR. She was textbook accurate.

She turned his head to the side and lifted his neck to make sure he wasn't choking on anything. After she cleared his airway, she went back to her compressions. Jean was calling 911 per Teresa's instructions. "If only I had some paddles with me," Teresa crooned.

She pumped out the words in rhythm with her compressions. She continued until after the ambulance arrived. The EMTs took over and tried to stabilize him. They even used the paddles on him, but it was too late. He was gone.

Jean was beside herself with fear, grief and shock. The EMTs decided to take her to the hospital along with her husband's body. She wasn't looking well, and they wanted to monitor her vitals after such a traumatic incident.

Teresa said she'd be right behind them and would alert her supervisor. After they were on their way, Teresa did what she usually did. She bagged the evidence, including the plate and silverware. Then she dirtied a clean plate and silverware and replaced them on the table and floor to stage a duplicate scene, just as Jean and the EMTs left it. Child's play, Teresa thought to herself as she put her car in reverse.

Chapter Twenty-One

The Hit List

Frantic calls were being placed. Officers were sitting in Donovan's club in Miami, but they were too late to save Tommy Nichols. With his death the bodies were stacking up. The press was relentless with daily reports. At best, Tommy Nichols' death was touted as sloppy police work. They would have to do better, much better if they were ever going to catch the duos, Santos and Donovan.

LaRue got ahold of Drake and filled him in on the events of the early morning. "We didn't get there fast enough. His blood is on us. All of us," he said with great remorse in his voice.

Katie was physically sick when she heard the news. She threw up once and lost her appetite until late in the evening.

"So, who's next, besides Katie?" LaRue asked Drake.

"If we follow the money, the next logical victims are Buddy Finch, Jane Mullins, and Megan Smith," Drake confirmed.

"Where does Finch live?" LaRue inquired.

Drake responded quickly. "Alabama. Decatur, Alabama. The local authorities are willing to work with us. You know the media is all over this and I don't mean maybe. They are posturing about how unlucky lottery winners are."

LaRue said with a mixture of gratitude and disgust, "They've all but harassed the rest of the recent lottery winners. Honestly, they may accidentally be helping us do our job. Because we lack enough manpower, the relentless thirst for headlines may be stalling some of these lottery murders. However, it did nothing to prevent Tommy Nichols' death this morning"

"Tommy Nichols lived in a gated community and required in-home nursing for the past two years. Nothing seemed out of the ordinary, not even to our guys who were surveilling the house. They saw a nurse arrive every morning and it was rarely, if ever, the same nurse. Our guys couldn't effectively run a stakeout if they stopped every nurse who arrived for the day. They knew about Santos, but no one matched her description," LaRue was exhausted.

"We did our best," Drake reminded him, fully aware that they would have to step up their game if they were going to thwart the rest of Donovan's attempts, including Katie's.

Detail was ordered by the local police departments to keep surveillance on Buddy Finch, Megan and Tiffany Smith, and Jane Mullins, hopefully they wouldn't be too late like they were with Tommy Nichols.

The Decatur police rolled up on Buddy Finch's home. He didn't appear to be there, so they sat on the house. They called his office using the guise it was his dental office calling to remind him of an appointment. Confirmed he was at work, they sent unmarked cars to keep eyes on him.

The stakeouts would only work for a day or so as Donovan's men were cunning and top professionals in the business of murder. A few cops sitting on a doorstep might slow them down, but for sure it wouldn't stop them from getting to Finch or anyone else.

If FBI agents planned on keeping these potential targets out of harm's way, they would have to assign round-the-clock bodyguards, and that would mean tipping their hand to Donovan. There just wasn't a good option.

It was a game of cat and mouse. Donovan knew the authorities were onto him and his men. So far, Donovan had been able to stay ahead of the FBI, mostly because no one knew what he looked like or whether he was in or out of the country. Currently, he was out of the country and awaiting news from Santos's whereabouts. She should have checked in by now.

Donovan and the rest of the world knew that catching him and his crew was job one for the FBI. They were on the run but for one last task, taking out Katie Lestler. That task now fell to 'Diamond' DeSoto.

Meanwhile, Mrs. Nichols was asked to allow the authorities to perform an autopsy on her husband. Drake and Katie were at the hospital trying to soothe her while encouraging the autopsy. They had no choice but to identify themselves and ask for her help in putting Teresa Santos behind bars.

Jean was beside herself with grief and now angered that the FBI knew they were possible targets and did nothing to stop her husband's killer. Neither Jean nor Tommy cared to watch or keep up with the news, as it just depressed them. Rather, they spent their time watching a lot of game shows and re-runs they grew up with.

Their children had tried to warn them, but they passed it off as media fear tactics and besides, they both had suffered from mild dementia. She was furious and distraught. She and Tommy lived quiet lives and had no intention of making any flashy changes to their lifestyle just because they won some money.

"You mean you all knew that we were next on this target list of yours and you did nothing to save my Tommy?" Jean shrieked. "How could you know such a thing and not even warn us that we were in danger? How is that even fair?" She fell silent with grief and streaming tears.

Drake started to speak, but Katie cut him off with a look and began talking with Mrs. Nichols. "We're so sorry for your loss. And it may be that your husband died from a normal heart attack, but we can't know unless we perform an autopsy," Katie urged as gently as she could. "We won't know anything for sure until we have your permission to do so."

"Mrs. Nichols," Drake cut in. "Our surveillance team didn't know that your nurse this morning was Teresa Santos. We only knew that you had daily professional home health care visits. They saw a nurse enter your home several times this week, so naturally they thought it normal when your health care nurse that entered your home this morning."

Drake continued gently, "Mrs. Nichols, please know we did everything we could to identify your assailant, Teresa Santos. However, she regularly changes her look and uses many disguises. If our agents had checked every nurse that entered your house this week, our whole operation would have been foiled."

Katie added, "By the time our agents knew to breach their cover, your husband was unfortunately, already deceased. Our team followed her but lost her when they were cut off by a passing train"

"Jean, if you want to bring your husband's killer to justice, we have to do the autopsy as soon as possible. Every minute we wait allows whatever chemicals she may have used to kill your husband to dissipate. We need to do this now, Jean," Katie pleaded.

Jean nodded her head yes as she turned to Katie and buried her head in her shoulder, sobbing uncontrollably. Katie comforted her, as at hospital staffer asked to interrupt her one more time to get her signature on the consent for autopsy paperwork. Jean dutifully signed the consent. The autopsy got under way.

Jean's son arrived shortly after and took over comforting his mom and continued asking questions that carried the same answers they'd just given to their mother. The family swore there'd be a lawsuit while Katie and Drake did their best to placate them before leaving to resume their search for Santos.

Teresa abandoned Kristy Hennessy's stolen ride and switched it for a stolen SUV from a parking garage. Then she drove to the Tampa airport and abandoned it. If she hurried, she could just catch a morning flight to Miami. However, she was stuck in Miami for a two-and-a-half-hour delay. Once in the air, her next stop would be Netzahualcoyotl, Mexico. From that point, she could go anywhere in the world. She'd be in wind until her next rendezvous with Donovan.

Meanwhile, Marty was on her way to Tampa to cover the news of Tommy Nichols. She arrived mid-morning and figured she could drive to Valencia Lakes with her good friends Janice and Beth, providing Beth felt up to it.

It was only about a half-an-hour jaunt to Valencia Lakes and she thought the distraction might be good for Beth. She caught an Uber to her house, hoping she would be home, and she was. Janice was there too. The trip to Valencia Lakes would give all of them time to catch up.

Marty had been on and off the air since 8:30 a.m. this morning when the newsroom got the hospital bulletin about Tommy Nichol's death from an apparent heart attack. The media didn't have an assassin's name or description, in fact, they didn't any solid leads at all. All they had was speculation until they got the autopsy report was being rushed. They were reporting that it was a potential lottery murder, but that it may have been from natural causes.

Marty's boss dispatched her and the film crew to Valencia Lakes, just like all the other media. He wanted her on site for any breaking news regarding Nichol's death. It would be a zoo, but such was the job.

When Marty arrived at Beth's, the greetings were long and genuine as they filled each other in on the latest news on the baby. Then the subject changed to the investigation. Beth led the way.

"Marty, we have news from Katie," Beth said. She launched into the news of Santos. Marty already had bits and pieces of the story, but nothing would be as solid as hearing it from such reliable sources. She'd have to verify with Katie, but that was just a text or phone call away.

Marty received a text from her boss, Joel, that read, *More details coming in. Call me.* She quickly called him.

"I've got an interview set up with Mrs. Nichols for 10:30 a.m. tomorrow morning," he told her. "She's barely holding it together, so keep it as short as possible. I wrangled an exclusive on this one, kiddo. I know you'll do it right. Gotta run. Talk with you after the segment." Joel ended the call and was on to more fires to put out.

It was only about an hour to fly from Tampa to Tallahassee where Beth, Janice, and John lived. It was becoming customary whenever Marty was in or near Tampa, she would try to make room for a quick visit.

Beth insisted that if she needed a car, she should take hers. It was quicker and less hassle than renting one, although Marty would feel a bit guilty if she ever took her up on it. She had an expense account and she was supposed to use it for her business and travel. She'd never borrowed her car and didn't really plan to. It seemed unprofessional, but she knew Beth had only the best of intentions.

"Why don't we book hour massages for tomorrow afternoon?" Marty invited. "We all could use it and I'm not sure when we'll have the opportunity again. If nothing else, we can lay by the pool and drink mimosas, well orange juice for you Beth."

Janice and Beth looked at each other and in unison chimed, "Umm. Yeah!"

"Great. I have a room at a luxury resort. They cater to their guests twenty-four-seven so ladies we can order room service at 2:00 o'clock in the morning if we want. We'll take full advantage of my expense account without any guilt."

"You're so on," Janice said.

It was only 4:30 p.m. when they pulled up for valet parking, and they couldn't wait to check in. It was a four-star resort, and just the sight of it relaxed the senses. Everywhere you looked it was tasteful, understated opulence. Their rooms were the economy rooms which would be deluxe suites in other hotels. They met in Marty's room before booking their massages and making plans for the evening.

Marty texted Katie but hadn't received a response yet. Unfortunately, Marty's lifestyle didn't lend itself to patience, so the gals booked last-minute massages and indulged in some R&R.

Drake and Katie arrived at the stakeout in front of Donovan's club. After they updated the schedule, they apprised the agents on duty, and arranged for a hotel. It wasn't a resort, but it wasn't a one star either. It was a three-star Hilton Inn. Before driving off, Drake spoke first about the elephant in the room.

"I think for your safety we should just get one room for the night. We know Santos was here earlier today, so there's a good chance she could still be in the area," he nudged gently.

"And then again, she could be out of the country," Katie said. "You know how these people operate."

Drake countered, "Diamond may have made us already. I really don't feel like arguing about this. I'm gonna get one room and we're ordering room service. The less exposure for you the better."

"If Diamond wants you, we're gonna make him come to us. That's why we set you up as bait in the first place, so let's make 'em come to us, Katie." His voice had gone from frustrated to tender in one breath.

Katie smiled a big grin that stretched across her face and she shook her head yes, in agreement with him. "Okay. You had me at room service." She giggled. "Drive," she whispered. Drake put the car in drive, and they decided they were hungry. They planned to order steak because they never knew when or where they'd have their next meal. They had to make it count.

When they arrived at the hotel, they kept things lighthearted as if they were on a weekend getaway, instead of a sting op. Katie asked if she could use the bathroom first and Drake obliged.

She took a quick shower and brushed her teeth. She was done in fifteen minutes. Her hair was still wet, but she didn't care. When she stepped out of the bathroom, Drake looked up at her with telling eyes. She was wearing her favorite pajamas. She looked spectacular in a casual way.

Drake forgot to breathe. He swallowed hard. "You look, comfortable."

"Thanks. I am. And thanks so much for letting me go first. I really needed that shower. It cleared the cobwebs." Katie declared as she dried her hair with a towel.

"You're welcome. I'm glad it made you feel better. You need a break from all of this, Katie. You really do." Drake couldn't help but notice how good she smelled. His defenses were waning, but she was still so vulnerable, he didn't dare act on them.

He choked back his feelings as he cleared his throat. "I ordered room service like you asked. Two steaks medium and baked potatoes with the works. There's a salad and dinner roll on the side. I figured we could order dessert later when we settle down with a movie. Sound good, kiddo?"

Her eyes sparkled in the room's florescent lighting. Once again, she flashed her dimpled smile and answered him with a quick giggle. "Yes. That sounds wonderful. I'm looking forward to it."

"Remember, don't open the door to anyone. If it's room service, I'll get the door, but they shouldn't be here for at least half-an-hour. I won't be long," he said as he shut the bathroom door.

True to his word, Drake was in and out within ten minutes. He came out of the bathroom wearing just a towel. Katie couldn't help but notice his defined body with glistening patches of wetness here and there. She wanted him more than she had wanted any man. Their jobs left little time for meeting new people, let alone dating.

It's only natural to develop feelings for your partner, right? Katie questioned herself. Adrenaline alone, would draw them together. But she held these thoughts in check. What if Drake's responding to the immediacy of the moment? Did he like me for sex, or did he like me because of the danger I represent? How can I know? She wondered.

What would it take to convince me that he wants me for all the right reasons and not for my vulnerabilities? She had to keep her distance until she had some answers, no matter how much she wanted to fall into his arms and his bed.

Knock, knock. "Room service." Drake bounded to the door with his gun drawn. He peered through the peephole, and of course didn't see anyone but the waiter. Drake opened the door and stepped outside of the room to inspect the dinner. When he was convinced the coast was clear, he dismissed the waiter and wheeled the dinner into the room.

Katie inhaled a deep breath. "Ahhh. That smells so good," she said enthusiastically.

"It does, doesn't it?" Drake agreed. They ate with pleasure in every bite and sipped the wine slowly. Neither of them wanted the moment to end. Good food, good drink, good company produced the desire for good sex. However, Drake didn't want just sex. He actually cared for Katie, which both surprised and scared him.

Katie said more with her facial expressions than her words. Tonight, their body language talked more than they did. They found a movie to rent and sat on the sofa, curled up in each other's arms. Katie felt safe for the first time in recent memory.

She wanted to stop time and freeze-frame this moment, but she was yanked back into reality when Drake reminded her that they needed a good night's sleep. They may not have caught Santos today, but there was always tomorrow, and they still had to find Donovan and Diamond.

There were two queen beds, so they didn't have to worry about sleeping arrangements. Secretly, they both wished there was one king. Fortunately, they would deal with their emotions on another day.

Tonight, was foreplay, Drake thought to himself. He rather liked that idea; it helped him control his baser needs. He was willing to take her on her terms, when she wasn't so vulnerable and being chased by a killer.

"Good movie, but we need to turn in," Drake reluctantly reminded her. "Don't worry, I'll be watching out for ya. I don't need a lot of sleep; guess that's why I chose to be an FBI agent." He chuckled as he stood up, stretched and yawned.

"I'm right behind you. Katie went to the bathroom one last time. Normally, she'd sleep in her clothes to be ready for anything, but tonight she trusted Drake and cautiously slept in her pajamas." She poured herself a final swig of wine. "Goodnight, superman."

"Goodnight, Wonder Woman," Drake replied. With that Katie snapped off the lamp and they listened to each other's breathing. Katie slept and so did Drake. However, his sleep was light and sporadic. He didn't want to sleep at all. He wanted to take care of Katie, but his body was tired and needed to replenish itself.

Katie woke up at 5:30 a.m. and Drake was watching her. She liked that he was watching over her. She smiled and stretched. "What time is it?" she asked sleepily.

"It's 5:30 a.m. I was gonna let you sleep another hour," he apprised her.

She shook her head 'no' as she sat up and ran a hand through her thick hair. "It's okay. I'm an early riser, remember?"

"Yeah. I know, but I figured you could use the sleep," he responded.

"Thanks. I really appreciate you. You're so patient with me, Drake. I'm one hell of a partner, aren't I?" she said as she rolled her eyes in self-loathing.

Drake smiled and shook his head. "Yes. You are one hell of a partner and I wouldn't trust my back to anyone else. You're a skilled marksman and you have good instincts, everything you need as a good agent."

Katie stretched her arms to her toes. "You're a great partner too, Drake. I can't imagine anyone else at my side, protecting me. Not that I'm shrinking from my duty. I'm determined to get at least one of them today." With that she threw back the covers got up and got dressed.

She pulled her hair to one side and secured it with a pretty barrette. Living in a man's world, she didn't have much opportunity to embrace her feminine side, so she took small opportunities when she could.

They ate breakfast via room service again, checked out and loaded up the SUV. They were ready to pursue Santos and Diamond.

LaRue called Drake. "We have law enforcement at every port and airport in the state. We're concentrating on the Miami airport as it's the most logical exit from the United States."

"That's great," Drake answered with surprise in his voice. He expected support from Miami-Dade County but had no idea they would mobilize a state-wide dragnet. Sure, it was a combination of FBI agents and law enforcement, which normally mix about as well as oil and water. But on this point, they would gratefully take what they could get.

LaRue continued, "We've been sitting on the airport since yesterday and haven't seen a trace of her or anything suspicious yet. We're due to change shifts in thirty minutes. However, I'm staying on to oversee the mission."

"We'll be at the airport by then," Drake announced with determination. While in the SUV, Katie was jazzed. Her excitement was contagious. Drake felt it in the air. They felt luck was with them today. They pulled into their parking spot, bounded out of the car and rushed into the Miami airport.

They had a rendezvous place with the Miami P.D. They hadn't sighted Santos yet, but they were hopeful she'd make her move today. Their task was compounded because Santos wore so many disguises. They needed to see past the facade and look for facial features, primarily her eyes. Drake got a Coke for himself and a large caramel macchiato for Katie, and they settled in for a long, but hopeful day inside the terminal.

Marty, Beth, and Janice had fully enjoyed their afternoon and evening of indulgent pampering at the spa. The food was delicious and so was the ambience of the hotel and rooms. But playtime was over. Marty had a job to do and Janice had to get back to hers. Beth could stay since she had her manager running the shop.

As instructed, Marty kept her 10:30 a.m. exclusive interview with Tommy Nichols' widow. Beth accompanied her and hung back from the shoot. Marty made introductions and the interview got underway. The film crew had adjusted the white balance lighting and was ready to roll.

Jean was very nice when receiving everyone into her home. She was understandably still in shock. She had been released under doctor's supervision. She was to follow up with her own physician as soon as she could arrange an appointment.

Beth was well received after Marty explained that Beth, too, had experienced the death of a loved one at the hands of Donovan. However, Tommy's cause of death was still unknown at this point. They would know more later that day.

Jean remembered reading about Beth's story and recognized Marty from TV news blurbs that aired during commercials. Jean wanted to do all that she could to help bring her husband's killer to justice. About fifteen minutes later, Marty and the crew started the interview. It was a live and exclusive interview, so the pressure was on.

"First, thank you for taking time to talk with us today, Mrs. Nichols. We're so sorry for your loss," Marty opened.

"I want to help in any way I can," Mrs. Nichols responded in a frail voice.

"Mrs. Nichols, can you tell me exactly what happened yesterday morning?" Marty questioned as gently as she could.

"Well, everything started out the same as usual. Tommy got up at five in the morning like he always does, *did*." Jean corrected herself and her eyes swelled. "Then he waited for me to get up at 6:00 a.m. and he had the coffee on. We enjoyed a cup or two and then the doorbell rang, and it was the nurse for the day," a single tear escaped.

"You see, Tommy was pretty much homebound, and we just don't get out much. My Tommy required some help at home with his meds and all, and he couldn't move around very well. But he opened the door and let her into our home." Jean sniffed twice before she could continue. Her hands were shaking.

Jean could hardly speak as she recalled the moments. "If only we had known we were in danger, just because we won some money in a silly lottery. We just didn't know." She tapered off for a moment to collect her thoughts of the terrible morning.

"What happened next, Mrs. Nichols?" Marty encouraged her to speak freely.

"Well, she came on in the house and we gave her a tour of our home, so she'd know where everything was and such. Then she volunteered to make us breakfast, eggs and toast, I believe it was." She was briefly gaining composure.

"We'd already eaten a piece of toast, but we wanted her to feel welcome in our home, so we said yes to her offer," Jean explained.

"So, was this your regular nurse, Mrs. Nichols?" Marty asked for clarification.

"Oh no, dear," she burst out. "She wasn't our regular. We can't afford a regular nurse. Our insurance only pays for so much, we're on a plan that gives us different nurses nearly every day." She was getting to the hard part now and the tears were swimming in her eyes, ready to spill over her soft wrinkled cheeks.

"So, you didn't think it strange at all that this was a nurse you'd never seen before? Is, that right?" Marty nudged.

"Oh, that's right. We never gave it a thought. We were used to having so many different helpers around that we never gave it a second thought. We didn't know my Tommy was in danger until after my Tommy was dead." She dabbed at her face and eyes.

"I'd read something about it and my son said something, but we didn't pay much attention to the news." As she thought about it, she scrunched her lips together in anger and continued, determined to let Marty know how angry she was that authorities hadn't told her their lives were in danger.

"Had we known, maybe we could have done something or at least kept our doors locked." She clearly looked agitated at the lack of notification that put their lives in danger. "We just don't bother watching the news very often. It's so depressing, ya know. Tommy's eyesight wasn't that good, so we didn't go out." Jean's mouth turned downward as she felt anger well up inside her.

Marty sympathized. "Then what happened after she fixed you eggs and toast?"

She urged. "Oh, dear, she had me make the toast while she finished up in the kitchen. It was just after that when Tommy started to eat that he began having heart attack pains. He fell off his chair and hit the floor hard. The nurse started giving him CPR and told me to call 911. So, I did."

"Did the nurse continue to give CPR to your husband until the paramedics arrived?" Marty asked.

"Oh, yes. She did. She never stopped trying to help him till the ambulance people got here. That's when they took over for her. They started to do the CPR on him too, but it was too late. My Tommy was gone right there on the kitchen floor." She wept and dotted her tears with a tissue while she spoke.

Marty paused briefly to allow Mrs. Nichols to compose herself. "Did you ride to the hospital with him?" Marty eased.

"Yes. The ambulance people wanted to have me checked out because they said I was in such a shock and all. They did a good job taking care of me. My son brought me home though, and then I agreed to talk with you people." Jean was quiet for a moment before resuming.

"I'm so angry we never knew we were targets of anyone. We just won the money, that's all. We were going to travel and set up college funds for our grandchildren. And now, I don't know what I'll do without my Tommy. I've lost my Tommy." Her tears spilled over her brimming eyes. She sniffled as her shoulders lightly shook. Her heartache was gut-wrenching.

"Mrs. Nichols," Marty soothed, "do you know what happened to the nurse after you left in the ambulance?"

Jean took a moment to answer as she dabbed her wrinkled cheeks and swollen eyes. "No. I don't know what she did. I don't remember anything after they put me and my Tommy in the ambulance. I don't know what happened to her. She did say she'd follow us to the hospital, but I don't recall seeing her there." She spoke in a dazed, confused manner.

"Is there anything else you want to tell us, Mrs. Nichols?" Marty was wrapping up the interview as Jean's emotions were raw and it was clearly getting harder for her to talk about yesterday's events.

"Oh, I don't know. Just that I want the person responsible for this to pay for what they've done. I don't know why anyone would want to kill my Tommy. He never hurt anyone in his life and now he's gone. Gone for good." She was shaking her head no in disbelief and had started to weep unconsolably. Marty quickly wrapped the interview. The boys cut the bright lights and started to tear-down the equipment.

"Good job, Marty," Sam later said. He didn't frequently give compliments, so she took it to heart when he did.

"Thanks, you guys. I assume we'll be live again tomorrow with the autopsy findings. Are you spending the night here?" Marty asked.

"That's the plan," Sam assured her as he and Max carefully loaded the van with the equipment.

"Well, get a good night's sleep. There's no telling when the expedited autopsy results will be in and, as you know, we have to be ready to go live on a moment's notice," Marty stated the obvious.

Marty tapped the back of the van twice and the boys drove off to their hotel for the night. Until she heard from Joel, they were staying in Tampa for follow-ups. They'd be there for sure until the autopsy results were in, unless there was another murder overnight. Katie was still out there with a contract on her life.

Chapter Twenty-Two

One Down, Two to Go

Beth and Marty hit some boutiques in the chic part of the downtown Tampa during their free afternoon. Then they grabbed a bite at a wine-bar restaurant with piano music to boot. It was a well-earned break after this morning's tough interview.

Marty quietly sipped her wine and Beth drank cranberry juice as they ate slowly while enjoying the piano music. The conversation was easy, avoiding anything to do with the headlines. "How much longer before you deliver?" Marty asked with concern.

"Five weeks to go and I'm ready for it to be over with," Beth responded with a genuine, bittersweet tone in her voice. "I'm bloated and it's hard to get around. Thanks again for taking me with you today. It's good to get out of the house before the baby comes. I'll be home most of the time after that for sure."

"So, it's Rori Elizabeth Phillips, for sure? That's such a strong name for the little fighter you have inside you," Marty said as she toasted her wine to Beth's cranberry juice. "Are you going to schedule a C-section or try to have her naturally?"

"I haven't decided yet. There are pros and cons to both. But I'll probably choose a C-section. Less wear and tear on Mom." Beth grimaced at the thought.

"Well, given all you've been through with this pregnancy, I don't blame you for choosing the less wear-and-tear option. Are you planning to breastfeed or go straight to the bottle, or do you know yet?" Marty was often in questionnaire mode. A job hazard, but all her friends had grown used to it. In fact, they half expected it whenever they were with her. It was kind of a good habit to let people get things off their chest, but occasionally it backfired.

"I think I'll go straight to the bottle. I know breast-feeding is best, but I'm not sure I'm up to it," Beth answered. "With Janice and John helping me out so much, I think it'd be easier on everyone if I just bottle feed."

"Sounds like you have made up your mind then," Marty replied as she grabbed the check. "This is on me."

"I guess I have." Beth alluded to her decision to bottle feed. She was satisfied knowing she'd settled another issue regarding Rori.

Teresa was starting to feel the pressure of the hunt. Her last-known face was plastered everywhere, and disguises that would alter her appearance enough to get through a good security check were getting harder to accomplish.

She was an hour into her two-and-a-half-hour delay. She was in the corner of a dark bar, nursing a glass of wine. She needed scotch but thought it might be too memorable if people started asking questions. She was wearing a dark wig that mimicked a long bob cut. It was attractive but not unusual. She was wearing chic-torn jeans, a deep purple leather jacket, a trendy T-shirt, and carried an oversized handbag for a carry-on.

She planned on getting a gourmet cup of coffee before boarding, mostly so she could blend in and stay awake in case some hotshot spotted her. She didn't wear the sunglasses and hat the way people disguise themselves in the movies, but she did wear a hoodie. She kept a low unremarkable profile and blended in as quietly as possible.

She got up to use the ladies' room and stretch her legs. She left cash on the table for her tab, exited the bar, and turned to the right for the closest restroom. She was 60' from the bathroom when she was spotted by a plain-clothes female cop.

The chase began slowly at first, but soon the pace quickened. Santos was darting and weaving in and out among the masses as she tried to put distance between herself and the cop. Unfortunately for Teresa, the cop radioed ahead for reinforcements and Santos was soon surrounded. The only choice left to her now was whether she wanted to be taken alive or become someone's bitch in prison.

Thoughts were sprinting through her mind. She knew Whit had rolled on them and was now in the witness protection program. She'd often wondered whether she could handle going straight. Killing efficiently had been most of her life's work. She was good at it and never got tired of watching the poison take effect. It thrilled her in a way she didn't understand.

Suddenly, cops were everywhere and had corralled her into a closed circle. She thought about the trite hostage-grab but decided against it. She was caught. As she reached for her gun, the police fired two shots, hoping they didn't hit a bystander. Luckily, the bullets plowed into Santos, and shortly after she raised her gun to her temple and pulled the trigger.

Teresa lay drowning in her own blood. She took minutes to die. The police were on her almost immediately, but there was nothing they could do. Hers was not an instant death, as one would imagine with a gunshot wound to the head at close range.

Perhaps it was poetic justice that she suffered a bit at the end as retaliation for the pain she had inflicted on her numerous victims throughout the years. Now her life ended unceremoniously.

Beth and Marty were shopping for a crib when Marty got the text from Joel to go live as soon as possible with the news that Teresa Santos was dead from her own hand at the Miami International Airport.

"What is it?" Beth asked. She could tell by the expression on her face that it was something big.

"Teresa Santos is dead, and I have to get on the air now. I'm meeting my crew in fifteen minutes. We have to go. I'll explain the details on the way." Marty and Beth hurried out to the car. They weren't far from the airport and even in traffic they arrived in fifteen minutes.

"This is a breaking news report. Live from Miami International Airport is Marty Saunders," Howard reported as he cut to Marty. He knew this was a career-defining report for Marty. She'd originally broken the story of the insurance conspiracy of the lottery murders and now she was about to report on the death of one of the major assassins involved in the conspiracy.

"Yes, Howard. I'm live at the Miami airport where moments ago Teresa Santos, wanted for the deaths of many in the lottery murders, was shot to death by her own hand rather than being apprehended and taken into custody. Just yesterday, she was suspected in the death of lottery winner, Tommy Nichols," She swallowed before continuing.

"Right behind me the crime scene tape marks the area where Santos was cornered this afternoon by undercover police. Santos was spotted by Samantha Jorge of the Miami police who radioed ahead to her team that she'd spotted Santos." Marty was so pumped; she could hardly get her words out fast enough. She continued unabated.

"They closed in around her attempting to arrest her. Ms. Santos put a gun to her head and shot herself. Sources say she died at the scene." Marty paused for Howard's next question.

"Do you know if they have found anything on her person or in her belongings that will get them closer to capturing Donovan Black, or 'Black Jack,' the alleged mastermind in the lottery murders?" Howard quizzed.

Marty's thoughts were whirling as she continued the interview. Now that Santos was dead, justice would never be meted out for Kristi Hennessey and possibly Tommy Nichols, not to mention the countless others that died during her reign of terror. Marty pulled herself back into the moment, answering Howard's question without missing a beat.

"It's too early to tell right now. Authorities won't say how close they are to apprehending Donovan Black. All we know for sure is that police are still sifting through the evidence here at the crime scene, and we'll keep you up to date on additional breaking details as they become available," Marty concluded.

With that she was clear, and she glowed knowing she'd just given one of the most memorable reports in her career. Better yet, she knew Katie could sleep a little easier tonight with one less assailant after her.

"That was Marty Saunders, reporting live from the Miami airport where Teresa Santos has been pronounced dead on the scene." Howard closed the report with happiness for Marty's career high. She was his protégée, and he was happy and proud for her accomplishments in her journalism career.

He moved onto other news. "When we come back, the race for the White House. What the latest polls are telling us, and flash floods saturating the eastern states. Stay tuned." Howard just had enough time to tell Marty "good job" via their closed mics.

Donovan was getting antsy. He needed to run and run fast. He had flown in and out of the country within the past twenty-four hours to arrange his and Santo's escape. He had a small passenger jet standing by for a quick exit to a non-extradition country of his choosing. He knew Santos had planned on going to Netzahualcoyotl, Mexico, where they had arranged a rendezvous, but that plan was now history.

Donovan had one nagging detail to take care of before he was in the wind. Katie Lestler. If it hadn't been for her, he wouldn't be in the mess, or so he thought. In truth, it was Beth and her unshakable quest to prove her husband had been murdered that had become his undoing. Perhaps he'd deal with her later. For now, Katie had to die, and it had to fly under the radar in this whirlwind media mess. His next call was to Diamond.

Katie had exhaled a big sigh of relief when Santos died. She and Drake were merely minutes behind the officers on the scene. Per protocol, there would be an autopsy to see if any clues could be harvested from her body. But at least the immediate threat to kill her was removed with Santos' death. However, according to Whit's information, Hector 'Diamond' DeSoto was still dispatched to murder her.

But for tonight, she could breathe easier for the first time in months. Drake still wanted her to stay on her toes. Just because one major threat was out of the picture didn't mean she was in the clear.

Chapter Twenty-Three

The Death of Buddy Finch

The news that police had eliminated one of the heinous murderers from the lottery murders was joyously received by the public. It didn't matter that she actually killed herself. In the public's eyes, she was dead because of the police doing their jobs. This wasn't a hate crime where sides were taken, but righteous indignation for justice brought on by public opinion.

Donovan had to get to safe ground before leaving the country. He had a safe house in Naples, Florida. Located on the Gulf of Mexico, it was secluded and low-key for the high standards of Naples.

The exterior wasn't as fancy as most that dotted the shoreline, and that was the way Donovan wanted it. However, on the inside of the house opulence was abundant. He liked classic sleek lines and modern furnishings. Nearly everything in the house was in a black-and-white motif. He liked high fashion and clean lines in his apparel too.

He dressed like a movie star wannabe. He detested anything less than perfection. Wherever he lived it had to be spotlessly immaculate. He held himself and everyone in his employ to the highest of standards. However, a top priority now was killing Katie, and he set about accomplishing that task.

Katie was genuinely relieved that Santos was dead, but soon she couldn't shake that nagging feeling of her own death looming in the distance. She tried as hard as she could to block it, but the frightening nightmares wouldn't stop.

On the one hand, she knew she had to see this case through to the end, yet she wanted to run away to an island with Drake and forget about the whole horror show. She knew there was no place she could run that

Donovan wouldn't find her. They didn't capture Santos alive and that meant Donovan's henchmen were stepping up to the plate to pick up where Santos left off.

Katie and Drake were currently staking out Donovan's club in Miami and once again found themselves staying in a local Sheraton. It wasn't fancy, but it wasn't a dive either. The sheets and towels were clean, and it came with a daily complimentary continental breakfast. They shared a room for safety and departmental budgets, and they were only too happy to oblige.

It was getting harder and harder to keep the relationship on a professional level. They both lay awake at night, wishing for more but not surrendering to their passions. Drake knew how vulnerable Katie was, and making a move now would only confuse her and compromise her safety. Katie knew it too. However, this further strained their sexual tension.

Drake knew about her nightmares. Sometimes she would bolt up in her bed and other times she would get up quietly and wash her face. He was never sure if or when he should say something, so he remained silent. He didn't want to interfere with the way she chose to confront her fears. Things were strained enough, and he didn't want to step over the line.

They later went to the medical examiner's office when the autopsy was in on Santos. The medical examiner, Dane Walker, explained the results to Drake and Katie. "Turns out she was wearing a vest beneath her clothes, and it caught the two slugs from the officers' guns."

"The shot she fired to her head hit the front of her skull and ricocheted, lodging in the frontal lobe of her brain. That's why she didn't die immediately. However, one of the bullets struck her on her side in between her vest and ribs and punctured her left lung. She died from exsanguination. She essentially drowned in her own blood and in plenty of pain," the medical examiner explained.

"Can you tell us anything else?" Drake asked as he and Katie were preparing to leave.

"No. Nothing of interest. She had several scars. Some puncture wounds and what appear to be previous bullet wounds. She had signs of a broken clavicle and a fracture in her femur. She was pretty beat up." Dane ended his evaluation and showed them to the door.

"Thank you, Dr. Walker," Drake said as he held the exit door open for Katie.

"Well, there's nothing there that puts us any closer to Donovan, not that we were expecting anything, but I was hopeful," Katie remarked as they drove off.

Whit's replacement, Hector 'Diamond' Desoto, had been dispatched to murder Katie. He wanted to do a simple hit, but Donovan was more careful than ever to make sure things looked like natural causes, especially since there were already three attempts on her life and the media were breathing down their necks.

It'd be tricky and would take all the ingenuity they had between them to devise a manner of death. Yes, this one was going to be very tricky. No matter what they decided, Katie's death was going to be heavily investigated.

The only choice left to them was to have Katie commit suicide. This would have to happen over a short period of time, optimizing on the three earlier attempts on her life. They theorized she might become very depressed having to always be on high alert, knowing that even if she quit her job, it wouldn't end the threat of Donovan. To say the least, it would be hard for her to enter a normal civilian lifestyle with a husband, kids, and a mortgage to pay.

Donovan's game was to have Diamond follow Katie and let her get a glimpse of him for a few seconds, everywhere she went. He'd only show himself to her, which would be a challenge since Drake was always with her. Additionally, he'd slip in and out of her hotel room, moving her things around so Drake would start to question her stability as well.

If all went as planned, the department would put her back on the nine-to-five schedule.

Diamond's job was to cause her to become so despondent that she would take her own life. They weren't far from that goal, had it not been for Drake. They were going to 'gaslight' her into suicide.

Buddy Finch, in Decatur, Alabama, fancied himself as a playboy minus the money until he got lucky and won part of the Florida Mega Millions. He opted for the installment plan, thus landing another soon-to-be-victim at the top of Donovan's hit list.

Megan Smith and Jane Mullins also had targets on their backs. But for now, all eyes were on Finch because his payout was sooner than Megan's. He liked fast cars and the fast lifestyle, so it'd be a cinch to take him out in a car 'accident.'

Buddy Finch was anticipating his money. He'd already purchased a new Ferrari and he expected the women to follow. Unbeknownst to many, he was a diabetic who wore his insulin pump beneath his clothing. He rarely drank and watched his diet. It helped him maintain a fast-paced active lifestyle. Although he liked to party, he stuck to sugar free sodas.

He called his mom once a week and sent her money even before he won the lottery. He planned on buying her a dream home anywhere she wanted just as soon as his money came through. His daily routine was easy. He was a loan officer at a local bank. He went to work every day, went home, changed clothes, and partied almost every night, then rinse, and repeat.

His father died from lung cancer when he was only eleven and he'd taken care of his mom ever since. He had a little sister three years his junior, and he doted on her. He gave her special attention whenever he could. He was trying to make up for the loss of their father.

Buddy shared a house with three guys. They split the rent, the food, and living expenses. That's how he had money to send home to his mom and sister every month. He wasn't obligated. He just wanted to make sure they had everything they needed. He knew his mom would never let him know if they were on hard times, so he nipped things in the bud.

All his roommates envied him for winning the lottery, but since Buddy wasn't a selfish person, they knew they'd see some of the money in the way of friendship. He was planning on buying a nicer home and keep his roommates with him without charging rent but sharing living expenses. He wasn't interested in settling down for some time.

While Finch was at work, Diamond hacked into his new Ferrari's computer system and his insulin pump. He would take him out on his way home. Diamond planned on putting him in a diabetic coma and steer the car into a railing.

Little did Buddy know he'd enjoyed his last weekend on earth. It was Monday evening at 4:30 p.m. He was wrapping up the end of his day. He hadn't a clue that he was wrapping up the end of his life.

"Mrs. Franklin, did you draw docs for the Anderson file?" Buddy asked. "They close on Wednesday at eight in the morning and I need the settlement on that as soon as possible. Here are the initial docs for the Hernandez loan. You can start processing it tomorrow."

"Oh, and where are we on the Larson loan? He wants an update." He was tying up the loose ends of a slamming Monday. He couldn't know these were among the last words he would speak to anyone. He grabbed a light jacket and headed out the door to his new Ferrari. He was looking forward to the drive home.

Buddy was sitting in the car and strapping on the seatbelt. He had his shades on and the top down. He was ready for the experience of his new car. He turned left and merged into the five o'clock traffic. All was right in Buddy's world. Little did he know Diamond was following him four cars back and biding his time to cause the crash.

Hacking a car's system was Diamond's favorite method for murdering his unsuspecting victims. It had worked well for the Donovan empire. Foul play was hard to prove, and the families of loved ones felt only the aftermath of grief inflicted by bum fate. The accident scenario served him well.

He devised his own system for hacking into car computers, insulin pumps, and just about everything else. He was more masterful at it than Whit, and his work was virtually undetectable when analyzed.

However, there were occasions when the on-board computers were looked at more closely. Often it depended on the type of vehicle and the nature of the accident. For example, things came into question if another car was involved or if the manufacturer had any recalls on a specific model. Because the Ferrari was a high-performance vehicle, the authorities would spend little time investigating the on-board computer. Speed was the reason for most deaths in imported cars such as these.

Because Decatur was known as 'The River City,' between Northern Alabama and Wheeler Lake, Tennessee, the traffic was getting congested on the exchange. This was the perfect place for Diamond to strike. With one click on his tablet, he first interrupted the flow of Buddy's insulin pump, which would send him into a diabetic coma. Next, he hacked the Ferrari and it locked up. All he had to do was watch his plan unfold and then just before impact he'd unlock the Ferrari and his insulin pump, and he could chalk up another successful kill to his name. It would appear Buddy went into a diabetic coma, lost control of the car and crashed, just one more tragic accident.

Buddy appeared to be swerving in and out of traffic as if he were just showing off in his shiny new sports car. But he was getting dizzy, had the shakes, and an instant sweat that carried a nasty, sweetish smell. Other drivers were cursing and gesturing. No one suspected he was desperately trying to avoid them and that he had zero control of his car and his body.

He did everything he could think of, including trying to shift into neutral, but that too failed. His shakes were getting worse. It was similar to Katie's accident. It was only a matter of time before he hit a wall or caused a multi-car pile-up.

He tried calling 911 and his mom to say goodbye, but his blood sugar was plummeting. The lights were dim and would soon fade forever. He knew in that moment that he was about to die. He plowed into a wire guard railing. Both he and the car were split into pieces.

Diamond drove by a little slower than the speed of the traffic to admire his handiwork. Yup. He was dead all right, and the mess would take hours to clean up. His job was done, and he was ready for a couple of drinks before he resumed his efforts with Katie.

It would take months before forensics could determine the cause of the accident. They knew he went into a diabetic coma before he died, but it was the catastrophic crash that killed him. For now, his autopsy read, cause of death, 'motor vehicle accident.'

The only life insurance Buddy had was from his bank for fifty thousand dollars. That might be enough to make it stretch for a while if it were properly invested. But for today, his mom and little sister had their son and brother to bury.

Chapter Twenty-Four

Chase Me ~ Catch Me

Beth was now in her eighth month and eager to feel Rori in her arms. She was especially ready to get Rory's death behind her. In fact, she wanted the whole lottery murders issue to be over for good.

She was folding Rori's clothes and finishing up in the nursery when unexpectedly the doorbell rang. She peeked through the peephole and was happily surprised to see Marty standing on the other side of the door.

Beth's house favored a country charm. It was an older home with vinyl siding instead of the popular stucco exterior. It had a wrap-around, screened-in porch, complete with a couple of swing benches on each side of the porch. The inside of her home gave off a warm and cozy vibe. It was only about fourteen-hundred-square feet, but she made it look bigger with strategic placements of mirrors.

Tasteful charm was everywhere in small doses. Her home was not at all cluttered. Her kitchen, done in red and green apple decor was separate from the living room. The rest of her home was done in earth tones and subdued matte-finished blue hues.

They sat down for some coffee, nibbles, and chat time. Beth had a variety of cookies and muffins. They were her latest cravings. As the baby grew, so did her appetite, and the nesting mode had kicked in too. Her house was spotless. "I see you almost every night on the evening news," Beth started the conversation.

"Yes. I'm still covering the story, but the world waits for no one. So, I'm all over the map, going wherever the stories take me," Marty said as she picked off a bite of blueberry muffin.

"What's new since the last time we talked during our night out on the town in Tampa?" Beth remembered with fondness, "Have you been able to find any lead that would get us closer to Donovan?"

"No. But on the bright side, Donovan's running out of bad guys, the ones he trusts anyway. First, Whit was captured, then Santos offed herself, and now Diamond's his go-to man. Donovan's sweating bullets as he tries to take out Whit, a feat that is getting harder by the minute as the clock ticks down to the trial start date." Marty gulped the last bite of muffin into her mouth.

"He's in the witness protection program and that's a fickle mistress," she continued.

"Sometimes it works and sometimes it doesn't." Marty dropped the bombshell as easily as she could. Beth knew Whit was going to be put in the witness protection program, but she thought it was going to happen after he witnessed at the trial.

"Well, we have to keep him alive. That's the only restitution I have for Rory," Beth begged. "Whit's testimony is my only hope," Her hands were shaking.

"It's okay, Beth. Easy now. We're doing all we can to keep Whit safe, but even if he does get taken out, we have the attempts on Katie's life that we can tie him to. I agree, we need Whit because he knows where the bodies are buried. Hell, he put them there. But remember Florida has life without parole as well as the death penalty. So, either way, Donovan's not going to be doing any more harm to anyone," she tried to comfort Beth.

"I may be new at this, Marty, but it seems to me if Donovan were put in prison, he still has enough people on the outside to do his biddings. Hell, no one even knows for sure what Donovan looks like, and the FBI hasn't been able to secure a solid lead on him yet. No. Whit has to die and so does Donovan. How did you put it before? We need the head of the snake, which is Donovan," Beth was outraged.

She was in obvious distress due to the direction the conversation was going. But Marty knew Beth was one-hundred-percent spot on. "Whit does have to testify and then he needs to die while in the witness protection and relocation program, or nothing would really change." Beth took a sip of tea. "Ideally, he needs to be put to death at the hands of the state. Both Whit and Donovan have to die if we ever want to see a real end to their destruction."

"There is a bright side to all of this, Beth," Marty said calmly, trying to placate her.

"What's that?" Beth almost spat the words out, not because she was upset with Marty but rather the justice system, and that Whit would never be prosecuted for Rory's death.

"The media, as you know, is not letting up on this unfolding story," Marty noted. "Whit rolled on Donovan and Stein when turning state's evidence, and the survival rate for such notorious criminals as Whit and Donovan are grim, whether in the witness protection program or in prison." Marty reached for Beth's hand and squeezed it.

Marty drove her point home and continued, "Whit's guilty, pure and simple, and his testimony will put Mark Stein away for life or give him the death penalty. With as many enemies as Whit's made throughout a vile career, *someone* has a contract or two out on him. Odds are he's going to die by his own sword."

"But right now, our focus is on Stein. Remember, the trial is all about getting a guilty verdict on Stein. He's the one who gave the order to kill Rory. Stein was Donovan's right arm because he erased the paper trail and laundered the money. Whit was just his top assassin." Marty paused while she took a drink of fresh lemonade.

Beth responded eagerly. "I want to see Stein pay for what he did to Rory, to our family. Rory never even knew I was pregnant. He knew nothing about this sweet little girl I'm about to bring into this world. He'll never get to see her, hold her, play with her, or watch her grow up. He's was cheated out of everything; don't you see that?" Beth was anything but calm. She had to stop and collect herself.

"I do, and you're not wrong," Marty reasoned with her. "Rory will miss all those things and the joy of raising her together with you. But don't you mean that all these things have been stolen from you, too? You have every right to be angry and hurt, Beth."

Marty empathized with Beth's pain and expounded. "The life you had planned is now gone. And you're stuck figuring out how to refocus and redefine your life, but this time as a single mom. I know you're scared, hurt, and tired of this whole mess, but hang in there, Beth. We'll get through this together."

Beth swallowed hard, took a deep sigh, and began sobbing. It was only natural for her to have these valid feelings and uncertainty about her future. Marty put her arm around Beth's shoulder and walked her into the living room so she could be more comfortable as she continued to weep.

Whit was hating life in the witness protection program. To him it was only slightly better than the cage. He was renamed William Wilson. He was now a construction worker for a large firm in Bellevue, Nebraska. He wasn't near a border, so jumping would be harder if he tried to go on the lam.

He had a wife, Debbie Snyder-Wilson, one child, William III, and a German shepherd named Sam. Debbie was an FBI agent assigned to keep tabs on him at home and to be an early alert should there be a mishap of any kind. The boy was Debbie's son, about a year old, so he couldn't accidentally spill the beans on Mom and 'Dad.'

They lived in a three-bedroom, two-and-a-half bath suburban home, and he slept in the guest room while his wife slept in the master. Of course, the third room was for William III and his dog. Life was a neat little package.

Debbie worked from home as a bookkeeper for a local recycling plant so she could keep close tabs on William and her son. She could communicate frequently and directly on a secure satellite line to the feds whenever she needed. She always checked in at morning and night.

FBI Agent, Bret Douglas kept eyes on Whit when he was on the job site. Douglas was the newest foreman on the crew, and everyone seemed to take a shine to him. He was affable and able to blend into his new environment easily. Between Debbie's twenty-four-seven watch and Bret's watchful eye, the new 'William,' alias Whit, didn't have a chance to breathe freely, much less get back to his old tricks. Bret stayed nearby in an older RV.

Whit was stuck. He knew it was only a matter of time before he would be the star witness in the trial, *if* he lived long enough to testify. He knew better than anyone if Donovan wanted him dead, he'd be dead before the trial. If by some miracle he lived, it would be a while before he'd have a chance to get back to his old familiar life.

Joel called Marty with new details of Buddy Finch's death. She hung up the phone and shared the news with Beth. She would have kept it from her, but she'd overheard too much of the conversation to blow it off. Marty sighed deeply as she reiterated the news to Beth.

"Beth," Marty eased.

"I know, you have to go," Beth interrupted with understanding. She had stopped crying when Marty's phone rang.

"It seems I have another exclusive interview with Buddy Finch's mother and sister." Marty hated the timing of the news. She had to leave right away to cover the story in Decatur, and Beth was in no shape to be left alone. She quickly called Janice to come over and be with her and perhaps spend the night.

As usual, Joel had already booked her ticket from Tallahassee to Decatur and the team were already in the air. They'd meet up at about the same time. It was never easy when everyone had to fly to do the assignment. The van was much better for down time between takes, but it wasn't always feasible.

"Beth, I caught a cab here but since I'm in a rush, perhaps I'll take you up on that offer to borrow your car just this once. Maybe John can come along so he can return it to you." Marty was a bit hesitant.

Marty continued, "I hate to impose, but I need to get to the airport by 3:40 p.m. It's 3:00 p.m. right now." Marty hesitated to ask, but it was her story and she had to be there on time for the go-live as soon as possible. "It's a lot to ask, but it's the fastest way."

"I have no problem with that, why don't we both go?" Beth said having recovered from her emotional turmoil now that she needed to help Marty. She grabbed her purse and keys. They were out the door in a flash. Technically, Beth wasn't supposed to be driving at eight months, but she could make an exception for Marty.

Drake first heard about Buddy Finch's death from Dave, although not by much. Marty would be broadcasting the latest details on tonight's news. He dreaded telling Katie. He knew she would take it hard and generate more fear. It was late afternoon and Drake was carrying a cup of coffee to her.

"Here. Why don't you sit down and take it easy for a minute." He started off as casually as possible.

"Thanks," Katie said as she rubbed her neck and arched her back. She eagerly sipped her warm but not hot coffee.

"So, what's up?" she asked with confidence. He had something important to tell her. She knew him well and she could always read his poker face when no one else could.

"I've got some news," he said with caution.

"Well, what is it? Out with it, I mean it," Katie demanded.

Drake drew in a big sigh and spoke. "Buddy Finch was in a fatal car crash this afternoon." He didn't get any further when Katie interrupted him.

"Finch was at the top of the list too," she said as she internalized the full impact of his death. Her turn was coming soon. "The two sisters in New Jersey, Jane Mullins, and myself are the last ones on his list before he's in the wind. I know the implications." She tapered off with a determined look on her face. She would never concede to becoming Donovan's next victim.

The crawl line across the TV read there had been another possible lottery murder. "Buddy Finch, one of winners of the Mega Millions was killed while driving home today. Full coverage at 10:00 p.m. on CNB." Howard was awaiting another live report with Marty.

She delivered the breaking news about the death of Buddy Finch and wrapped it up as quickly as possible.

She closed her mic and took it off. She was fumbling with her phone. She was wondering how Katie was holding up. She needed all the support she could get as the trial grew closer.

Katie eagerly took Marty's call. "Hi. I've been hoping to hear from you. Do you know anything that we don't?" Katie asked with anticipation.

"Like your accident, there weren't any skid marks or evidence of an attempt to stop or even slow down," Marty said.

Katie's thoughts were racing. Inside she was thinking, *only this time they accomplished their objective.* "Finch is dead, and they are coming for me next," Katie emphasized. She was more fearful than she thought possible.

"Are you still in Decatur?" Katie asked.

"Yes. I plan to be here for the next few days or until we hear back from the medical examiner's office." Marty reiterated her broadcast. "Finch was just getting off work and was driving home when things went haywire. A couple of witnesses thought he was just showing off in his Ferrari, but some thought he had lost control, and some thought he looked like he had passed out."

"So, it really was like my accident," Katie said. "Too bad he didn't survive for so many reasons. He could have told us if he lost control of his car like I did. His death is awful and unnecessary. He was so young, and his poor family." Katie empathized more with every death and the nagging knowledge that she was next.

Marty continued, "It might take a couple of days to get the autopsy report. Tomorrow I have to interview the family and witnesses that want to volunteer their information for free. A lot of them are selling their information to the tabloids. It's disgusting."

Changing gears, Marty turned to Katie's well-being. "What about *you*? How are you doing, Katie?" Marty knew she was a basket case, but she'd never let it show.

Katie half-lied. "I'm holding up fine. I'm coping with it every day and staying busy," she answered. She was right about the coping during the day while at work, but not so well at night.

Her usual nightmares were picking up steam, and she wanted to know how to shut it out and remain focused on the case and not that she was Donovan's next target. The call ended with well wishes and the promise to keep each other updated.

Chapter Twenty-Five

Gaslighting

Marty called Beth as soon as she hung up from speaking with Katie. She had planned to keep her in the loop, even though there wasn't anything they hadn't already covered.

Finch's funeral was packed. It was standing room only. Some people thought him a bit obnoxious at times, but his effervescent personality gave him a warmth and charm that few could resist. His mother and sister were distraught almost beyond consoling. They wept quietly but with no drama. They laid him to rest in the cemetery next to his father.

In the meantime, Diamond was back to torturing Katie by making sure that only she saw him during planned sightings. They had his mug shot and a description from Whit, so they had a rough idea of what Diamond looked like.

Once, when Katie was coming back from the bathroom in a restaurant, she thought she saw him paying his check. Another time, she spotted him around the corner where she and Drake parked. Together, they got out of the SUV, but Drake took a minute to retrieve some paperwork when she spotted him.

"There! Did you see him, Drake?" Katie queried.

"See who?" he responded.

"Diamond!" she exclaimed. "I recognize him from his mug shot. I keep seeing everywhere. It must be him. He's biding his time planning my death." She was almost hysterical.

"I didn't see him, Katie, but I believe you did. It's just like Donovan to have his henchman torment you." He assured her he was on her side.

These were the kinds of sightings she would glimpse that made her question her sanity. Katie was so confused she didn't know what to think or whom she should trust. Who would believe her, other than Drake?

Diamond didn't let any grass grow under his feet. He was simultaneously planning the deaths of Megan Smith and Jane Mullins, as well as Katie's. He thought of it as multi-tasking. He really enjoyed tormenting Katie with his gaslighting technique, making her think she was slowly going insane. He had a job to do and dead bodies to deliver.

The FBI task force began to question Katie's stability and her acuity to see this case through. That is, everyone but Drake. He believed her and that was the end of it. If she said she was having sightings of Diamond, then that's what she was witnessing.

Donovan was getting jumpier by the minute. He wanted to stay in the States to keep a bead on Diamond and his efforts. He decided to have one of his lesser henchmen murder Jane Mullins. He wanted Diamond to focus all his efforts on Megan Smith and Katie.

The mass media exposure was weighing heavily on Donovan. The pity was Donovan enjoyed living in the United States. He had an unusual love for this country, which was uncommon for a man in his line of work. As long as he could continue to fly under the radar, he was reluctant to leave.

Diamond's tricks were starting to work on Katie. He took a silver pendant necklace from her dresser and returned it in plain sight a week and a half later. He moved her contact solution and hairbrush. Once, he took a pair of pants from her wardrobe and returned them via the valet service. She was sure she hadn't used the valet since she hadn't worn them yet.

These kinds of disappearing and reappearing pranks began to take their toll on her. On one occasion, he stole a bottle of Calvin Klein for women and replaced it with a similar-looking bottle, but the fragrance wasn't even close to that of Calvin Klein. Drake observed her slowly unraveling.

One night around three in the morning, Drake found Katie in the bathroom sitting on the floor, rocking back and forth with her knees drawn up to her chin. She hardly looked up when he entered the bathroom. He sat down beside her and took her in his arms. She sobbed lightly into his shoulder for several minutes.

Then she looked up at him. She was sniffing from crying. "Thank you," she uttered softly as he gave her some toilet paper to blow her nose. She was grateful for his comfort.

He'd been reluctant to go to her during the months they'd been together. He was afraid she'd be embarrassed for showing her emotions or that she'd reject his offer of comfort to her.

She felt good in his arms, like she belonged there. She wondered about his intentions. The heat between them grew thicker with each passing day. But they couldn't afford to jeopardize their professional lives. He let go of her for only a moment, as he leaned forward to retrieve more toilet paper, so she could wipe the tears from her pretty face.

"Thank you," she repeated as he prepared to listen to whatever she wanted to tell him. "You must think I'm crazy too. I keep finding things I've supposedly misplaced and then they turn up in places I'd never leave them." She was bewildered.

She poured out her heart. "I alone keep seeing Diamond and next I'm sure it'll be Donovan. That wouldn't be too bad, huh? We'd get a two-fer in all this mess." She was talking softly at first, but quickly led to a crescendo by the time she finished. Her nerves were frayed, and she needed some deep sleep.

Drake spoke calmly as he cupped her face in his hands and spoke directly into her eyes. "I don't think you're crazy. Donovan and Diamond will stop at nothing to get in your head. Don't let them," he encouraged her.

He contained his emotions. "Know I believe you, no matter what. They're trying to make you doubt your judgment, to mess with you, and if you don't get some serious sleep soon, you're going to weaken your defenses. It's simply physics at this point."

Drake got to his feet and offered his hand to help her up. "Let's get you to bed. Sleep in my arms tonight and don't worry about Diamond or Donovan. I've got you and I'm not sleep deprived. You just focus on getting some deep sleep." And with that he gave her a kiss on the forehead and lifted her to her feet. No matter how hard he tried, his feelings were getting the better of him.

He helped her into bed. She pulled the covers around her and gratefully laid her head in the nook of his arm and shoulder where she fell soundly asleep within minutes. It was the first good sleep she'd had since the last time she slept in his arms. She had forgotten what a good night's sleep felt like.

"I can't thank you enough for helping me get some sleep last night," she shared as room service knocked on the door. Their expense account of daily per diems didn't allow for such luxuries, so Drake paid for it out of kindness and the need for a decent breakfast.

Katie removed the lid from her plate. "Eggs Benedict? That's my favorite. How did you know?" Her questions were rapid and almost playful.

"You ordered them at our last catered department meeting, and I noticed how much you seemed to enjoy them." He was playful too.

"I can't believe you remembered that. That had to be months ago. Good memory." She admired his attention to details.

"Good observation, you mean," he corrected. "I just pay attention to the details that interest me."

"Well, thank you again for noticing my breakfast preferences and for a good night's sleep. I feel refreshed and ready to go, but I could sleep like that for days," she admitted.

"Well enjoy because we have a busy day," he said as he nodded to her breakfast. "We're taking a different tact. We're going to nail this bastard if it's the last thing we do."

Drake was convincing, "We know he's been in and out of the room for weeks. Someone had to see him coming or going, and today we're going to find a witness and arrest him when we catch him at his own game. We're gonna turn the tables on him, Katie."

"How exactly? Turn the tables on him? How?" Katie was onboard with the new approach but didn't follow him on how they were going to go about it.

"We start *dogging* him," he explained. "You go about your day as planned. Check in with Dave and hang with one of the stakeout teams today. I'll stalk the hotel room and question the staff for information."

Katie interrupted. "But we've done all that before and it hasn't produced a thing. What are you going to do differently this time?"

"I'm glad you asked. We've been playing this by the FBI handbook, by our rules. It's time we start playing by his," he grinned.

"Exactly what do you mean by that, Drake?" Katie questioned with piqued interest.

"It means we use whatever force is necessary to get Diamond and Donovan," he said. "They must have little piss ants running around for them. Snitches. We go after them this time. They're easily persuaded to talk when you apply pressure or cross their palms. We've been hoping the press and social media would help flush them out, but all that gets is false leads. We need more, and we need it now."

"Katie, your trial's getting closer and I don't want to see you go through another night like last night, although I did enjoy holding you while you slept. I think that's the best way for you to sleep until this thing is over." He finished half-hoping she wouldn't mistake his kindness for a pass and half-hoping she would. He was pleasantly surprised she didn't object to his suggestion that she would be sleeping in his arms until this ordeal was over. Katie let the sleeping remark go by and addressed the piss ants. "Why can't I go with you to put the pressure on these guys? Diamond has to know we're a team and we don't split up."

"Because you're the target, Katie," he said with deep feelings. "I don't want to parade you in harm's way. I want you back with the team, staking out Donovan's club. Alternate between teams if you want but stay out of the way on this one. The last thing I want is for Diamond or Donovan to get to you."

Katie was quiet for a moment as she absorbed his words. She nodded her head, indicating complete acquiescence to his plan. "I just want this to end. I'll do anything you want me to do, so long as it gets us closer to catching them."

They finished breakfast, grabbed a cup of coffee to go, and were out the door. Drake drove her to the stakeout at Donovan's club. There were two cars there, one at the front entrance and one at the back. She'd sit at the back entrance today. At this point, the only way to keep Katie safe was to leave her in the hands of FBI agents.

Early one morning while Katie was uncharacteristically sleeping, and without drawing attention to himself, Drake installed several mini surveillance cameras around the hotel, especially the entrances, and around their room. Drake knew Diamond wouldn't be expecting the additional cameras. After all, he already knew where the surveillance cameras were and had adeptly avoided them.

Drake was hoping this would be his undoing. Also, it would prove that Katie was telling the truth about the sightings of Diamond and that he was playing a dangerous game of cat and mouse with her. It would end the whispers among the ranks.

He reviewed the current footage and noted the times when Diamond came and went and from which entrances. The film only went back twenty-four hours, but Diamond appeared four times in one day. Yahoo. They had proof it was Diamond tormenting Katie and it would clear her name. Diamond was going down and soon.

Chapter Twenty-Six

Rori

Beth was in the shower when she noticed blood trickling down her legs. She had been experiencing pain but thought it was Braxton Hicks contractions that begin before real labor, until she saw the blood. Her water had broken, and the baby was coming soon. She hurried out of the shower and called Janice, who rushed right over.

Beth called her doctor and the hospital while Janice was on the way. Beth was still bleeding when Janice arrived. The contractions were closer and now all-consuming. She was in complete agony. Her doctor had an ambulance on the way, and she and Janice were whisked to the hospital with an OR room on standby in case they needed to do a C-section.

Beth was crying from pain and fear. She had done everything right during this pregnancy. Sure, she had been under tremendous trauma from the loss of Rory, but she'd followed her doctor's orders to a 'T'. She couldn't chance losing her baby, Rory's baby.

The ambulance arrived at the hospital in eight minutes and she was rushed to the ER. Her doctor was waiting with his team of nurses. They got busy working to stop the bleeding and stabilize her. Her baby was in distress, and she was rushed upstairs to the waiting OR. Knowing her situation, the doctor was determined to save her and the baby with a C-section.

Janice called John and Marty. John arrived within minutes, but no one had an update yet. The minutes ticked by. Janice left a phone message for Marty. "Beth's in surgery. Her water broke this morning when she was in the shower. She was bleeding out when the ambulance arrived. She's in the operating room now and we don't have any updates yet, but we'll keep you posted."

Marty's return phone call finally came. "I'll be right there as soon as I can hop a plane," she advised. She was at home in D.C. and she hurried to book her flight, then called Joel to let him know what had happened and where she could be reached.

Marty and Joel made previous arrangements to let her be there for Beth when the time came unless she was on a breaking story. The birth of Beth's baby was of human interest to the continuing saga of the lottery murders. It was a hopeful event amid all the tragedy this story had presented to the world.

Marty caught the red eye and would be in the air for a couple of hours. She had booked her rental and it would be waiting for her. She couldn't get there fast enough. She was praying for a miracle that Beth wouldn't lose the baby and that she too would be fine.

"I've got to stop the bleeding," the doctor told his head surgical nurse. "There it is. Clamp. I think we've got it." They were in the middle of a C-section and the cord was wrapped around the baby's neck. The doctor was working together with his team to bring this baby into the world while keeping the mother alive and stable.

Janice and John were trying to keep each other calm, patient, and positive. Waiting was the hardest task of all. They were looking forward to Marty's arrival, hoping it would be in time for the birth. It gave them something to distract their attention from the looming unknown.

Rori was two weeks early. The survival rate is very favorable at 38 weeks, but there is always an increased risk for both the mother and the baby when delivery is premature. Her doctor knew how stressful Beth's pregnancy had been and he was more concerned than usual with this delivery.

Finally, after working on the baby for ten minutes, he delivered a small but otherwise healthy baby girl. The nurses administered two Apgar tests that are taken on all newborns to summarize the overall health of the baby.

The tests check for appearance, pulse, grimace, activity, and respiration. Rori scored below normal the first time around. On the second test, they double checked for changes and accuracy. Rori had mostly healthy scores. Her skin tone was a little yellow, indicating possible liver issues. She was cleaned and readied for her mother's arms as soon as she woke up from the surgery.

Beth asked for her daughter the minute she was awake. That first touch and first time they looked at each other, Beth's life was forever changed. She would keep these moments locked in her heart forever. Her doctor came into the waiting room to give Janice and John the good news.

Dr. Patel announced the news, "You're now officially an aunt and uncle."

Janice beamed, "When can we see them?"

"Just as soon as there is an available room. It shouldn't take long. But I'll let her know that you're here and are waiting to see her and your new niece." Dr. Patel said his congratulations and disappeared behind automatically opening doors. About a half-hour passed before Janice and John could see the baby and Beth.

Janice couldn't have been more excited. "Let me see that sweet baby girl," she said in a high-pitched happy tone.

"How ya doing, hon?" John asked as he came into the room after his wife. By this time, Rori was in Janice's arms cooing and snuggling around her neck. It was a happy bittersweet moment.

Beth was missing Rory more than any other time during her pregnancy. They tried so hard to get pregnant for five years, and now she had Rori but faced a life without her husband.

Marty arrived around three in the morning, eager to see both Beth and the baby. She had stopped by the downstairs twenty-four-hour gift shop and picked up some flowers for the mom and a stuffed giraffe for Rori. As soon as she saw them, she knew how much Beth meant to her.

She had become a close friend over the past several months and knew she was going to spoil that precious little girl to the fullest. Marty was listed as a sister, so she was allowed to see Beth. They made special arrangements with the night shift that would allow her to see Beth whenever she arrived.

"How are we feeling?" Marty asked as she set down the vase of wildflowers and handed the giraffe to Beth. She sat on the edge of her bed.

"We're doing well. And better now that you are here. What took ya so long, globe trotter?" Beth asked rhetorically.

"Ha. I was actually home if you can believe that?" Marty quipped. "I almost don't know why I bother with a house. I'm so seldom there. I guess I just like the security and roots it represents. But enough about me. Where's Rori?"

"She's in the nursery. They're going to let me feed her in a few minutes, so your timing is impeccable. They have her in an incubator. They don't think it will keep her from coming home with me right away. She's jaundiced, but they say it's common and not to worry." Beth looked tired but totally happy. "They're going to send me home with a portable incubator for her liver."

"It's common for preemies who need to finish fully developing." Beth's voice sounded sleepy.

"Do they know how long she'll have to use it?" Marty asked with concern.

"Not yet, but they think it'll be only for a couple of weeks. Turns out I might have been further along than they thought. But the good news is that she's healthy and beautiful. She's just so beautiful. She looks like Rory." Beth began to tear up with these words. It was like she was in a dream. Surreal. She could hear herself speaking, but there was no reality.

Marty squeezed Beth's hand tightly. "I'm here for you, Beth ... for both of you. You know that." Just then the nurse came in with Rori and placed her in Marty's arms as Beth requested.

It was silent while they all absorbed the moment. "Beth, she really is beautiful." That's all Marty could say without breaking down. She felt Beth's sorrow and loss. She knew how much had been stolen from her, and they both teared.

Marty spent what was left of the night with Janice and John. They shared how happy they were with their new niece. Since Marty was considered part of the family, she proudly wore the title of Aunt Marty, which sounded more like an uncle's name. But she didn't care. She was just happy to be considered part of the family.

Marty's family was scattered across the country like most are these days. Her parents lived in Greenville, South Carolina, while her brother lived in Buffalo Grove, a quaint and affluent suburb of Chicago. Her brother was a trial attorney, which came in very handy for Marty's journalism and reporter career. He was married with three children, and they had the happy little chunk of life that most people only dream of.

Beth and the baby came home two days later. Beth was staying with Janice and John for the first couple of weeks. She needed to establish a feeding schedule and keep up her strength so she could recover from losing so much blood during her delivery.

She hadn't needed a transfusion, but her doctor put her on a week's bed rest to err on the side of safety. As it turned out, Marty stayed two nights before being called on assignment. It seemed the police had made an arrest.

Chapter Twenty-Seven

Diamond Strikes

Katie pulled into her parking spot at the hotel, turned off the engine and started to exit her vehicle when Diamond grabbed her from behind. He had a gun to the back of her head as he pulled her from the car. It was one of the few times Drake wasn't with her, but she assumed he would be behind her in short order. She realized she may have made a fatal mistake in leaving the stakeout without him.

Diamond had been waiting for Katie to arrive. He wasn't sure if Drake would be with her. He was expecting to kill him, but much to his delight, Katie arrived alone. This job was going to be easier than he had anticipated.

Diamond slammed Katie up against the side of the car. "Do exactly as I say, and I won't torture you." Katie struggled to free herself, but it was no use. He was bigger than she was, and he used his body weight to pin her against her car and limit her movement.

She was now face to face with her nightmare and was straining to reach her gun. She knew once she was out of the public's view, she was as good as dead. If only she had listened to Drake. He had to stay behind until the relief team took over surveillance at Donovan's club. She assured him she'd be fine since he'd be right behind her.

Diamond ripped the gun from Katie's shoulder holster and the .22 caliber from her ankle strap. "Now hand over your cell phone," he hissed. He was a ruthless and notorious killer, although thug-violence wasn't his usual pattern for hits. Usually he made a professional hit, two taps to the back of the head, but true to the lottery murders, he made the deaths appear to be accidental or from natural causes.

"What's your game this time, Diamond?" Katie asked as calmly as possible.

"Shut up! Bitch!" Diamond wasn't much for conversation when murdering his prey.

"What are you going to do to me?" she pressed, trying to draw the attention of any passersby.

"I said, *shut up*," he growled as he pushed the gun into her left temple. "Come with me. We're going into the hotel like we're friends. Got that? And don't try anything." He shoved the gun in her back. "You hear me, bitch?" Katie could hear his anger as she felt his hot rancid breath hit her senses hard. She nodded her head in acceptance to his terms.

He straightened his clothes and put his arm halfway around her waist with his gun concealed in his hoodie pocket. She knew if she tried to make a move and he pulled the trigger, there was a good chance she'd be a paraplegic for the rest of her life.

Her thoughts were racing as she wondered what was keeping Drake. Diamond had to know he was right behind her. That's when it hit her. What if he managed to kill Drake first? Oh, God! I'm gonna die tonight, and the thought of losing Drake was like a punch in the gut.

It hurt so much to think that Diamond got to Drake. She was on her own. What about her parents and brother? How will she survive this attack? Her mind was jumbled, but she remained aware of Diamond and his gun. They arrived at her hotel room door. He forced her inside the room.

Drake rarely let Katie out of his sight. He had sworn to protect her. She'd spent the day at the stakeout like they planned, while Drake followed up on his new surveillance videos. He usually met up with Katie and the agents at the stakeout around five. But on this night, their relief detail agents assigned to sit on Donovan's places were delayed, so Drake hadn't arrived yet.

Katie still insisted on driving back to the hotel for a much-needed shower and rest. She'd been bored to death at the stakeout. She contended that Diamond wouldn't make a grab for her in a public parking lot in the light of day. She couldn't have been more wrong.

Drake arrived at the front entrance stakeout car to see if the relief team had made it to the stakeout. When he got there, he found dead agents, the two on the day shift and the two relief agents. He didn't have time to waste. He tore off to the hotel. Katie was all he could think about.

Drake called for backup while he darted among traffic. He knew Diamond had Katie and he would gladly kill her, but he didn't know if he would torture her first or execute her immediately. He couldn't let his mind go there. He just had to focus on the traffic and hope he could reach her in time.

Diamond shut and locked the door behind them and shoved her down on the sofa. Then, oddly, he went to her refrigerator for a beer. "Here." He tossed one to her. "Start drinking and where do you keep the hard stuff?" Diamond quizzed, as he slammed cupboards, looking around the kitchen for her liquor. The hotel room had a kitchenette, complete with a full-size refrigerator and stove.

"It's in the cabinet over there." She pointed with her head to a top-end cupboard. "It's in there," she said with a mixture of calmness and defiance. He had poked around their room plenty while gaslighting her and knew they kept beer and wine in the refrigerator, but it was hit and miss on the hard stuff. They put it wherever it was handy, not necessarily in the same place.

"*Drink*," Diamond ordered as he selected a bottle of scotch, then poured a single for himself and a double for Katie. "Drink up," he chided exigently.

Diamond wanted Katie's death to look like a suicide by a mix of alcohol and drugs, so he had to get her good and drunk before pouring the crushed pills down her throat. After all the trouble she'd caused, he wanted to see her squirm.

Katie was thinking fast. She remembered her training and her experience. She'd been in tougher situations than this before and believed she could get out of this one too. She watched as Diamond slammed back his scotch. "Drink faster," he commanded.

"Why should I. You're just gonna kill me. How are you gonna do it, Diamond?" she antagonized. She knew men like Diamond thrived on their ego, and she played to it.

"Slow," he grinned. "I plan to kill you nice and slow, so you can think about that boyfriend of yours. Did he make you feel safe? Too bad he's not here to save you now. Now drink," he demanded, as he poured her another double.

"Let me guess," Katie said as she tossed her hair back to see him better. She ignored her inference to Drake. She couldn't think about his loss right now. She had to focus. "You're gonna ply me with alcohol, get me drunk and have your fun killing me at your discretion. Am I right?"

Because she was an FBI field agent, she regularly took DHM, Dihydromyricetin. It's a drug from an ancient Chinese remedy, which allows a person to consume about 20 beers in two hours and fully recover from its effect within 15 minutes. Agents were required to keep this drug in their system as a fail-safe for just such an occasion. She definitely had the upper hand. But this time the situation was real and the consequences of her focus and ability to stay sober would determine two things.

Firstly, she needed to convince Diamond that she was drunk while she remained somewhat sober, and secondly, she had to find a perfect time to attack him and turn the tables in her favor. Doing both successfully would determine if she remained alive. Perhaps he was playing with her, but Diamond continued to drink with her... his one for her two.

"You've caused me nothing but trouble, and I'm gonna make your death painful and slow." He tipped the bottle into his glass. "I want you to feel the life draining out of you as the darkness swallows you," he sneered.

"I thought you needed to make my death look like a suicide. You've tried everything else. What do you have left for me now?" Katie questioned to stall for time.

"Yeah. You've been a real pain in the ass, you have," Diamond was belligerent as he continued. "Because of you we lost Santos. For that you'll pay."

"Was she a friend of yours?" Katie gouged. "I thought your kind were all hired hands, no room for fraternizing and all. Was she your girlfriend?" she mocked. Katie was pushing his buttons. If he lost control, she had a shot at overpowering him.

"Shut your mouth. Drink and shut up," he demanded as he stood over her, pouring her another full glass.

Now was the time to make her move. He was directly over her. She shoved her knee deep into his crotch and ground it for maximum effect. He dropped the bottle and his gun. He momentarily writhed in agony.

She tried to put distance between herself and him, but he was too fast for her. He recovered quickly, enduring the throbbing pain in his groin and the effects of the alcohol. He managed to grab her ankle as she was going for the gun.

They fought hard and wrestled to overcome each other. Katie was tough. She got in a few good blows and a couple of roundhouse kicks before he subdued her. He had her in a headlock and dragged her into the bedroom.

Drake was almost there. He tried calling Katie's phone, but it dropped to voicemail every time. The phone was dead, and he feared Katie was too. He pushed down harder on the accelerator and blocked the thought from his mind.

Diamond threw Katie on the bed. He forced her mouth open, but she bit him hard. At that point, he punched her in the face, and she was out cold. Finally, he had a moment to catch his breath. She had given him so much grief, he was only too glad to watch her die. He took a small packet from his pocket and shoved its contents into her mouth, forcing it shut. It wouldn't take long now.

Diamond knew he'd run out of time and needed to get out of there as fast as possible. Drake might be there soon. He was on the fire escape just as he heard the Dade County police break down Katie's front door. It was too late for his escape. He could follow Santo's' lead and shoot himself or he could make a break for it, but either way he knew the place was surrounded.

"Police. Call out!" Officers found Katie with a faint heartbeat, and the paramedics were close behind. By now the SWAT team was on the scene and it sounded like a siren circus. Paramedics arrived and went to work on Katie. It took several minutes to stabilize her.

"Her heart has stopped. She's crashing." One of the paramedics was calling for the defibrillator. "Charging at two hundred and sixty joules. Clear." He shocked Katie.

"No response," replied another paramedic.

"Try again, three hundred joules. Clear!" He hit her again.

"We have sinus rhythm," another paramedic confirmed. During the ride in the ambulance, they had to shock her heart again. She was taken to the emergency room where a crash cart was on stand-by.

Drake arrived at the apartment only moments after the ambulance left. He immediately drove to the ER, which took about twenty minutes.

They were still working on her, so no one could see her, not even an FBI agent. Her condition remained critical.

Diamond made it down the fire escape into the waiting arms of the Dade County P.D. He was apprehended before he could give a second thought to suicide. It was a glorious day. The FBI had finally captured another most-wanted fugitive.

Drake was still at the hospital when he heard the news that Diamond had been captured. It was a big relief, but there was still no news on Katie's condition. At this point, Drake figured that no news was the same as good news. They tell you right away when the patient dies.

Chapter Twenty-Eight

Four Attempts and Counting

The paramedics found an empty packet of pills near Katie and took it with them so they could identify what she had ingested. She was still unconscious.

The medical staff pumped her stomach. Katie started waking up as the siphoning began. It was awkward and painful. She was sore, but she had been through much worse. She stabilized shortly thereafter, and she was able to answer questions. She still thought Drake was dead.

Diamond lawyered up the second the feds came into the interview room where he had been taken after he was captured. They tried to cut a deal with him like they had with Whit, but Diamond kept his mouth shut most of the time.

"You do realize the moment your attorney gets here the deal is off the table and is gone for good?" Dave pressured. Dave was the head of the FBI task force as well as Drake and Katie's handler. He was intimidating, but to no avail. "We don't need you to get a conviction at trial. We have Whit and Katie's testimonies, and that's all we need to make the case against you and Donovan stick."

With that comment Diamond spoke up. "First, you have to find Donovan and that ain't gonna happen," Diamond taunted. "He's in the wind."

"You realize you'll be going away for the rest of your life unless you get the death penalty, don't you?" Dave tried to bait him into making a deal before his attorney arrived. However, he clammed up and never spoke another word until after his lawyer showed up, and even then, his lawyer spoke for him.

Drake walked into Katie's hospital room. They were keeping her overnight for observation. *"Drake!"* Katie called out. "You're *alive*." Her voice was raspy, and her throat was hurting from the siphoning hose that was down her throat less than an hour ago.

"Of course, I am," he reassured her, walked up to her and gave her a lingering kiss on her forehead. "What made you think I was dead?" he asked with knitted wrinkles in his brow.

"When you didn't show up within a few minutes, I figured that Diamond had gotten to you first," she said with an obvious sigh of relief. "I'm so glad you're not hurt. I couldn't bear having to break in a new partner," she teased.

"We got him, Katie," Drake happily announced Diamond's capture.

"We got Diamond?" Katie questioned with hope.

"We got 'em," Drake said with assurance and a smirk.

"We did? Where? When? How?" She fired eager questions. "I want details." She was almost doing her happy dance in bed. She wanted to throw her arms around Drake's neck and never let go. She wanted to wake in his arms after a long night of lovemaking and sleep.

"Yeah, we caught him coming down the fire escape into the waiting arms of the police and our agents," he pronounced with a giant grin on his face. "We did it, Katie. We got Diamond, and now there's just Donovan to go, and you know he's gotta be sweatin' bullets after this. He's gotta be wondering if Diamond's gonna roll on him like Whit did." Drake was happy and hoped the news would ease her mind.

"Yeah, he does," Katie agreed with Drake, and a broad smile broke across her tired face. She was briefly silent as she soaked in the information and its ramifications. She closed her eyes and thought about a day when she didn't have to fear for her life. It was a distant but happy thought.

"The only health you should be worrying about now is your own," Drake stressed. "I can't imagine all that you've been through. You really need your rest, and I'm gonna stay with you tonight and make sure you're safe."

"We don't know if Donovan has any other henchmen hiding in the wings." Drake didn't want to take any joy away from the capture of Diamond, but he wasn't about to let down his guard now.

His words stung as she entertained the idea of another hit man gunning for her. However, she was so relieved that Drake was alive and with her that she listened to what he had to say.

Katie responded, "What do you mean about 'other' men waiting in the wings?" Katie shook her head as if she knew of no one else trying to kill her other than Diamond. She knew that Donovan had other players, but she didn't think any of them were as adept at killing the way Diamond and Whit were.

"I can see you need to rest," Drake said. "I'll go back to the hotel and get a few clean clothes for you, so we'll be set for tomorrow when you get out of this place. I'm staying with you tonight. By the way, you're not starting to like hospitals, are you?" he teased. "Tell the truth. It's the whole breakfast in bed thing, isn't it?"

Katie started to protest but then realized how happy she'd be if he stayed with her during the night. Nights in a hospital play tricks with the mind. "Get out of here," she choked out. "And hurry back." He let the door shut behind him. For her continued safety, an officer was posted at her door until Drake got back.

Drake promptly returned to Katie's hospital room with her things. He picked up a pizza and a small salad. It hurt going down her throat, but it was well worth the pain. They watched a bit of TV together and talked about the trial and how it might play out. They talked about everything but the elephant in the room, which was their feeling for each other.

The nurse made her nightly round at eleven o'clock. It was time for lights out and a good night's sleep. Katie always found it easier to talk in the dark whenever she was unsure of herself.

"Drake," she began, "I can't thank you enough for staying with me tonight. It's probably not necessary since we have Diamond. I think Donovan's given up on me by now, too much publicity and all." Katie chose her words carefully.

"It's necessary," Drake emphasized. "I don't want to risk another thing happening to you. You matter too much to me."

"Is that as a partner or as a friend?" Katie cautiously approached the subject at hand.

"It's both," he hedged. He didn't want to scare her off, so he didn't know how much he should reveal. "I value you as a person, an agent and friend, a close friend," he said with softness in his voice.

"I value you as a close friend too, Drake." Katie could feel knots forming in her belly.

"I like you, Katie. I have feelings for you, and they go beyond friendship. I meant it when I said you are my close friend. I mean you're that, but more too." Drake fumbled for the right words.

Drake was stumbling all over himself and wondering if he was getting his meaning across. "I'm not sure if I'm saying this right, Katie but you matter to me romantically, emotionally, and physically. I care what happens to you and I want to be part of your life, not just your partner." There. He'd said it.

Katie was biting her lip with joy. She had no idea that his feelings went so deep. "I care for you that way too, Drake," she confessed. "I want to be with you, but how is that going to work in our professional lives?"

"Let's just take this one step at a time," he suggested. "Okay? Let's just get through the trial and we'll talk again. In the meantime, we should get some sleep. You're exhausted and you need to rest your voice." He got up from his chair and went over and kissed her goodnight. It was the kind of kiss that lingers long after it's finished.

Donovan was up in arms. Never had he encountered anyone as hard to kill as Katie Lestler. He did have a few other gorillas working for him, but they weren't as reliable when it came to hunting down FBI agents. Donovan knew he no longer had a shot at taking her out, at least not now. He refocused his efforts on killing Whit and Diamond.

By now the media had swarmed the story regarding the capture of Hector 'Diamond' DeSoto, and Marty was ready. She broke the story on the ten o'clock news with breaking news segments during commercials and a crawl line during regular programming. Tomorrow was going to be a good news day as the details of Diamond's capture came in. She caught a fast sleep and was ready for a go-live an hour before airtime.

Whit was stuck in a holding pattern and dreaded it might last the rest of his life or at least until after the trial, which was now less than a week away. If he lived to testify, he would land wherever they planted him, and he wouldn't have any say in the decision.

So far, there hadn't been any attempts on Whit's life while in the protection program, but the trial was approaching, and the FBI weren't taking any chances. Sequestering their witness provided Whit's optimum chance for survival. The feds decided to videoconference his testimony during the trial, knowing it would only take one clean shot and the star witness would be dead.

Whit didn't hold much hope that he would live to a ripe old age. Once his FBI agent detail was over, his day-to-day protection would end. He would be someone new, somewhere else, and be largely responsible for his own safety.

Since Diamond's capture, the lottery murders story was world-wide, and Marty wondered how Katie was holding up. Because Katie was an FBI agent, the public knew nothing about her. The bureau kept it silent while Marty was in the thick of the storm, struggling to keep the facts from sensationalism and distortion. Supposition sold print and viewership increased when the truth was stretched beyond recognition.

Drake and Katie went back to the apartments in Tallahassee for the pending trial. The FBI had luckily secured an apartment for them and still kept them under surveillance due to Donovan's ongoing threat to Katie's life.

The first night Drake and Katie went out to dinner for a change. By now they were sick of room service. They went to a small but elegant French fare restaurant and enjoyed two bottles of fine wine with their Chateaubriand steak dinner. The meal and wine were decadent. They took an Uber back to the apartment and would pick up the SUV tomorrow. For now, they deserved a break from the madness that had consumed them.

The trial was upon them, and the real danger seemed to be past. They could no longer deny their feelings for each other. Perhaps it was because they were forced to work so closely together or that imminent danger begged for a port in the storm, or they wanted to celebrate the capture of Diamond. Whatever the reasons, they didn't care. They knew how they felt about each other and longed to be with each other.

Drake opened the door and the minute it was closed, they began kissing softly at first, then deeply and hungrily. Clothes hit the floor as Drake pushed her against the wall. With her legs wrapped around him, he picked her up and carried her to the bed. Their passions exploded as they made love all night long, taking short breaks for water, wine, and cheese.

The morning sun peeked through the blinds and cast shadows on Drake's body. Katie was awake at six-thirty, which was sleeping in for her. Drake stirred awake and smiled at her as he brushed a shock of hair from her cheek.

"Good morning," he said. "How'd you sleep?" He knew the answer.

"Umm. Great. When I actually slept. How 'bout you?" She returned his smile and giggled. She seemed to do that a lot around him. He could always make her laugh, even in the darkest moments.

"Wonderfully. I had you in my arms all night. I've been wanting to do that for so long," he confessed.

Katie got up to use the bathroom then came back and sat on the side of the bed, wondering if she were dreaming again or was she really that happy.

"What now? I'll bet you're hungry." He smiled again as he eyed her in his shirt.

"I could eat… or not," she teased. With that he pulled her into his arms. Breakfast came later.

The media vans and uplinks littered the lawns and parking lots as close to the courthouse as they could get. Most arrived a couple of days early to cover the pre-trial in the Mark Stein case and the effects it was having on the community. It was all the buzz in a city of Tallahassee with about a two-hundred-thousand population. The city just wasn't prepared to handle the influx of people who were to attend and cover the trial.

Marty was in almost constant contact with Beth, Janice, and John. They had driven into Tallahassee for the trial. They made hotel arrangements immediately after the trial date was set, knowing if the case came to trial, it would be a zoo trying to scramble for a room at the last minute. They booked extra rooms in case they needed them.

Beth had booked the rooms at the Residence Inn Marriott near the state capitol as did Drake, Katie, Marty, and her crew. Drake and Katie took one of the extra rooms in order to have a comfortable hotel for their newly found affection rather than using the FBI apartment. The group was eager to talk about all that had happened since they'd seen each other and watch the trial get underway.

Marty met Beth, Janice, and John in the lobby for drinks. They hugged, then ordered drinks and appetizers. Beth handed Rori to Marty so they could get reacquainted. She was five weeks old and as cute as could be. She had big dark blue eyes and soft pink skin. Her smile was adorable, and she had Rory's dimples.

"Beth, she's beautiful and so tiny." Marty was captivated by this adorable little girl. "How is she doing as a preemie?"

"She's off the incubator and has put on almost a pound since her birth weight." Beth was beaming.

It was obvious Rori was the apple of her eye. Janice and John were glowing as well. "She's keeping all of us on our toes," Janice said, smiling as she spoke. "We don't get much sleep, but that's all right. She's worth it," she said as she lightly touched Rori's cheek.

The drinks and appetizers arrived, and Marty gave Rori back to her mother. Beth was wearing a sling for the baby as they were still bonding. Beth could enjoy her fist drink in nearly a year because she wasn't breastfeeding. She ordered a simple glass of Chardonnay as they all munched and talked.

"Marty, bring us up-to-date on the latest with the trial. Do you think Diamond and Whit will live to testify?" John asked while taking a bite of a stuffed mushroom cap.

"Not to be overly optimistic, but yes, I do," Marty asserted. "I think Whit will make the trial now that he is going to videoconference his testimony."

"But what about Diamond?" Janice asked. "Is he going to cooperate? He has to know they'll put him away for life, if not to death."

"He knows, but I think Diamond would rather take his chance in prison than be known as a snitch," Marty answered with a strong sip of a gin and tonic.

"Well, there's no way the jury is going to acquit him," Beth insisted. "There's too much forensic evidence, plus Whit and Katie's testimonies will put Diamond away for good."

"He's being treated as a hostile witness," Marty explained. "He's guilty for the deaths of Buddy Finch, the four FBI agents and the attempted murder of Katie. His trial's gonna be on down the road."

"It gets so complicated," Janice said. "Can you explain what we'll be hearing during this trial? I know we'll have a separate one for Diamond and the insurance companies, but those will come after this one. Right?"

"You're correct," Marty began to clarify. "Let me lay it out for you because I have trouble keeping it straight too. There's a lot of people, but the primary players in the criminal case are Mark Stein and Whit. His real name is Jason White."

Marty continued, "As you know, Whit's going to confess murdering six victims besides Rory and the attempt on Katie. That much we know for sure. Then he'll testify against Donovan and Diamond, which puts more pressure on everyone to catch Donovan."

"What's a *hostile* witness mean?" Janice asked.

"Diamond didn't cut a deal with the district attorney, so he'll be treated as a hostile witness, meaning the prosecutor will have to try to trip him up. He'll have to answer all questions posed to him at which time he'll give up as little as possible while attempting to protect Donovan. We're hoping he'll tell us where Donovan is hiding out, but so far, he's remaining loyal to him," Marty explained.

"But Whit gets a free ride for this," Beth said with a monotone pain in her voice.

Marty nodded her head and sighed deeply before answering. "Yes. He does. He won't pay for Rory's or anyone else's deaths. That was the deal he made. It sucks, but that's how the DA sees this as a win." Beth went quiet and patted Rori's back.

"There's still something I don't understand," John interjected. "How is this trial going to give us Donovan? I thought Whit said he doesn't know where he is."

"You're right," Marty agreed. "It doesn't give us Donovan unless Whit decides to tell us."

"He's given up the house and club in Florida, but Whit swears he doesn't know where he is right now. And maybe he doesn't. Heaven knows, the FBI can barely keep track if he's in or out the county," Drake inserted.

"So, that's it?" Beth interrupted. "We just hope he'll decide to tell us when it suits him? What else does he need to bargain for? I thought he had to tell the FBI where he is in order to get his deal. He's getting off scot-free for everything else."

She was sick to her stomach. She didn't know if the conversation, the wine, or both made her ill. She couldn't afford to get sick. Rori was depending on her and she wasn't going to miss this trial for anything.

"Beth," Janice said. "You don't look so well. Do you want to go lie down while I take care of Rori?"

"No, thank you. I'm just not used to the wine. I'll have some more appetizers. Thanks," Beth responded. The drinks and appetizers soon became dinner and led to lighter conversation. By the end of the evening, they all managed to have a good time talking about Rori and their mutual interests.

Janice and John excused themselves right after dinner, citing they were tired and wanted to relax before the trial started tomorrow. It wasn't a blow off, as they really were tired from the stress of taking care of Beth and the baby. More importantly, they wanted to give Beth and Marty some one-on-one time. They knew how close they'd become and wanted to let them catch up.

The two went to Beth's room to put Rori down for the night and have a chat. They kicked off their shoes, had some more wine and curled up on the sofa.

Marty started. "Have you given any thought to what you want to do now?" she queried lightly. She didn't want to upset her with the sadness of Rory.

Beth answered, "I have. I still don't have any definite plans, but I've been offered a lot of money for my story. I'm sure you know about the sharks in the water. But given that we no longer have any steady income, other than the shop and our savings, I'm giving it some serious consideration. I've been promised that the story would be told exactly the way I want it, but you know reporters." They laughed.

"That sounds reasonable," Marty responded with a snicker. "Your story is unique, and it affects the whole country and everyone who has ever played the lottery or has been interested in insurance annuities."

"So, you don't think I'm trying to profit from my husband's death?" Beth bit her lip and tears welled in her eyes.

"No. No, I don't think you're trying to profit from the loss of Rory. Of course, not. I think you're being very brave to let anyone write your story. Most people wouldn't be strong enough to relive the horror, but you, Beth, you're different," Marty bolstered. "You're that one-in-a-million solid rock that could do this and bring dignity and perhaps some closure to this whole thing." Marty was encouraging and sincere.

"You really think I should do this?" Beth asked for verification.

"Yes. I think it's a great thing you're doing," Marty stated. "You know if you don't control this, someone out there is going to make up their own version of this nightmare and cash in on your pain. I mean, it's not like you're trying to play to the sympathy card. You already have that from the public," she reminded her.

Marty continued, "People view this whole thing as an outcry. This way, if you're in on the whole process, you have some control over what and how your story is told. You'll get the truth out there and that will bring you a lot of peace. Maybe not as much as you need, but some. I know it's not the same as having Whit pay for killing Rory, but it's something and you partially get to control it. That's worth it, Beth. You should do this." Marty inspired Beth with her words of wisdom and truth.

Chapter Twenty-Nine

Opening Statements

The FBI moved Whit daily from one safe house to another. As far as their neighbors and co-workers knew, he and his family were on vacation. However, Debbie's son was temporarily put in FBI custody to keep him safe.

Given how much Donovan's men liked to take over the controls of computerized vehicles, they drove low-tech, non-computerized cars to transport Whit from location to location. They didn't want history to repeat itself.

They checked daily for Lo-Jack tracking devices and used satellite phones and land lines to secure the sites and protect Whit. The FBI knew if someone really wanted to risk his life for Whit's, it was more likely than not that Whit would die. But they were taking as many precautions as possible.

Whit was surrounded with a detail of seven agents. Four on the outside of his place and two on the inside, plus Debbie. The only problem with a videoconference was that someone with the know-how could hack into anything. Therefore, they used a VPN, or virtual private network, and changed the IPS signatures daily. Whit was as safe as they could make him.

Mark Stein's trial of the century began promptly at ten o'clock and Beth, Janice, John, and Marty all met downstairs for breakfast. Rori had eaten and was wide awake for a few moments. Everyone doted on the star of the breakfast show. However, after all that activity and food, she readily fell asleep in her carrier. Beth had everything she needed for the day, including the diaper bag, sling, and carrier. She was ready for anything.

They were on pins and needles as they walked into the courtroom and took their seats. Because Beth was the surviving spouse of one of Whit's victims, she and her family had reserved seating at the front of the courtroom, as did Katie and Drake.

Beth would testify about the phone conversation before Rory's death, and Katie would testify regarding Whit's two attempts on her life. She couldn't count the ones by Teresa or Diamond. The group exchanged hellos with Katie and Drake and discussed quietly where they would all meet for lunch and then dinner back at the hotel.

"All rise. This court is now in session with the Honorable J.M. Stokes presiding," the court clerk announced. "You may be seated." It had begun.

There were three large TV screens situated strategically around the courtroom. The first was in front of the jury box, the second faced the judge and the third faced the rest of the courtroom. They were placed to minimize obstruction of view.

When it was time for Whit's testimony, the TVs' would be turned on and off simultaneously. This truncated courtroom distraction and allowed the minimum amount of viewing time for Whit's testimony. Whit had a green screen behind him so it wouldn't divulge his location.

Federal Prosecutor Shawna Ferguson had an impressive win record, even though most criminal trial attorneys were favored for the win. She had to prove the defendant was guilty, whereas the defense only had to prove a shadow of doubt.

Luke Jackson, the defense attorney, was well-known nationwide. He had a team of great legal minds assisting him. After all, talking about big insurance meant talking big money for big minds, and only the very wealthy could afford Jackson and his team.

Whit's testimony was expected to turn the whole insurance industry on its ear and rewrite insurance laws. The charges and publicity weren't fair to the thousands of honest insurance agents who had spent their careers serving the public with much-needed life, health, property and casualty insurance, and investment policies.

Marty and her team were covering the story outside the courtroom and witnessing the drama play out during sessions. She and her crew occupied the same hotel as the others. It made travel and communication much easier. They would be stationed there throughout the trial for daily on-site live coverage.

The media were so thick around the courthouse and designated media areas that the satellite dishes looked like salt-flat mounds. Expectations were high. People were expecting to hear horrific stories about deaths ordered by Mark Stein. The jury was sequestered for the duration of the trial.

Shawna Ferguson got up to deliver the opening statement for the prosecution. "Good morning, ladies, and gentlemen. This is no ordinary trial as you all know from the media and the politics in this election year. The state is seeking a guilty verdict against former Florida State Attorney General, Mark Stein.

"Your verdict will set a precedent for serious reform of the insurance industry and consequences of all those involved, namely, Mark Stein, who perpetrated the biggest insurance scandal in all of history." Shawna continued undaunted.

"The people will show a preponderance of evidence that the defendant knew of and orchestrated the murders of seven individuals who did nothing more than win a lottery. Furthermore, we'll show the defendant duped insurance agents to invest clients' winnings in straight life annuities with installment payout plans for fatter commissions." Shawna was determined to get a conviction and bring down big insurance.

"He hoodwinked the sale of these annuities because they offer the security of a regular pay out plan with the quid quo pro, that upon the death of these annuitants,' the unpaid monies become the sole property of the gluttonous insurance companies." She had rehearsed her opening statement for weeks and it was paying off.

She kept going. "This scam was perpetrated by the defendant and seven insurance companies as a last-ditch effort to remain solvent in an uncertain economy by collecting copious monies from the influx of lottery winnings. We are here today to topple this egregious conspiracy, starting with the conviction of Mark Stein."

"In conclusion, "Shawna put her hands on the banister of the jury box for emphasis, "we'll hear testimony from FBI Agent Katie Lestler regarding attempts of her life that were ordered by the defendant." She paused momentarily to gauge the impact of her words. "We will send the message to Mr. Stein and big insurance that they can't get away with murder," With that she took her seat.

Luke Jackson, the defense attorney, got up from behind his desk and approached the jury box. "Good morning. We are here today to advocate that Mark Stein, while acting as Florida's attorney general, did not know about the atrocities that were taking place during his administration."

Jackson ran his hands down the front of his suit coat before continuing. "He may have acted with ignorance, but not with malice. He had no knowledge the insurance companies named in pending civil suits were committing these heinous crimes. My client acted in the good faith, counting on the individual integrity of said insurance companies to guide their moral compass." He took a deep breath as he strutted in front of the jury. His hubris knew no bounds.

He continued with arrogance, "The defense will prove 'reasonable doubt' regarding Mr. Stein's alleged directives advising agents to sell straight life annuities with a regular payout plan Furthermore, he did not order the preposterous allegation to execute any lottery winners. Those decisions were made by the sole discretion of the insurance companies, their leaders and their agents."

"Face it, ladies and gentlemen, If we were to be totally honest, we've all made a few bad calls that have landed us in hot water without our knowledge of maligning individuals behind the scenes." Jackson boasted.

He cleared his throat. "Now in those instances, you are no guiltier than my client who sits before you today." Jackson pivoted slightly and gestured to his client with an open hand. "He simply had no cognition that anyone would ever conceive a conspiracy to murder innocent people with the quest of keeping their money in order to remain solvent." He mockingly chuckled. "No, ladies and gentlemen. It's simply not true."

He wrapped up his opening statement. "There simply is no evidence to prove that my client had any prior knowledge of this conspiracy until he found out about it with the rest of us. Thank you." And he took his seat. The prosecution called its first witness, Katie Lestler, to the stand.

Chapter Thirty

The Trial

"The opening statements were delivered today as the trial of the century, the people vs Mark Stein, former Florida attorney general, gets underway." Howard was leading off the evening news with the number-one story for a good deal of the foreseeable future.

"We have Marty Saunders on location. "Marty, what can you tell us about day one of the trial?"

Marty began, "Yes, Howard. We're live in Tallahassee where Mark Stein is being tried for the murders of seven lottery winners, plus the attempted murder of FBI Agent Katie Lestler and the murder of Rory Phillips, who was murdered in February of this year."

"Marty, any word today on whose opening statement was the strongest for the jury to consider?" Howard asked.

Marty shivered with nerves. "No. Not really. It seems to be about equal right now. However, the beginning testimony of FBI Agent Katie Lestler, had an impact on public opinion. Seems everyone is liking what she has to say, and she seems exceptionally credible."

"What about the mood of the courtroom, Marty? Is it as crowded as it looks?" Howard was leading her through the interview.

"Oh, yes. It's wall-to-wall people. It's standing room only and the crowds are being controlled and some turned away. Security is very tight, especially given the nature of this trial. Emotions are high and running hot," Marty relayed.

Howard changed gears. "Marty, we know authorities are still looking for Donovan Black, who allegedly is the mastermind of this diabolical scheme. Is there any update regarding his whereabouts or when he might be brought to justice?"

"No, not yet. Police are working around the clock trying to bring him in, but so far, no word. Back to you, Howard." She steered him away from Donovan. She clearly wanted the public to know the intent of the trial was to dispense justice for Mark Stein. The interview was over, and Marty was done for the day.

Howard finished and went on to the national weather story. When Marty was clear, she and her crew extracted themselves from the crowd and rejoined their group back at the hotel.

"Well, that was day one," Katie exclaimed. "I can't imagine how much harder tomorrow will be. I know they barely got past my name and my occupation before court was adjourned, but I felt the eyes of Stein and the jury on me."

"You did fine, Katie," Beth reassured her. The others at the table agreed.

"You did great," Drake said softly. "And you're gonna do great for the rest of the trial. Believe in yourself."

"That was a weak opening for the defense," John declared.

"I know," Janice agreed. "I thought so too. His strongest argument was what, that he didn't know any better, but trusted the integrity of the insurance companies? Please. I'm appalled."

"What a joke," Katie threw in her two cents. "Gee, the I-didn't-know-so-I'm-not-guilty defense. As if he didn't tell the agents to sell those annuities. It's pathetic."

"And it's only day one," Janice said as she squeezed Beth's hand. She knew how draining this ordeal was going to be for her, yet it would give her some measure of closure if Whit lived long enough to testify. They finished dinner and dispersed until they met for breakfast the next morning.

Meanwhile, Megan Smith was looking over her shoulder for the cloud that was Donovan Black, who might still be trying to have her killed. She knew via the news that Diamond had been captured and that Mark Stein's trial had begun.

The payment would be wired to her bank account, so there was concern about her account being hacked. However, with both Whit and Diamond in custody, chances were minimal. Also, she figured the threat against her life must be low given all the publicity about the lottery murders, but she wasn't going to take that chance, and neither were the police or the FBI.

Megan Smith had three law officers assigned to her; two of them were assigned by the local police department to watch the perimeter, while one was designated as her bodyguard. His name was FBI Agent, Raymond Masters. He'd been on the force for eleven years and hadn't seen anything to equal the scope of this manhunt for Donovan.

Masters slept during the day when the women were guarded by his partner, Brad Donner while they were at work or school. He kept watch while Megan and her sister, Tiffany, slept in their bedrooms. The policemen used unmarked cars while surveilling their apartment complex in the Van Vorst Park area of Jersey City.

With such a large a bounty on Donovan's head, the leads were coming out of the rafters. A whole team of FBI agents were tasked to sort false leads from the reputable ones. However, Donovan's orders had already gone through. He was so full of vengeance, he wanted to send a message. He wanted to break precedence and convince the authorities that he was untouchable.

Megan Smith was looking forward to opening her own advertising company and helping her sister pay for veterinary school. They both had big dreams and they wanted to live to fulfill them. They weren't gonna go crazy with out of control spending when they got the money; rather, they were planning a vacation to get away from all the stress and publicity.

So far, the nights passed without incident. Yet, nights were the most dangerous time for them and the most obvious choice for an assassin to make his move, so sleep came uneasily.

The best thing the girls could do was stick to their routine. After all, doing anything out of the ordinary might make them an easier target for Donovan. This made it easier for the FBI and law enforcement to anticipate the actions of Donovan's men. The question still remained. Where was Donovan and did he have any more hired guns to take out Megan? Had he fled the county? No one seemed to know.

Donovan had been in and out of the country several times since the conspiracy began and hadn't killed that many people, considering the multiple lottery winners. He wanted Whit dead by any means necessary. If that meant killing everyone around him, that was fine too.

Killing Whit was a pretty tall order for the man Donovan hired to kill him. Jane Mullins could wait a bit since her first payment was months down the road. But the clock was ticking on Whit and Megan Smith.

Only twenty days remained to kill Megan Smith and thirteen days to kill Whit before he was slated to testify. Meanwhile, the seven insurance companies were crumbling beneath the burden of the state's retribution and the public's outcry for reform.

Donovan had several business accounts in foreign entities to launder his money. He'd already paid half the amount of money up front for the designated hits on Whit and Megan. His new hire went by the name of 'Train.' His real name was Antonio Francisco. Now he was on Donovan's payroll and Whit and Megan's trail. Only a bullet would stop him.

It was day two of the trial. Katie was once again called to the stand. She was reminded of her oath and took her seat.

"Ms. Lestler," Shawna began. "Were you traveling home in your 2021 Chevrolet SUV in an eastbound lane on the evening of May 12th of this year?"

"I was," Katie responded.

"Can you tell us of the events that took place that day?" Shawna prompted.

Katie crossed her legs. "Yes. I was driving home when suddenly my car was out of my control. I couldn't control the wheel, the brakes, or the accelerator. I couldn't even shift the gear into neutral or turn off the engine," Katie recalled. "I was trying to gain control when I called 911."

She cleared her throat, looked at Drake and continued. "I told the operator what was happening and gave her my location. It was during rush hour and I was eastbound on Benton Street. The dispatcher asked if there was anything I could ram such as a trash dumpster or barrels. I told her there was nothing like that in the downtown area. I was swerving to avoid cars when suddenly I was T-boned." She took a sip of water and stole another look at Drake and Beth.

"What happened next, Ms. Lestler?" Shawna prompted.

"I survived the crash at an impact speed of about 33 miles per hour. I had a ruptured appendix, spleen and a deep cut over my left eye." She pointed to the scar. "And my ribs were badly bruised." Katie winced as she recalled the pain.

"And you said that neither the accelerator nor the brakes were responding and that you didn't have control of the steering wheel. Is that right?" Shawna asked to verify.

"I tried pulling the hand brake, but it didn't help much," Katie replied.

"And do you know who hacked into your car's system?" Shawna was moving forward in a careful process.

"Yes. I mean the Jason White," Katie answered matter-of-factly.

"How do you know it was Mr. White and do you know who ordered this attempt on your life?" Shawna probed.

"He confessed in exchange for the witness protection and relocation program and said the defendant ordered the attempt on my life." There. Katie felt she'd unlocked an important part of her testimony.

Shawna tilted toward the second attempt on her life. "What happened while you were in the hospital, Ms. Lestler?" Shawna was pushing for the most copious details of her hospitalization.

"Mr. White attempted to kill me again," she half-whispered with a sting in her voice. Drake winked at her and she continued.

"It was the second night of my stay in the hospital. It was in the wee hours of the morning, around 2:30 a.m. or so, when I saw a male nurse advance toward my bed. He looked at my chart for a moment and then he approached me with a syringe. I knew by the way he was acting; he wasn't a real nurse," Katie insisted.

"How did you know that?" Shawna questioned.

"It was when he approached me. He didn't act like he belonged there. He acted like he was trying to belong there. He said he was going to give me a shot of Ativan for anxiety, but I already had my round of pills. I knew it was too early for my next dose of sedatives, plus, I was on a morphine pump, so I knew he wasn't a nurse." Katie cringed inside as she relived the event.

Katie continued without prompting from Shawna. "Then I recognized the snake tattoo on his arm. We had witnesses from the accident that identified him with a forearm tattoo of a coiled snake with red and green eyes, so I knew it was him." Her eyes often darted to Drake for reassurance.

"When did you shoot him?" Shawna pushed.

"When he was about to inject my IV. That's when I looked him in the eyes right before he started to inject it." Katie's voice was escalating now, knowing that once again her emotions had gotten away from her.

"And what happened after you shot him?" Shawna was putting together a jigsaw puzzle piece by piece.

"I shot him the first time and he fell on top of me," Katie explained. "He was still trying to inject my IV when I shot him again. This time he crumpled to the floor. Blood was everywhere." Katie closed her eyes to shut out the haunting memory.

Katie was reliving that horrible night but was stating the facts with as little emotion as possible. "I know this must be very difficult for you, Ms. Lestler, but if you could elaborate about what happened that night." Shawna was as gentle as she could be but drilled to the facts.

Katie took a breath and gave a half smile. "The hospital staff came in and took him out of the room. They helped me take a shower and moved me to a different room," she answered with vivid memory. Her hands were trembling so hard, she had to hold them in her lap to hide them from the courtroom. Her strategy wasn't working.

"I see. That must have been very traumatic for you," Shawna sympathized.

"Yes. It was, but we're trained at the bureau how to handle these kinds of things." Katie was falling back on her training now.

"What kind of things do you mean, Ms. Kestler? Do you mean shootings?" Shawna pressed.

"Yes. That's exactly what I mean. We have access to professional help if we feel we need it." Katie twisted the Kleenex in her hand.

"Did you feel you needed it?" Shawna wanted to address the credibility of her witness. This was bound to come out in cross-examination, and she wanted to get ahead of it.

Katie continued before she had time to think about what she was saying. "At first I didn't, but it was required as standard procedure whenever there is an officer-involved shooting."

Shawna pressed on, "Did you ever seek the help of a professional therapist or physicist after the initial mandatory requirements?"

"I did later. I had four voluntary sessions with a therapist, and I was cleared for duty after a short absence. The time off allowed for the healing of my wounds." Katie winced as she remembered how much her bruised ribs had hurt her.

"And today, Ms. Kestler, do you still feel you're fit for duty?" Shawna had to establish her current ability to effectively do her job.

"Yes. I do." Katie spoke with the conviction that she was ready for duty and certainly ready for this trial. Shawna moved away from the hospital inquiry and started down the path to Stein. "Again, can you repeat who issued the hit on your life?" Shawna alluded to the defendant.

"It was Mark Stein." Katie glanced at him for only a minute as she was sickened by the sight of him. Katie was relieved and ready for this line of questioning.

"How do you know it was Mr. Stein?" Shawna quizzed.

"Like I said, Mr. White confessed it was him, and there's a money trail that traces back to the defendant," Katie answered with confidence. The words left a long overdue pleasure. Even though she'd already testified to Whit's attempts on her life, it felt good to implicate Stein.

"Your Honor, the people enter Exhibit A." The bailiff took the evidence from Shawna. It was a paper trail of Stein and Donovan's withdrawals and deposits of varying amounts into offshore bank accounts.

"Is there any other evidence against the defendant implicating him in the attempts to murder you?" Shawna escalated her questioning. "What other evidence do you have against the defendant?" Shawna shot a smirked look at Jackson. "There are phone records indicating Mr. Stein had placed several calls to burner phones," Katie said.

"Were you able to trace these calls to any of the assailants?" Shawna pressed onward.

"Yes, we were," Katie responded.

"What did you find?" the prosecutor asked.

Katie answered, "Unfortunately, the nature of the burner phone tracks calls placed by the defendant, but we can't prove to whom they were made. Burners only show the phone numbers of calls placed, but not the recipient. Often, criminals scramble the phone numbers by routing them through several cell phone towers in order to make it impossible to know from where the suspect placed the call. We recovered three burner phones and the defendant's personal cell phone."

Before Jackson could object, Shawna quickly followed with evidence. "Let the people show Exhibit 2, your Honor the phone records of Mark Stein, Jason, Whit, White, and Hector 'Diamond' DeSoto."

Shawna continued, "How do you know it was Mr. Stein's personal phone?" She wanted to be clear on this point.

Katie answered easily. "Because the message log shows Mr. Stein's outgoing calls and text messages made to Mr. White." There was a murmur throughout the courtroom, especially in the jury box. The questioning was getting intense, and Katie's answers were clear.

"Do you know what was discussed?" Shawna pressed.

"We believe that during these calls, Mr. Stein ordered Jason White to kill me." Katie felt relief with each passing question but was also afraid of Donovan's retaliation.

Jackson was quick to his feet. "Objection. Speculation, your Honor."

"Sustained. Tread lightly, Ms. Ferguson." Judge Stokes was engrossed as much in the testimony as anyone in the courtroom.

"Your Honor, the people submit exhibits B through J. Mark Stein's confiscated cell and burner phones of the defendant." Shawna handed a cell phone to Katie and continued.

"Do you know for sure that your murder was the topic of the conversation? Can you please read the last text message on the defendant's cell phone?" Shawna questioned, knowing the answer.

Katie eagerly obliged. "Take out Lestler. Usual means. Confirm." Again, the courtroom moaned in light of concrete evidence.

"Is there any other evidence that Mr. Stein hired Mr. White to kill you?" Shawna asked. She was locking down the death sentence for Stein.

"Yes, Mr. White confessed when he turned state's evidence when he rolled on Mr. Stein." Katie looked at Drake and briefly smiled.

Shawna was going for the trifecta of evidence. She'd linked the cell phone evidence to the money trail.

"You mentioned the money trail. Can you give more details about this?" Shawna pursued.

"Yes. Prior to the attempts on my life, there was a three-hundred-thousand-dollar deposit into White's offshore bank account. It came from a Cayman Islands bank account belonging to Mark Stein." Katie was stating a fact, fully aware that she'd scored a blow to the defense.

"Thank you, Ms. Lestler. No further questions." Shawna shot Jackson a 'gotcha' look and took her seat. "Reserve the right to recall the witness." Shawna had locked down the evidence that directly linked Whit to Stein. Her job was done on that point.

Luke Jackson had premature silver hair and was in his late forties. He was handsome with an oblong jaw and a high forehead. His hairline was low, and his hair thick. He had blue eyes and a tanned skin. He was intimidating in an ostentatious way.

"Ms. Kestler, you are an FBI agent. Is that correct?" he began.

"Yes. It is," Katie responded.

"So, might it be safe to say that during your time as an FBI agent that you may have acquired a few enemies along the way?" he pushed. "Is that possible?"

"Objection. Calls for speculation." Shawna was right on top of Jackson.

"Sustained," the judge ruled.

"Sorry, your Honor. I'll rephrase the question. Have you made an enemy of anyone during your time as an FBI agent?" Jackson asked.

"I may have. But none come to mind," Katie responded reluctantly.

Jackson was going to circle back to this, but first he had to defuse the text messages. "Regarding the cell phone text messages which read, take out Lestler, usual means, confirm. Was there any specific mention of murder in that message, Ms. Lestler?" Jackson was smug.

Katie couldn't believe how Jackson was spinning the text message but had to answer. "No. There's not any specific wording, but it certainly alludes to it." Katie rushed to get in her whole answer, which was dripping with sarcasm.

Jackson smiled at her sarcasm and was mad at himself that he hadn't truncated her statement before she got in her inuendo. "Perhaps my client was suggesting Mr. White should ask you out on a date," he hypothesized. Jackson was grasping at straws and he knew it. Yet, he was paid to mount a defense. "So, in fact, there's no mention of murder in those text messages. Is that true, Ms. Lestler?"

Again, Katie tried to get her words in. "Yes. But we'd never met, so it's highly unlikely that he was arranging a date."

"Just yes or no, Ms. Lester," Jackson instructed before she could disarm his question. Changing gears, he moved toward the money issue. "You said the FBI has a paper trail you traced back to my client, namely a deposit of three-hundred-thousand into Mr. White's offshore bank account. How did you determine it was for your alleged murder?" Jackson was ramping up for his defense.

Katie leaned forward and answered the question. "It was based on text messages and the fact that it was wired into an offshore account. The amount of money was also an indicator."

Suddenly, she realized it was the combination of evidence that would convict Stein. Her answers were leaving room for a shadow of a doubt, no matter how far-fetched Jackson's theory suggested. Her stomach flipped as she looked desperately at Drake for reassurance.

Jackson took a deep breath and puffed his chest. "So basically, all you have is your interpretation of the text messages and a sum of money deposited into Mr. White's offshore account. You have no actual evidence that this was for a murder-for-hire circumstance. Is that true, Ms. Lestler?"

"Objection. Calls for supposition," Shawna insisted.

"Sustained," Judge Stokes ruled.

Katie was cornered. "It's the comb …" She was cut off by Jackson.

"Just stick to answering the questions, Ms. Kestler," Jackson warned.

Katie wanted to finish her statement but reluctantly answered the question. "No. But we have the full confession from Mr. White," Katie spat the words into the mic.

"Ahh. Good. We'll get to that, Ms. Kestler." Again, Jackson ran his hands down the lapels of his expensive suit as he readied for his next round of questions. "Let's move to the subject of White's confession."

Jackson was coming down the home stretch. "You have only the word of a known criminal, namely, Jason 'Whit' White, that he was hired by my client, Mr. Stein, to murder you. Correct?" Jackson was impugning Whit's credibility.

"Yes." It was a simple answer that was creating a small measure of doubt for Stein.

Jackson marched on with his defense. "He confessed to the seven murders, and we know he attempted to murder you. Do you agree, Ms. Lestler?"

"Yes. We have his sworn confession and my testimony that he tried twice to murder me." Katie crossed her leg in discomfort wishing she could be finished with her testimony.

Jackson paced over to the jury box to buy some time to regroup. "Would you say that Mr. White is an honorable man or is his pattern of behavior questionable?" Jackson was trying his best to tear apart Whit's confession by driving home that fact that he's a notorious criminal and liar.

"He's not an honorable man," she answered hesitantly. She didn't know where he was going with this.

"In fact, he lies for a living. Wouldn't you say, Ms. Lestler?" He knew Whit's confession and his attempt on Katie's life were his biggest hurdles in this trial. Jackson was closing in.

"Yes. He does, but…" Katie shot a look at Drake, hoping he could help but knowing he couldn't.

"Great!" Jackson exploded, perhaps to awaken those in the court room whose thoughts might be wandering. "Now let's tackle the two attempts on your life. You claim Mr. White shut down your vehicle while you were driving in the downtown area. True?" He pretended a burp.

"Yes." Katie was holding her breath, trying to study him and know where he was going next.

"So, on the day of your unfortunate accident, you claim my client, Mark Stein directed Mr. White to shut down your vehicle to stage an accidental death. Is there any direct evidence proving this or is it also just an interpretation of the facts by you and the FBI?" Jackson was trying to fracture Katie's credibility. He wanted to the jury to conclude she was unstable.

"We have evidence and my testimony, in addition to his confession." As the words left her mouth, she realized the method to his line of questioning.

Jackson quickly bantered, "But does the evidence prove it was my client, Mark Stein who ordered this attempt on your life?"

Katie was cornered. "Well, no. But it's Mr. White's conf…" Jackson cut her off again.

"So other than Whit's confession, you have no proof whatsoever, that it was specifically my client who shut down your car. Is that true?" Jackson was clearly pleased with himself.

Katie had no choice but to answer. "Yes." She blinked hard and looked at Drake. She felt her perspiration bead on her forehead and under her arms.

"Of course." Jackson took a quick breath for emphasis as he quipped his triumph with cockiness. "Now about the second attempt on your life. He clearly did try to murder you, Ms. Kestler, but the question is why?"

"Is it possible Mr. White was hired by someone other than my client, to murder you, for instance, a former fugitive you apprehended? I caution you, Ms. Lestler, you're under oath and have previously stated that it's possible you may have made enemies in your line of work as an FBI agent." Jackson was pacing in front of the jury.

"It's possible, but not probable." Katie rushed her answer before Jackson could cut her off.

Jackson was livid that she kept over-answering his questions. "Again. I caution you, Ms. Lestler. Reign your answers to a simple yes or no. When I want your elaboration, I'll ask for it," Jackson spat out.

"The witness will answer the question," Judge Stokes instructed.

Katie sighed deeply and loudly before answering reluctantly. "Yes. It's possible." Katie was sick that he pinned her down with that one question.

"No further questions, your Honor." With that Jackson glanced at Shawna with a take-that attitude as he walked back to his seat. He was feeling proud of his defense, and his pomposity showed.

Chapter Thirty-One

The People vs. Mark Stein

Katie was shaking by the time she took her seat between Beth and Drake. Each took her hand and squeezed it reassuringly. Both soothed her, but Drake was her closest friend and now her lover. She took comfort in his touch.

She knew she'd given up a reasonable doubt with her last words, yet she was hoping with all the evidence they had, plus Whit's testimony, that Stein would be behind bars for life or execution. Both she and Beth would never see him pay for his sins. It was a burden and a bond only they shared.

The next two weeks were testimonies from automobile experts and the accident investigators, members of the victims' families, some of whom would come later in the trial, and, most importantly, the insurance agents who were instructed to push straight life annuities for their lottery-winning clients. The state was laying its case brick by brick, not missing a single detail.

Meanwhile, Megan Smith was counting down the days to her freedom. Two more days to go until Megan would be out of the woods and have financial security.

"State your name for the record," the clerk instructed in a matter-of-fact manner.

The life insurance agent took the stand. "Rick Townsend," Shawna proceeded to question the witness, knowing that his and other life insurance agents' testimonies would pin Stein to the wall. "You work for the Assurant General life insurance company that's been indicted for fraud against lottery winners. Is that right?" Shawna asked directly.

"Yes," Townsend replied, leaning forward into the microphone.

"Please tell the court how and when you were instructed to sell lottery winners straight life annuities for bonus compensation," Shauna prodded.

"They sold them before I got there," Townsend noted. "We were told our commissions would double if we sold them to lottery winners and anyone who had a sudden windfall of cash. It was a standard of practice by my company."

"Standard of practice," Shawna emphasized. "Does that mean that all agents were automatically coerced into pushing lottery winnings into straight life annuities? Why was that?"

"Yes. That's exactly what I mean, because they needed the influx of lottery dollars to remain solvent in these uncertain time because when the annuitant dies all the monies revert to the company," he stated with hesitation.

"Did you increase your sales of straight life annuities?" She was leading him to put in place a graphic picture of how the agents were coerced to sell these annuities.

"Yes, I did. I was providing for my family." Townsend didn't want to come off as the pawn he was.

"Did you know the instructions were directed by the defendant?" Shawna wanted Stein to get his comeuppance.

"No," Townsend explained, clearing his voice before answering. "I didn't." Townsend was sweating bullets. He was in the process of cutting a deal for himself, but so far nothing had been pinned down.

"And did you sell a straight life annuity to Rory Phillips after he won part of the Mega Millions lottery?" She was getting down to the brass tacks of this trial.

"Yes, I did. But I didn't have a choice." He loosened his tie a bit. "Like I said, it was a standard of practice in our company to sell straight life annuities whenever possible." He had no choice but to incriminate himself. He was already arraigned for several charges to be heard at his trial.

"And did you know that sale would facilitate the murder of Rory Phillips?" Shawna was showing there was no culpability on the agent's intent, allowing him to remain a credible witness.

"No. I didn't. I would never have sold it had I had known it would lead to the murder of anyone." The agent showed genuine remorse for his misdeed. With this question, she drove a giant spike into Stein's coffin.

"No further questions, your Honor." Shawna had extracted what she wanted from Townsend.

It seemed that Jackson had no place to go. He swaggered up to the witness stand. "Mr. Townsend, you testified that you didn't know my client allegedly instructed your insurance company to sell straight life annuities for financial gain or any other reason, really? Correct?" Jackson was vainglorious. He was securing a path to reasonable doubt.

"That's true," Townsend again leaned forward into the mic.

"So, from your testimony, selling straight life annuities was a standard of practice at Assurant Life Insurance company. Is it safe to say that this mandate could have come from your insurance company, rather than the defendant?" Jackson was setting him up.

"I suppose it's possible but ..." Townsend started to respond before Jackson cut him off.

Jackson taunted, "You said you had no prior knowledge that the sale of a straight life annuity would lead to the death of Rory Phillips, and that you had no choice in the matter when it came to funding Rory Phillips's winnings. Right?"

"Yes." It was a tricky question with a simple answer. Townsend reluctantly replied.

"I have no further questions, your Honor." With that, Jackson sat down with a smug grin on his face, hoping he'd created a modicum of doubt in the minds of the jury.

"Permission to redirect, your Honor?" Shawna asked.

"Proceed," the judge agreed.

"Mr. Townsend, you mentioned that there was a written agreement between your company and you, in which the winnings would be funded only by a straight life annuity as a standard of practice. Did I understand that correctly?" Shawna wanted to be very clear on this matter.

"Yes. That's correct," Townsend admitted. He was tired of answering the same question.

"Then you really don't know if the directive came from your own company or the defendant. Correct." Shawna was laying a path of conspiracy in which the leader was Stein.

"That's correct," Townsend hoped this ended his testimony. "No further questions." She shot a 'you're going down' look at Jackson as she prepared to call her next witness.

Shawna had one more insurance agent to call to the stand, Jay Beckett. With the testimonies of the two insurance agents and Whit's testimony, Shawna would lock down the prosecution's victory.

Beckett, the president of Life Assured Insurance, was sworn in. In his testimony, Shawna procured that Stein instructed his agents to sell straight life annuities for the express purpose of keeping the winnings for the company's financial gain and to remain solvent in turbulent times.

Jay Beckett was also brought up on fraud, accessory to murder and a litany of other charges. His testimony crippled the defense's strategy of claiming ignorance of this practice.

After Shawna secured Beckett's testimony it was Jackson's shot. Jackson was swaggering after his last victory with Townsend. "Mr. Beckett, did you know that my client was behind the mandate insisting that the lottery winnings be invested into straight life annuities?"

"No." Beckett's answer was expected.

"No further questions, Mr. Beckett." Jackson took his seat.

Jackson was treading lightly, being sure to frame his questions for only this witness. He only had one move. He tried to establish that Beckett had no tangible knowledge that his directives came from Stein. It was a shoestring defense, but it was all he had.

Marty and her crew reported the news daily and turned down countless offers to be on the morning talk shows and late-night comedy TV circuit. There would be plenty of time for that after they covered the real news straight from ground zero.

'Train' was busy tracking down Whit's 'location du jour.' It was only hours before he would begin his testimony. Train had till dawn to take him out.

Whit was being held in a double-wide trailer on Wednesday night, the day before he took the virtual witness stand. Things were going as planned and security was as tight as they could make it. There was an ambulance onsite along with a make-shift emergency room in case one of Donovan's men got to him.

The FBI located Whit in Quincy, a suburb of Tallahassee just off I-75, in case they quickly needed access to a major hospital. All precautions had been taken and all background checks had been made twice to verify that everyone on site had a legitimate reason to be there. Everyone, except Train.

He embedded himself as a nurse much like his old pal, Santos. He used the same methods for creating a verifiable false identity. It got him there and right on time. Now all he had to do was create a diversion. He knew exactly what he was doing.

Train liked fire. They were easy to light without much trace evidence. This time he used 9-volt batteries and steel wool pads to spark a few trashcan fires that would blossom if placed in the appropriate areas, and ta da, instant accidental fire. His goal was accomplished. He had his distraction.

The first fire broke out in the kitchen. Then a secondary broke in the back of the trailer. Most trailers go up fast, so the agents on duty reacted hastily. Four of them surrounded Whit and he became the nucleus of the agents. Train was ready with a .38 Special and a silencer.

The other three agents on the perimeter were moving through their training and using their expertise to secure the area. They knew the fires were set deliberately, and this was the diversion tactic they'd been waiting for.

Beth, Marty and Katie sat around having drinks. John took Rori up to bed and left the girls to talk.

Beth began, "Katie, I think you did very well on the stand. Jackson backed you into a corner with that 'have you made any enemies in your line of work' bit."

"I know," a furious Marty chimed in. "I know how rough this is going to get and my heart just goes out to both of you."

Beth bolstered, "I know the defense keeps going for the shadow of a doubt in the minds of the jury, but we have a ton of evidence against them and, with Whit's testimony, we'll nail Stein and Donovan." Beth wanted Whit to live long enough to take the stand but worried because it was the night before he was to testify, and she knew firsthand how ruthless Donovan could be.

"Do you know what we should expect from Whit tomorrow?" Marty asked, turning toward Katie.

"Not really," Katie answered. "It'll depend on what the prosecution leads with. But I'm betting she'll get right to it before something happens to him."

The first FBI agent took a hit to the head. The second to the neck. Whit was in his human huddle, being shuffled to the ambulance that was racing to pick them up. A third agent took a couple of rounds to the Kevlar vest she was wearing. The back doors of the ambulance swung open, and Whit was shoved into the van as fast as lightening, and then he was gone.

Train failed to get his kill. But the compound was ablaze. Sirens could be heard as a fire truck pulled up and firemen were scrambling to hose down the blaze. The trailer was gone but the garage was still burning. Smoke was thick and Train disappeared into the night.

Day 20 began. The courtroom had a palpable air of urgency that was electric. The anticipation of Whit's testimony was what the world was waiting to hear. This was no longer just a ground-breaking story in America, but around the world.

People were waiting for justice. There was a ferocious appetite for the gory details of the seven murdered victims. They had already heard in detail of Katie's near misses. Now they wanted to hear more about those who weren't so lucky. Many people were calling the 'lottery murders' dead giveaways.

"All rise," the clerk announced.

Testimony would begin, and Megan Smith and Whit were still alive. The rules of conduct were read for the courtroom, followed by the procedures for the closed-circuit TV testimony.

Katie and Beth shifted uncomfortably in their seats.

Rori was being a bit fussy, so Beth stepped out for a moment until she soothed her into a quiet mood, and she fell asleep in her arms. She stepped back into the courtroom just as the TV monitors clicked on. Before them was the face of the enemy, Whit.

Chapter Thirty-Two

Confessions of the Soul

Whit was wearing a dark blue suit blazer, a dark purple and blue tie, a white shirt, jeans with pressed seams and black sneakers. He looked as presentable as any serial murderer could.

He was sworn in, and Shawna got up for the prosecution of the century. She had practiced this day over and over in her mind and rehearsed it in her office. Her ability to question this witness would either determine the punishment of a malicious murderer, Mark Stein, or set him free. She had to eliminate all doubt in the jury's minds.

She felt her perspiration as she began questioning the witness. "Mr. White, you've confessed to the murders of seven lottery victims and the attempted murder of FBI Agent Katie Lestler. Do you agree with that statement?"

"Yes," Whit replied, already aggravated with her first question.

"How did you obtain the names of these victims?" Shawna pressed for immediate incrimination of Stein.

Whit was ready for this question. "Through my contact, Mark Stein. Seven indicted insurance companies were in bed with him."

"I see. Walk me through that process, Mr. White," Shawna prompted.

"There's not much to tell. Mr. Stein, supplied the lists of lottery winners and to the seven insurance companies and then dispersed the names to his hit men, including me. He then spread the murders among the insurance conspirators, so we wouldn't draw attention to any one company." Whit hated every minute of explaining the mundane.

"And this process worked well for the past ten years or so?" Shawna knew she was laying the groundwork.

"Yeah, until my hit on Rory Phillips," Whit stated blandly. "His wife wouldn't shut up about it being a murder instead of a freak accident. That broad ruined it for all of us. She wouldn't shut up and let it go." Whit was obviously pissed.

Beth smiled through her tears. She was proud she'd insisted Rory's death was murder, and now she was nearly face-to-face with the man who killed her husband. It sickened her.

"How did the defendant contact you to kill Rory Phillips? Did you ever meet in person?" Shawna circled back to the guilt of Stein.

"No! We never met in person." Whit was emphatic. "He always texted me a hit name and address and any medical issues, so if they were sick or anything, I could play into that and make it look like they died from natural causes. But because Phillips was healthy, I made it look like an accident," he answered with a shrug.

Shawna would come back to this, but first she needed to lock down their relationship. "There's a lengthy thread of texts on these phones, Mr. White. But for the sake of time, please clarify for the court, how you communicated with the defendant."

"He texted me the hit," Whit replied with a sigh.

Shawna rushed her next question with sarcasm. "You're testifying that both, you and Mr. Stein never met in person to arrange the details of Mr. Phillip's murder? Is that correct? Are you sure about that, Mr. White?" Shawna was establishing Whit's lack of credibility.

"Yes." Whit put his foot down for emphasis. "We never met in person. How many times are you going to ask me that?" he answered defiantly. "He hired me with a text for the Phillips job. Like usual."

"Mr. White, can you please identify Mr. Stein?" Shawna wanted Whit to point to Stein.

Whit shifted uncomfortably in his chair and took a long drink of water. "Sure," Whit answered. "He's sitting over there with his attorneys."

"Let the record show that the witness has identified the defendant." Shauna directed the court reporter and continued with her prosecution. "Then, what if I were to tell you that Mr. Stein confessed that you and he met in person for an updated list of hits, that included Mr. Phillips?" Shawna taunted.

You could see visible sweat beading on Whit's brow and upper lip. "Well, maybe I misremembered. Yeah. That's right. I just forgot, that's all."

"You 'misremembered'. So, I'll ask you again, Mr. White, how did Mr. Stein hire you, in person or by text?" Shawna was maddened by his lie but ran with it.

"I just told you. We met in person for the Phillips job." Whit's temper was showing.

"Now, that you've stated you met in person, would you care to rephrase your statement, Mr. White? You are under oath." Shawna continued, knowing Whit had no redeeming qualities.

"What if I told you that the people have obtained a text conversation you exchanged with Mr. Stein?" Shawana was excising the truth from him much like a tumor would be extracted.

"Like I said, we met in person. I don't recall any text messages." Whit was getting confused and could hardly keep up with his lies.

"So exactly when did you meet with the defendant to set up the hit on Rory Phillips?" Shawna was weaving her case.

"We met in January of this year. That's when he gave me Phillips' name and when he needed him taken out." Whit was obviously upset by having to detail everything.

Whit adjusted his tie while beads of sweat started streaming down his face. Truth was, unbeknownst to Whit, Stein had gotten lazy and started using his personal cell phone for texting while Whit assumed he was using his standard burner phone.

Stein reasoned he'd never get caught and if he did, he'd just remove the SIM card and ditch the phone. Too bad he didn't have time to do that before the FBI obtained a warrant to search his home and office. The warrant was based on the money trail.

"Objection, your Honor. Where is the prosecutor going with this?" Jackson was losing his patience.

"Sustained. Make your point, Ms. Ferguson." The judge was short with her.

"Your Honor, the people refer to evidence Exhibit K, Mr. Stein's cell phone," Shawna stated as she handed it to the clerk. "It contains the phone calls and text messages of their conversations from Stein's cell phone and Mr. White's burner phone."

"So, to be clear, you did receive a text to 'confirm the murder' of Rory Phillips. Correct, Mr. White?" Shawna was closing in.

"Yeah. Maybe I got one or two text messages." He'd been caught in another lie and the whole courtroom knew it, and that's the way he wanted it. He figured if he perjured himself on the stand that his credibility would be shot, and they might question his entire testimony. He hoped this would sway Donovan to cancel his execution. He wanted out of the witness protection and relocation program. It was as bad as prison.

Shawna was upset by his lies but ran with what she could. "Do you remember the text messages? Do you need me to refresh your memory, Mr. White?" Shawna almost had Stein's fate sealed. "It read, 'Confirm R. Phillips, tonight at Rory's Tractor Trailer Repair.' Did you respond to this text with a confirmation of Mr. Phillips' murder?" Shawna smiled as he delivered his answer.

"I might have." His tone was menacing and so was his attitude.

"Did you or didn't you, Mr. White." Shawna's anger took over.

"Okay. I did." Whit had admitted it. There it was. The few occasions Stein used his personal cell phone for hits and confirmations that the hits had been carried out. Both Stein and Whit were caught with their hands in the cookie jar.

"Did it simply read, 'Done,' Mr. Phillips?" Shawna's question was simple but damning.

"Yes. It did." Whit shifted his weight and crossed his arms. It was the hard evidence needed to convict Stein beyond a shadow of a doubt.

She had done it. She brought out the diabolical nature of this heinous criminal, Mark Stein, while Whit hung himself with his own words. The defense had nowhere to go. The more vile the offense, the more the jury would want justice for all his victims.

Shawna continued with the sound of victory in her voice. "Mr. White, please describe for the court how on the night of February 14th you went about killing Rory Phillips?" Shawna had been waiting to pose that question for several long months and she was about to receive the answer in open court. This was the moment everyone had been waiting for, the sinister and gory details of his actions.

Marty took Beth's hand and they exchanged looks of apprehension. They knew what was coming, and Beth wasn't sure she could bear hearing Whit describe her husband's murder. Yet, it was like a train wreck; she couldn't turn away. She needed to hear the truth, no matter how painful. She was glad she wasn't pregnant during the trial.

Whit began after he cleared his throat. "I entered Phillips shop and confronted him." He paused again for a sip of water. "He was on the phone, and we struggled for a minute before I overtook him. I knew how I was gonna take him out for a few days. I had Stein's order to make it look like an accident since he didn't have any health problems."

"How did Mr. Stein know which winners were healthy and which ones had a medical condition?" Shawna probed.

Whit crossed his leg over his knee and answered the question directly. "He got the info from the MIB, the Medical Information Bureau in D.C. I don't know who his contact was, but he clearly had someone in his pocket."

"What happened next, Mr. White?" Shawna was leading him as she had planned.

"I'd cased the place for days, waiting for a cabover to come in for repairs. I figured it was the easiest way to make it look like an accident." He drank a sip of water again. "Phillips struggled a bit, elbowed me in the ribs, a kinda gutsy move for having a gun at his temple. It didn't faze me cuz' I was expecting it." Whit enjoyed recounting the murder in detail. He showed no contrition. He continued with a lilt in his voice that didn't go unnoticed by the jury.

Shawna interrupted briefly, "What kind of shop do you mean, Mr. White?"

"The one he owned; a semi-tractor trailer repair shop," he answered.

"He tried to kick the gun out of my hand while I was forcing him to climb onto the engine. I accidently fired my gun when he tried to back kick it from my hand, and I clipped him in the upper leg." Whit coughed again; years of smoking had caught up with him. You could hear the audience moan. He shifted in his seat with an obvious grin as he bragged.

He continued, "The cabover hung open for repairs so I raised it to tipping center. Then I took out one of the safeties so all I had to do was strike the other one when I was ready to crush him to death. I like to take my time with my vics. I whistle while I work."

Beth cringed with tears as he described the details of Rory's death. It was as ugly as she imagined, and Rory did know he was about to die. She reasoned that his last thoughts must have been about her and how to save himself. But it was worse when Whit said it and removed all doubt.

"Please continue, Mr. White. Did you receive payment for this murder? And if so, how much and how did you receive it?" Shawna was coming down the home stretch.

"Oh, I got paid and it went into a Swiss bank account. We switch up banks to make things harder to track. I got half up front and half when it was done. Yeah. I got paid all right." He shrugged. "I got a three hundred thousand for the job." He sighed with sickening satisfaction as he relived the event.

"And can you please tell us who paid you to execute Rory Phillips?" Shauna was pinning him down.

"The defendant, Mark Stein." He said it again. There was no coming back from that confession. All eyes were momentarily fixed on Stein, then back to Whit.

Shawna switched gears. "Let's discuss the two attempts to kill FBI Agent Katie Lestler. Were you hired to murder Agent Lestler?"

Drake took Katie's hand in his and held it tightly. He knew Whit had to cop to his deeds, but he hated that Katie had to relive the events in open court.

"Yes," Whit answered again with aggravation in his voice.

"And was it Mr. Stein that gave you that order?" Shawna queried.

"Yeah," he answered smugly.

There it was. A confession from a witness stand is the most powerful tool there is. Sure, Whit had turned state's evidence and perjured himself twice, but his confession was one of the strongest elements in the case.

"When did he hire you to kill Agent Lestler?" Shawna wanted him to clarify his answer.

The petty details were wearing thin for Whit. "Well, I don't have an exact date but around the middle of May, I think." Whit answered.

Shawna was undaunted. "And can you tell us in detail about the first attempt on her life?" It was difficult to fully deliver her examination when she was in front of a monitor. It was so impersonal.

Shawna could feel her perspiration beading on her forehead again. The fact that they were discussing murder and attempted murder didn't make the exchange any easier. Furthermore, the fact that he was unwilling to divulge much detail made her job that much harder. He was definitely a hostile witness even though he'd cut a deal. She needed the jury to visualize these crimes in detail if she were going to get a guilty verdict.

Shawna crossed to the jury box while Whit continued answering. "I took control of her car. The details were easy. Shutting down a car is as easy as a few clicks. I accessed the GPS and the VIS that controls everything from the horn to the ignition system," Whit explained.

"Excuse me, Mr. White. Could you please tell the court what VIS stands for?" Shawna had no idea what he was referring to and she was pretty sure no one else did either.

He continued in monotone. "It stands for vehicle immobilization system. Dealerships and lenders are using it more and more when people fall behind on their payments. They call it the payment assurance program. They use it to track subprime buyers. That's why they can make high-risk loans." Whit stopped to take a breath. He knew he had to follow through and give up the information she was seeking.

"Please continue, Mr. White," Shawna insisted.

"Like I was saying, I took control of her steering wheel, the whole electronics, and ignition systems. I wanted to do more than just shut her down. I wanted her to hit something or someone, so it looked like an accident. It was just dumb luck that she got T-boned by another car," he said with sick smirk.

Whit didn't divulge the fact that he was driving the SUV or that he took his tablet with him after shutting down her car. He kept that tidbit for himself. "I hopped the train to get away. I jumped off right before the first stop and got away."

He continued his answer. "Good luck on my part. But it didn't do the job. I took another run at her in the hospital when she was recovering." He remembered the night too well.

Whit continued without prompting. "She's hard to kill. I didn't know for sure if she was on to me yet. I assumed she was. I knew the FBI were there in plain clothes, sitting around in the waiting room and whatnot. Oh yeah. I saw 'em," he said braggingly.

"What'd you do next?" Shawna whisked a stray piece of hair from her cheek.

"I got a pair of scrubs and pretended to be her night nurse. I entered her room and crossed to her chart at the end of the bed. I pretended to read it and then I told her it was time for Ativan, an anxiety medicine. I had a syringe in my hand." He stopped abruptly for show as he demonstrated a mock injection.

"What was in the syringe, Mr. White?" Shawna was leading him through his confession.

"It was filled with sux. I planned on smothering her with a pillow. I wanted to watch her die. I wanted to watch the life and fight drain our her." He was still kicking himself for failing to accomplish his mission.

"And what is this sux that you're referring to? Is it succinylcholine?" Shawna continued.

"That's right. It paralyzes the body, but not the mind. It shuts down the central nervous system and disappears pretty quick from the body." Drake shifted in his chair and uncrossed his arms, while Whit continued his testimony. "She wouldn't be able to struggle, and this time I'd make sure she was dead. I wanted her to suffer for all the trouble she'd caused me. But she shot me before I could do it." Having to admit that fact stung his pride.

Shawna wanted the jury to really hear this part of his testimony. She crossed right up to the monitor and stared at him as he answered. She wanted to expose the true nature of a real monster. She wanted the entire jury to focus on Whit. And they did.

"And where did you get this drug?" Shawna pressed.

"I had easy access to it in the hospital," Whit grinned big at that.

"And you say she shot you before you could finish the job. Did she shoot you again during the struggle, Mr. White?" she asked, knowing the answer.

"Yeah. The first time was in the chest near my heart. I fell on top of her, and as I started to get back up to finish the job, she shot me again, in the shoulder this time. That's when I hit the floor, and I don't remember much after that until I was waking up in the recovery room. I remember how badly I wanted to get out of there," he admitted. "But they had me handcuffed to the bed and heavily sedated."

"What happened after that?" Shawna probed for more information. She poured herself a glass of water and eagerly sipped it.

Whit mimicked her actions. "That's when I was cut a deal of total immunity for my testimony and here we are today." Whit had a smirk on his face that screamed defiance in the face of justice. The jury saw this along with the whole courtroom.

"One last thing, Mr. White," Shawna was closing in. "You mentioned your gun went off accidently and caught Mr. Phillips's in the leg. Do you still have that gun, or did you get rid of it?"

"The feds took it before I could toss it." He was upset that they confiscated Rory's gun; he wanted it for a souvenir.

"Did they match the recovered bullet to your gun?" Shawna asked, knowing the answer.

"Yeah. They did. Like I said, that's when I decided to cut a deal," Whit was tired.

"That'll be all, your honor." Shawna proved her case against Stein, and everyone knew it. It was too bad the defense couldn't settle in a capital murder case with a state's evidence trial. She would have had at least three offers by now.

It was the end of the twentieth day of the trial and Whit's testimony for now. The trial was the lead story on every news cast and talk show. The testimony of Whit was as detailed and sensationalized as possible. Even Marty had trouble keeping the glitz out of the report, mostly because Whit was so arrogant and hostile; he made it hard for the story to be anything other than salacious reports.

Dinner that night was buzzing. "In my entire career, I don't remember a story like this," Marty said. "Nothing even comes close, and I've interviewed a lot of criminals in my day. You've all seen my one-hour segments on Eye-to-Eye and Early Morning News. I can't believe his hubris. He's been nothing but odious during this whole trial."

"Neither can we," Janice said, answering for everyone. Rori was awake and playing with her giraffe.

"Now that his testimony's over, I don't know what I feel," Beth said with no obvious emotion. She seemed distant. No doubt her thoughts were on Rory and the fear he must have felt knowing he was going to die and there was nothing he could do to stop it, no matter how many guns he owned.

Beth suddenly spoke up. "The rat bastard should never have been able to cut a deal. I know he's supposed to give us Donovan and Stein, but all we have now is Stein, and it doesn't seem to be nearly enough after what we heard today."

"I hear that," Sam said, as he raised his glass in a mock salute with a 'no' shake of his head and disdain in his voice. Max raised his glass in agreement but said nothing.

"I would love to know he gets what's coming to him in the witness protection program," Janice said. "Does that make me a bad person?" She inquired with real confusion and inquiry in her tone.

Beth answered as she stared at nothing. "I don't think it makes you a bad person, it just makes you human and humane. Something we don't see in Whit is remorse. He's arrogant, antagonizing and nothing like we're used to."

Beth focused her eyes on Janice for a moment before continuing. "He has no attrition so none of us can't relate to him. It just doesn't compute that there is that much evil in the world until you're forced to confront it up close and personal."

Beth was struggling out loud to process the ordeal. Later, Beth and Marty sequestered themselves again for some heart-to-heart, but Beth was exhausted, so they went to bed early that night, but no one slept well.

It was now day 27 of the trial. Shawna called Beth to the stand to elaborate on her phone call with her husband just before he died and to provide a personal side of the story.

Beth was so nervous she could feel herself shaking. Shawna dove right in to get Beth off the stand as quickly as possible and limit her pain.

"Can you please tell the court what happened when you talked to your husband on the phone just before he died?" Shawna wanted Beth's testimony to bolster Whit's testimony.

"It was February 14th of this year," Beth said while looking at the jury. "It was our eighth anniversary and when he got home, I was going to tell him that we were finally pregnant. We'd been trying for quite a while." Her voice cracked.

"I called him to get an idea of when he might be home, so I could time my cooking to match his arrival." Beth took a breath. "I'd made a romantic dinner and I didn't want to burn anything. We didn't want to fight the crowds on Valentine's Day." Her voice tapered off.

"Please continue," Shawna prompted.

Beth took a long sip of water, "Well, while we were on the phone, he said he had to check on the work of a new hire and that he heard a noise in the shop, and he was going to check it out. There had been a lot of break-ins in the neighborhood and I told him to just call the police and come home. But he insisted on seeing for himself."

Beth had a sting in her voice as she continued, "Anyway, he told me he had his gun with him while he was headed to the shop to check things out. That's when he must have encountered Mr. White and well, you know the rest." Beth trailed off. The memories were far too agonizing for her.

"I know how hard this must be for you, Mrs. Phillips, but please tell us what you heard." Shawna was very mindful of her pain and eased into her questioning.

"I heard the phone drop. I heard the alarm ringing in the background. That's when Mr. White murdered my husband." Beth was in tears and her whole body was shaking now. She couldn't go any further.

"Thank you, Mrs. Phillips," Shawna said as she handed her a tissue. "Your witness." She shot a dagger at Jackson.

It was Jackson's job to discredit the witness. He had his work cut out for him. "Mrs. Phillips, other than the testimony of Mr. White, do you know beyond a shadow of a doubt that my client, Mark Stein, played a role in your husband's death?" Bear in mind Mr. White had perjured himself on the stand twice.

"Well, no. But ..." Beth didn't have a chance to answer before Jackson shut her down.

"A simple yes or no, please, Mrs. Phillips." That was his favorite tactic. Jackson was hoping this would put a reasonable doubt in her testimony.

"No!" She answered, enraged at being played as a grieving widow and not for her knowledge.

"That's all, your Honor." Jackson sat down and slouched a bit in his chair.

"There will be a 15-minute recess." Even the judge was disgusted by Jackson's arrogance. He needed a break and was sure the rest of the courtroom did too.

Chapter Thirty-Three

Train Kills

Diamond changed his mind and was now ready to give information because he was hoping for a lesser sentence, due to his cooperation with authorities. He too wanted to cut a deal. Much of his testimony mirrored Whit's regarding Stein's involvement to murder Katie.

He admitted to gaslighting her over several weeks in order to convince her colleagues, superiors, and Drake that she had experienced a nervous breakdown and was certainly capable of committing suicide.

Mounting a defense was a tall order given the colossal evidence stacked against him. Jackson had nowhere to go but impugn his testimony with the same reasonable doubt that he'd raised with Whit.

Jackson endeavored to break Diamond's testimony insisting he had a fuzzy memory and couldn't be certain that he met with Stein when planning Katie's murder. But Shawna batted back alluding that no one else would know of the 'gaslighting' plan.

The rest of the trial went rather smoothly. It wasn't the drama that the courtroom previously witnessed. It was mostly experts testifying about various details of the trial.

Megan Smith was following the news more closely than most. Her life depended upon it. It was now the two days before she was to receive her money and she was jumpy. She and her sister, Tiffany, were eating dinner at home. Nothing fancy, just chicken.

"The good news is that Whit and Diamond have testified and that means you're not in danger anymore, doesn't it?" Tiffany asked with hope.

"I certainly hope so," Megan replied, trying to bolster both of them. "I don't know why they'd have a reason to kill me now. Everyone knows that they are in custody, and I can't believe, I don't want to believe, they would want me dead now that everything is out in the open."

"We still have officers or agents watching us and an agent keeping watch every night," Tiffany said optimistically.

"That's true and I did see the two of them out front before I came in tonight, so I'm sure there's nothing to worry about. We've made it this far, kiddo," Megan hugged her little sister. They went to bed early.

Train confronted and killed the agents outside. Then he slithered inside the house and stealthily sneaked up behind the agent, Raymond Masters and took him by surprise. Train snapped his neck.

While Megan lay sleeping, Train sliced open her throat, allowing the blood to drain from her and leave a horrific mess. Donovan said to make it messy to send a message that no one was out of his reach. But perhaps the worst assault was that he didn't have to kill her sister too. That was just for fun. Donovan seemed untouchable and for today, it was true.

Marty broke the news of Megan and Tiffany's deaths to her viewers. The media were trying to sort out details and taking up airtime with a lot of redundant information about how they'd bring the latest in this developing story. However, due to the cruel and gruesome brutality of their murders, the media and tabloids were all over the story. Sensationalism abounded.

If Marty said it once, she said it a dozen times, she and all the world were sickened by the news of Megan Smith's death, but the senseless slaughter of her sister was more than people could take.

The FBI tip lines were blowing up and operators couldn't sift through them fast enough. People wanted to cash in on the two hundred and fifty-thousand-dollar bounty on Donovan's head. It was like a zoo fighting to hear the tipster and get the information down in a timely manner. The noise volume was almost unbearable, even with headphones. People wanted justice. And it was only day 29 of the trial.

Chapter Thirty-Four

Reasonable Doubt

The key to the defense hinged on proving reasonable doubt that Mark Stein had no knowledge of or directed the hits on the seven victims plus the attempt on Katie or that he encouraged life insurance agents to push the sale of straight life annuities. A daunting task at best.

Luke Jackson and his team of high-priced lawyers had their work cut out for them. The prosecution had presented a nearly flawless argument, and they needed to debunk the credibility of the witnesses and neutralize the preponderance of evidence.

They couldn't put Stein on the stand, as they couldn't knowingly perjurer a client. The only witnesses they could call to the stand was Whit and Diamond. This would be a short defense. Once again, all eyes and ears were on the monitor watching Whit squirm in his smug demeanor. Jackson stood up and crossed to the screen to grill Whit.

"Mr. White, you've testified that Mark Stein hired you to kill seven lottery winners and FBI Agent Katie Lestler. That's true, isn't it?" Jackson puffed his chest like a gorilla in mating season.

"Yes," came the answer from the man who sat in front of the green screen. It seemed to be a red herring for what was to come.

Jackson pushed forward. "Did he just call you up and order the hit like he would say, a Big Mac?" Jackson taunted. He figured he could throw a little sarcasm Whit's way since he so willingly threw it to anyone who questioned him.

"Of course not," he answered as he shifted again in his chair and crossed his arms. He could feel small sweat beading in the palms of his hands. He'd already lied about the communication methods and whether or not he'd met Stein.

He was hoping his plan would work. Sure, he'd be kicked out of the witness protection program, but he figured he'd be kept in isolation in prison and would eventually escape. He hoped that neither Donovan nor Stein would get to him behind bars. It was a flimsy plan, but it was the only one he had.

Jackson was going for the jugular and hoped Whit's confession wouldn't hold water with the jury. "In your previous testimony, you perjured yourself twice regarding how you were hired to commit these murders. This certainly speaks to the lack of your credibility, doesn't it?" Jackson asked rhetorically as he advanced.

"So, then how do you know you beyond a shadow of a doubt that you were talking directly with Mark Stein?" Jackson questioned while hoping to find another crack in Whit's story.

"I've talked with him before on several other hits and it's always the same voice," Whit replied.

That was the statement Jackson had been going for. It established a reasonable doubt. Kudos for Jackson. "Isn't it 'possible' that you were talking with someone else, perhaps Donovan Black, the alleged master mind behind this entire conspiracy?" Jackson added, pursuing the conveniently unavailable Donovan.

"It's possible, but not likely," Whit answered in defiance.

"Objection. Calls for speculation," Shawna interrupted. "Mr. Donovan isn't on trial here." She made her point to stick to the facts.

"Sustained. Tread lightly, Council." Judge Stokes was empathetic to Shawna.

"Withdraw the question." Jackson took a new tact. "Regarding the text message you received that read, 'Confirm R. Phillips tonight at Rory's Tractor Trailer Repair,' you believed it came from my client, don't you?"

Whit volleyed, "Yes. I did."

Jackson thrust his hand in his suit pocket and stood in front of the jury and pointed at the witness with his open hand. "However, he could have indicated a social event for the two of you, perhaps a dinner date?" Jackson was struggling to win one point in the defense of his client.

"Yeah. Sure, it's possible, but it wasn't no social event," Whit snickered with displeasure and a huff.

"Good. It's possible. We're making progress," Jackson agreed as he ignored the last half of his answer. "Chalk one up for me." His pompousness knew no bounds even in the face of defeat. "Now, there's the matter of the two attempts to murder, umm, FBI Agent Katie Lestler."

Jackson pushed forward, "So, in truth, it's just hearsay and your testimony that the call to kill her actually took place? Correct? I caution you, Mr. White, as we know you're not the most truthful person in this courtroom today, don't we?" Jackson said rhetorically and irreverently.

"You can say that, but that's not how it went down," Whit was belligerent.

"But the fact is, Mr. White, you can't say for certain, beyond a shadow of a doubt that you were communicating with my client. Can you?" Jackson was speaking directly to the jury and he had them exactly where he wanted them.

"No. Not with one-hundred percent accuracy," Whit conceded with disdain.

"No further questions, your Honor. The defense rests." The monitors went dark.

"Does council wish to cross?" Judge Stokes asked Shawna.

"No. Your Honor." Shawna was pleased with her case and Jackson's weak defense.

Now all that was left were the closing arguments. The judge ordered a recess until the next morning at 10:00 a.m. Marty recapped the day's proceedings, noting the prosecution had presented almost irrefutable evidence that Stein ordered the hits and the sale of straight life annuities.

Beth and Marty retired to her room. Rori was cooing while playing with a mobile as their discussion got underway. Marty sounded hopeful. "All we have are closing arguments for tomorrow. It's going to be a relief to all of us when they come back with a judgment. I know it will be guilty. The prosecution did a stellar job securing a guilty verdict. I can't see it going any other way."

"Neither do I," Beth agreed. She wasn't over her testimony. It pulled the scab off a wound that was slowly healing.

Marty piped up, "I'll say it again, Beth. When you were on the stand, you did an excellent job. I was proud of you. You said just the right things and you spoke from your heart. That must have cut you so deeply to rehash all that's happened." Marty was tender with her words.

"It was very hard. I'm sorry I broke down on the stand," Beth said as tears welled in her eyes.

"Why?" Marty was stunned. "You told the truth and there's no shame in crying for your husband, whether it's on the witness stand or anywhere else."

"Are you sure I didn't look like a fool?" Beth asked for reassurance. "I felt so weak when I cried, and that's not at all who I really am. Normally, I'm a very strong person, but when it comes to recounting Rory's death, I have a hard time holding it together. I struggle with that." She blew her nose. "I still cry. I can't seem to get over this hurdle. How do I strengthen myself?" she implored as she threw her tissue in the trash can.

"Let yourself cry," Marty responded. "It's how you heal. The crying may stop, or it may never stop, but you should let it out. I think in time you'll be able to talk about it, but it's far too soon to put that kind of pressure on yourself. It's hasn't been a year yet and you're kicking yourself for crying? I don't think so."

"Maybe you're right," Beth responded. "I'm gonna get past this. I'll get to where I can talk about Rory and remember only the good times we shared together. And I get to tell Rori all about her daddy. I hope I don't cry for her sake."

"I hope you do, at least sometimes," Marty offered. "That way, she'll know it's okay for her to cry too. It's because you have Rori that you'll heal. It takes time, but you *will* heal." Marty gave her a warm hug.

Chapter Thirty-Five

The Verdict

Shawna prepared her notes for the closing arguments. She had studied for this closure every night during the trial, adjusting it with each day's new findings. She now had all the pieces to the puzzle and was ready for the closing of her life. This was her biggest case, and certainly the highest profile case, she'd ever had or probably would have, and she was ready.

She was dressed in a dark, blue suit with a red, silk blouse underneath her blazer. She wore two-tone navy and red heels. They sported a gold stiletto and a peep toe with a dash of red splashed across the top of the shoe. Her hair was loosely pulled up with wisps strategically framing her fine-featured face.

Her lipstick was an understated red, not too shiny or noticeable; rather, it blended masterfully without being overbearing or a focal point on her face. She looked powerful and ready to seal Stein's fate. She was as polished as they come and just as confident, without cockiness.

Jackson was in a world of hurt. He knew how weak his case was and how guilty his client was. He still had to do his best. That's why he was getting paid the big bucks, and he needed to deliver on this one. He hated losing. It was the biggest case of his life as well, and he simply had to win, otherwise his career as a trial attorney would be irreparably damaged.

Shawna approached the jury box. "Good morning, ladies and gentlemen. Throughout this trial the prosecution has proven beyond a shadow of a doubt that the defendant, Mark Stein, is guilty of causing the murders of seven lottery winners and the attempts on the life of FBI Agent Katie Lestler." She felt powerful and psyched. "We have proven the defendant knowingly coerced the sale of straight life annuities to unsuspecting lottery winners, most of whom had no idea of the impact of these sales." Shauna added.

Shawna was just getting started. "You've seen the forensic evidence and heard the testimonies of numerous experts and witnesses. We've tracked the exchange of three-hundred-thousand dollars into the offshore bank account of Jason 'Whit' White. We have his confession stating he got his money and his orders from the defendant."

She advanced, putting her hands on the jury box and looking in the eyes of each of them. "We've heard the testimony from the widow of Rory Phillips that her husband was in danger the night of his death, to which Mr. White confessed to killing him. We've heard from FBI Agent Lestler that Mr. White attempted twice to kill her per the directive from the defendant, Mark Stein. In short, we proved our case." She marched onward with a parable.

"I'm reminded of a common story about a man and a snake. It seems they were trying to cross a rough terrain or road, if you will, and the snake asked the man to pick him up and take him across the road. But the man refused. 'You're a snake,' the man replied. 'Ah, but I'm a good snake. I won't hurt you,' said the snake," Shawna continued.

"So, the snake proceeded to cajole the man until he broke down and took the snake across the road, and the snake promptly bit the man. At that point, the man said, 'But you promised not to bite me!' To which, the snake replied, 'Ahhh, but you knew I was a snake and I don't change who I am just because you believed my lie.'" Shawna was pacing in front of the jury, then stopped to make her point.

"And with that, ladies, and gentlemen, I remind you that the nature of the defendant, Mark Stein, is that of a murderer." Shauna drove her point home.

"I ask you to convict this man, this snake as we know him to be, who masqueraded as the attorney general for the state of Florida. He was elected to protect our citizens, not to murder them. His actions are unconscionable." She was closing in with her last punches at the defense. She had the jury where she wanted them.

"So, when you're in your deliberations, please consider the facts and remember the true nature of the defendant. His victims were innocent. They did nothing more than win some lottery money and that act put a death sentence on their lives." She looked intently at the jury until all eyes were upon her and simply said, "Thank you," With that, she crossed to her table and took her chair.

Jackson stood up. He was pompous as always and checked his French cufflinks while approaching the jury, as if this case were a slam dunk in his favor. He had a 'fake it, till you make it,' attitude.

"Unlike opposing council, I don't have a charming parable to tell you," he began. "I simply want to drive home the facts. There simply is no hard evidence to prove that my client is anything but innocent."

Jackson loved to add theatrics and melodrama to his delivery by punching certain words as he spoke. He especially depended on them when he had little chance of a win. "We cross examined the witnesses and the only response we received was that no one could prove beyond a reasonable doubt, that my client contributed to these murders either in person, via email, phone, or texts."

He proceeded as he slowly paced in front of the jury. "Furthermore, my client had no knowledge that any insurance agents were encouraged to sell straight life annuities. That directive came from the insurance companies as *a standard of practice.*" He was giving it all the fire power he had in his arsenal, which was flimsy at best. Jackson paused briefly before giving his only illustrations.

"Take, for example, Mr. White. When it comes down to my client, he communicated only in hypotheticals." He adjusted his tie and collar before continuing.

"We proved that the directive, 'Confirm R. Phillips tonight at Rory's Tractor Trailer Repair,' did not prove or imply the murder of Rory Phillips." Jackson's chest was puffed, and his demeanor was dismissive as he ran his hands up and down his tasteful suit jacket.

Jackson pushed on, "For all we know it was a social invitation. Did he make some bad choices? Of course! Who among us hasn't made a poor choice that perhaps you've regretted deeply in this sojourn we call life?" Jackson stated with an awkward grin on his face. It was reminiscent of the Grinch in the children's' show, *How the Grinch Stole Christmas.*

He proceeded with a shake of his head and a hand over his heart. "There simply is no irrefutable proof that ties my client to these murders or the attempted murder. As for the confession of Jason White, he was caught in two lies on the witness stand. How can we trust his testimony to be anything but hearsay? It's hardly credible." There was that oily smile of the Grinch again. Jackson was reaching with his argument and he knew it. He was winding it up.

"For all we know, it could have been anyone," Jackson paused for effect. "There was never any identification shown. Therefore, I simply ask you to acquit my client based on the facts that there is reasonable doubt that my client committed these crimes." He cleared his throat.

"And I remind you that where there is reasonable doubt you simply must acquit." He pressed his hands together like praying hands, briefly bowed his head and said, "Thank you." He nodded his head to Shawna as he sat down and waited for the judge to adjourn the jury for deliberations.

It was the moment of truth when the jury would review all the evidence and decide the fate of Mark Stein. The facts remained in the court of public opinion that he was guilty beyond a shadow of a doubt. But how the jury would find him remained in question. It was the waiting game now.

The jurors took a preliminary vote to see where they were initially on Stein's guilt. It came back ten guilty and two not guilty votes. They didn't have far to go to get a unanimous vote. The foreman began the review of the notes and the physical evidence. It was going to be a long night.

Back at the hotel, everyone met for drinks, including Marty's crew. They seemed to be on the same page that Stein was guilty. "Now all that remains is the capture of Donovan," Marty remarked. "I don't know if we're making any headway in that direction. Drake, do you or Katie have any updates on him?"

"I don't," Drake said. "I haven't heard anything. Have you, Katie?"

"Not a word. The last we knew he was still being pursued and the tip line was blowing up." Katie was sick that they weren't any closer to finding him than they were three months ago when they released the bounty on him.

"Who is leading the charge on finding him?" Janice asked. She was speaking to Drake and Katie. "I'm wondering if there has been progress that you don't know about. Maybe the authorities are waiting until this trial is over."

Katie replied, "Dave is heading the task force. I suppose it's possible, but I can't imagine why he would want to keep that information from us. That's been our detail since I was offered up as bait." She bit her lip when thinking of what being bait had caused her.

Once again Beth and Marty sequestered themselves to Beth's room. They had more to talk about tonight. They felt relief that the testifying was finished. Rori was a delight as she was awake and ready for attention.

"How long do you think the jury will take? Beth asked as she held Rori above her head playing with her. You've covered lots of trials and I'm just wondering if you can tell by their demeanor how long they might take?" Beth asked, hoping Marty would have some kind of guesstimate.

"I really can't tell. I seriously doubt if it will take very long. The evidence against Stein is overwhelming. They had your testimony, plus all the others and Whit's and Diamond's confession. I can't believe it would take very long." Marty squeezed Beth's hand. After handing Rori to Marty she tucked her knees under her while changing positions and relaxing into the couch. "The prosecution did an impeccable job presenting overwhelming evidence that flies in the face of reasonable doubt."

"I hope you're right." Beth paused as she looked at Rori bouncing on her lap. "I've been thinking of what we talked about before. You remember the possibility of me telling Rory's story. I think I'm gonna do it."

Beth kissed on Rori while continuing. "I've been approached by several publishers already, but I think I'm gonna go with Penguin Random House. They've offered me the best deal and a ghost writer to help me." Beth was sharing from deep in her heart. "I want to do it for Rori more than for myself."

"Why is that?" Marty knew the answer but wanted Beth to acknowledge it out loud.

"Because it will provide financial security to raise her and a college fund for her down the road. Plus …" she trailed.

"Umm, hmm. Go on," Marty encouraged.

"Like you said before, I'll get to control what's said and maybe that'll help me get more closure, so I can move forward with my life." Beth bit her lower lip.

"I think this is a smart move for you. And you're right about everything. You'll get to control what's being said, how it's being said and, to some extent, when it gets said. It'll give you financial freedom so you two can take vacations and come to visit me. After all, I am her aunt, you know." At that, they both laughed and clinked their glasses together for a toast.

It took two days for the jury to return a verdict. The court had reconvened for the reading of the century. "All rise for the Honorable J. M. Stokes," the clerk announced. As the jury entered the courtroom, the judge was just as eager to hear the verdict as anyone.

"Ladies and gentlemen of the jury, I understand you have reached a verdict," the judge spoke.

"We have, your Honor," the jury foreman answered, then handed the verdict to the court clerk for the judge to view first. He then gave it back to the clerk for the reading.

"Will the defendant please rise?" the judge requested. With anticipation swelling in the courtroom, the clerk read aloud the jury's verdict on each count for seven murders and the attempted murder of Katie. There were gasps and sighs of relief as it was announced Stein was guilty on every count.

The only people unhappy with the verdict were Stein and his legal team. Looks of relief were exchanged among Marty, Beth, Katie, Drake, John, and Janice. They could hardly process the magnitude of this verdict. Marty was about to tell America and the world the good news.

A death sentence was almost a certainty in the minds of most. The judge would decide Stein's fate at a later date. The choices were life without parole or the death sentence, but either way there would be lengthy appeals by Stein's legal team, which had done a bang-up job the first time around.

The courtroom was buzzing with chatter. The media were all over Shawna and Jackson with microphones being shoved in their faces as they were exiting the steps of the courthouse.

Howard was ready in New York with the anticipation of the broadcast. "We have breaking news. The verdict for the trial of the century is in. It's guilty on all counts for Mark Stein, former Florida attorney general. Reporting live on the scene is Marty Saunders."

"Marty, what can you tell us about this breaking news?" Howard was as proud of Marty as he was of his own daughter.

Marty answered after a brief delay. "Well, Howard, there are a lot of happy people filled with relief from the guilty verdicts. The jury took only two days to render guilty on all counts. This is expected to spark widespread reform throughout the insurance industry, which has suffered unduly at the hands of a few." Marty was just getting started and was happy to report the guilty verdict.

Howard launched the all-important question. "How will this impact the insurance industry?"

"Jason White's testimony exposed the entire conspiracy, and the insurance companies involved are being sanctioned. Straight life annuities are expected to be re-examined, and the legality of them is being called into question." Marty's emotions showed as she anticipated Howard's next question.

Marty took a quick breath and continued professionally. "I want to point out that most insurance agents never consider offering the straight life annuity option to their clients, solely because it doesn't allow beneficiaries, even though it pays out the most amount of money. This case has seriously and unjustifiably tarnished them."

"How do you think this will affect the political environment?" Howard was covering every base.

"It's too soon to tell, but it will probably become a platform for many political candidates." She kept up. She felt a sense of pride knowing her friends helped orchestrate these upcoming changes and caused the conviction of Mark Stein.

"Do we have any word yet when Stein will be sentenced?" Howard's question brought her back into the moment.

"Not yet," Marty responded. "But it should be soon. The judge in this case wants to sentence Stein as soon as possible. I'm sure he's looking at his docket."

"Do you know if Jason 'Whit' White and Hector 'Diamond' DeSoto will be targets in prison?" Howard asked, knowing it was on the minds of everyone following the case.

"That may depend on the capture of Donovan Black and whomever killed Megan and Tiffany Smith and their bodyguards. However, Donovan allegedly has the power to execute Mr. White and Diamond from inside or outside of prison. Both are still at large with one of the biggest manhunts ever launched." Marty was secretly hoping they all would get their comeuppance.

Howard was winding down the interview. "Any word on the capture of Donovan and the unknown assailant that murdered Megan and Tiffany Smith and their bodyguards?"

"Nothing new to report. The manhunt is still underway, and authorities are confident they will find them soon." Marty was only too aware of how important it was to capture them. Katie's life was still in danger until they were caught. Marty wrapped the interview, grateful to Howard for leading her through it step-by-step. He was a good mentor and father figure.

Marty was now available for the morning talk shows and the late-night circuit. She had plenty of work to do and doubted she would do any of them. Max and Sam took the lights and camera down and met back at the hotel.

"Cheers!" Everyone raised their glasses in victory. Marty declared victory. The mood was joyful. Big insurance just took the biggest hit in its existence. Even though there were only seven companies involved, it directly impacted the reform of all insurance companies. It was still down the road a piece, but it was coming.

"To the end of straight life annuities." Beth raised her glass to a toast and the others followed.

"Ah." Marty said as she raised another glass to recognize the role Beth had played in all of this. "This has been a long time coming, Beth." Marty hugged her. "We did it. *You* did it. You made this happen. If it hadn't been for your persistence, none of us would be here today. And think how many lives you've saved because you stuck to your guns. You did this for all of us, Beth. Here. Here."

Beth felt a cry coming on as she fought to control her tears. "Thank you. I couldn't have done any of it without your help. You all were strong for me and were always there to help me when the going got so tough. We did this together."

Janice squeezed her sister's hand. "What are your plans now that all this is over?"

Beth hedged her answer as not to include the book deal just yet. She didn't want Janice or John to talk her out of it, citing too many stressful memories. She had resolved to do the book for all the reasons she had discussed with Marty.

"I don't have any immediate plans. It'll be a year in February, and I promised I wouldn't make any rash decisions until then. But at this point, I know one thing for sure. I don't want to leave my family and start over somewhere else. I want Rori to grow up with her family around her." Beth was committed to staying where she was. Beth was committed to staying where she was.

John raised his glass for one last toast, "To family, by birth or choice."

Katie chimed in with one last dangling piece of the puzzle that still hadn't been resolved. "Here's to finding Donovan and whoever murdered Megan and Tiffany Smith and their FBI agents."

Drake piped up, "But we have his name. It's Antonio Francisco, goes by Train. We just got the text right now. Train blundered when he failed to kill Whit. This means Donovan will put a price on his head, too."

Katie spoke next. She and Drake had received identical text messages. "Speak of the devil," she said. "We're dismissing Whit from the witness protection program for perjuring himself on the witness stand. But get this, he managed to escape when he was in route to prison. So that leaves Whit, Donovan, and Train in the wind." Katie, visibly upset, waited for their response. Her hands were trembling.

"With Whit in the wind again, Donovan may use him to re-up his operations, probably something different this time, but equally diabolical,"

Drake inserted. "Whit cost him millions, if not billions, and he'll either kill him or put him back in business to work it off."

"You're right, this case won't truly be over until we catch them," Marty said. She was all too aware of this. Her concern for Beth was simple. She couldn't fully move on without the resolution of their capture, and she knew Katie wouldn't be safe until then either.

Drake and Katie looked at each other, holding their breaths momentarily. They both knew that their nightmare wasn't over, but they still had each other, and knew they'd pull Katie back into desk duty until they caught all of them.

Life for Katie and Drake would continue to be hard and nerve-racking, but now they'd face it together, as partners and lovers. If they only could catch a break with the manhunt they'd feel some relief, but not knowing if Donovan was in or out of the country left a pretty big turf to cover. No, they'd have to wait for one of them to come after Katie again.

As for Beth, John, and Janice, they would continue to support each other and help bring up Rori. The friendship Beth and Marty had forged would continue throughout the years as well. For now, the only focus for all of them was getting back to a normal routine and moving forward with their lives.

That night, Donovan's plane landed back in the U.S. He had a score to settle with two FBI agents, Drake Sommers, and Katie Lestler, and Beth Phillips, a newly widowed mother for causing him the loss of his lucrative income and a life on the run.

THE END